He fought for her. He bled

Famous bad boy DJ **Anton Trask** stays out of other people's business. He learned that lesson long ago and paid for it in blood. But when the stunning Fiona Garrett shows up at one of his nightclubs asking for his help, his world is thrown into chaos. He and Fiona grew up together at GodsAcre, a remote doomsday cult in the mountains. She was fifteen years old when he busted her out of that hellhole, but she's all grown up now. Anton hates losing control, but Fiona's sultry eyes, soft red lips and gorgeous body make his heart thud and his temperature rise...

Pursued by a ghost...

Fiona Garrett is on the run from a brutal killer that the whole world believes to be dead. She hates asking Anton for help once again — she owes him her life already — but no one else could possibly believe her. Still, Fiona is unprepared for the effect Anton has on her...his hard body, the hypnotic glitter of his dark eyes, the raw male power he exudes. He sparks a desire inside her that she'd never imagined — and she can't control the flames.

Anton wants to leave GodsAcre and all its demons in the past, but he and Fiona have no choice but to face them head-on as danger ignites all around them. All he can do is keep her close to him.

And the closer she gets, the less he ever wants to let her go...

Visit me at my website, http://shannonmckenna.com for news and updates, but the best way to stay in touch is to subscribe to my newsletter! Here's the link, http://shannonmckenna.com/connect.php, so you'll never miss a new book or a great promo! Plus, look out for a special gift from me to subscribers...a free Obsidian Files novel!

HELLBENT

THE HELLBOUND BROTHERHOOD
BOOK THREE

SHANNON McKENNA

PRAISE FOR SHANNON McKENNA

"Blends an intensely terrifying psychic thriller with a mind-blowing erotic romance."
—**Library Journal**, on *Fade To Midnight*

"Blasts readers with a highly charged, action-adventure romance . . . extra steamy."
—**Booklist**

"Pulse-pounding . . . with searing sex and raw emotions."
—**Romantic Times**, 4 ½ stars

"Shannon McKenna makes the pulse pound."
—**Bookpage**

"Shannon McKenna introduces us to fleshed-out characters in a tailspin plot that culminates in an explosive ending."
—**Fresh Fiction**

"An erotic romance in a suspense vehicle on overdrive . . . sizzles!"
—**RT Book Reviews**

"McKenna expertly stokes the fires of romantic tension."
—**Publishers Weekly**

"McKenna strikes gold again."
—**Publishers Weekly**

ALSO BY SHANNON McKENNA

The Hellbound Brotherhood
Hellion
Headlong
Hellbent
Heedless (Coming Fall 2020)
Havoc (Coming Spring 2021)

The Obsidian Files Series
Right Through Me
My Next Breath
In My Skin
Light Me Up

The McClouds & Friends Series
Behind Closed Doors
Standing In The Shadows
Out Of Control
Edge Of Midnight
Extreme Danger
Ultimate Weapon
Fade To Midnight
Blood And Fire
One Wrong Move
Fatal Strike
In For The Kill

Stand-alone Titles

Return To Me

Hot Night

Tasting Fear

Anthologies

All Through The Night

(with Suzanne Forster, Thea Devine and Lori Foster)

I Brake For Bad Boys

(with Lori Foster and Janelle Denison)

Bad Boys Next Exit

(with Donna Kauffman and E.C. Sheedy)

Baddest Bad Boys

(with E.C. Sheedy and Cate Noble)

All About Men

(a single author anthology)

1

Hellbound Nightclub
Seattle, WA

The lightshow that accompanied the first set in the nightclub downstairs sliced like a razor straight into Anton's aching head, but he didn't allow himself to close his eyes or turn away.

Don't flinch. Only pussies flinch from pain. Jeremiah's harsh, drill sergeant voice echoed in his mind.

Get the fuck out of my head, old man. You're dead and gone.

The past had no hold on him. He repeated that to himself often. Most of the time, it was true.

It didn't feel true today. Not after going back to Shaw's Crossing for his foster father Otis's funeral. That trip last week had stirred up a shitload of toxic memories.

He stood by the viewing window that covered the entire wall of his private office and stared down at the gyrating crowd below. He focused upon the young DJ on stage doing the opening set. The kid had talent. He was young and green, but he instinctively knew how to manipulate a crowd. It was still early, but the dance floor was packed.

The spectacle didn't soothe his jagged nerves the way it usually did. The whip scars on his back itched and throbbed, and his hand was burning like a hornet had stung it. He wore a big pendant on a heavy chain around his neck, and when he looked down, he saw that he'd been squeezing it in his fist so hard, the sharp studs and gems on the white gold cylinder had left purplish-red marks in his palms.

Anton leaned his hot forehead against the glass to watch the dancers below. Years back, when he'd worked as a bouncer in the Vegas dance clubs, he'd discovered that he liked the club scene. That anything-goes vibe chilled him out. GodsAcre, the remote mountain enclave where Anton and his brothers grew up, had been a ruthlessly controlled environment, and their leader Jeremiah's extreme, fucked-up, rigid moral and religious code had been rammed down their throats every damn day.

Being the contrary bastard that Anton was, he'd become a DJ. He'd built up a following, gotten famous, and then more famous. He had toured the world, produced his own music. He eventually opened his own nightclub. It was a success, so he expanded the enterprise. Now he had a chain of notorious dance clubs all over the West Coast. The perfect antidote to all the hellfire and brimstone he'd spent his childhood listening to.

He'd also gotten rich in the process. Which did not suck.

Down on the dance floor, the writhing masses were cutting loose, letting go of their inhibitions. Jeremiah would have said they were piling onto a train that was headed straight to hell. That Anton was selling them express tickets.

So be it. Everyone could go to hell in his own special way. Yay, freedom.

His phone buzzed in his pocket, jolting his rattled nerves. He pulled it out to check. A text message from Eric.

When are you getting your ass back here? Bristol wants to tell FBI, CDC and the press about the death pen. We don't have much time. Researching the latest in biological weapons. Nothing yet, but my skin is crawling. Call me.

Damn. Biological weapons? Seriously?

Anton had blasted out of Shaw's Crossing at the first opportunity, right after Otis's funeral. So had his youngest brother, Mace. But not Eric, his middle brother. Eric had insisted on lingering there, to wrap up loose ends, he said. To take care of business.

His brothers knew perfectly well that was bullshit. Eric was all hung up on a woman who lived there. The same one he'd been wildly in love with seven years before. Things had ended very badly for him back then. A massive clusterfuck, in fact. Eric had barely survived it.

But had his little brother learned his lesson? Oh, no. Not him. That stubborn idiot was drawn to Demi Vaughan like a moth to a flame. He just couldn't wait to self-immolate.

And once Eric had gotten himself wound up with Demi again, the two of them had then proceeded to almost get themselves killed by a band of murderous thugs up at the moldering ruins of GodsAcre, the long-defunct doomsday cult in the mountains where they had been raised. It was miraculous that they'd survived at all, the way they told it.

None of it made sense, but according to Eric, the Trask brothers were now honor bound to go back to that godawful place and figure out what the fuck had happened before more people died. They had to figure out what those people digging holes up at GodsAcre could possibly be looking for, and stop them from finding it. According to Eric, GodsAcre was their responsibility. Their property. Their fucking sacred charge.

Eric had always been afflicted with a pain-in-the-ass hero complex, but Anton himself was not so afflicted. Why should saving Shaw's Crossing be their job? What had the people in that place ever done but kick their asses and make them miserable? Let the town implode, if that was to be its fate. Fuck that place.

The Trask brothers owed those people nothing.

But no. At Otis's funeral, all it took was one look at Demi Vaughan, and Eric's goose was cooked.

And now his brother had evidently convinced himself that the device he'd seen the thugs use in the GodsAcre attack, this 'death-pen,' was a weapon made for mass murder.

The fuck? Granted, Eric and Demi had been through ten different kinds of hell, but even so, that sounded nuts.

Of course Anton wouldn't abandon his brother. He'd go back there and offer what help he could. And Eric was hardly defenseless. Anton had posted two of his best security men to cover them until he and Nate Murphy, his head of security, could get back there to offer their support. Anton had only dared to tell this strange tale to Nate, and so far, Nate was handling it well. Anton was grateful for that.

But the whole thing made him so tense, it was impossible to concentrate.

A nearer source of light assaulted his eyes as the door to his office opened. Nate leaned inside. "Anton," he said. "That hot redhead's back at it again. She says —"

"I said to get rid of her," Anton snarled.

4

Icy silence followed his words. Anton turned to see Nate lounging casually against the doorframe, waiting to reply. He appeared to be relaxed, but his eyes were hard.

"You get a free one today," Nate said finally. "One free one. Just because you've been bereaved, and your brother got attacked, and it's been a weird week for you. But for future reference, remember that I am not your fucking butler."

Anton blew out a sharp sigh. "Yes," he said curtly. "Message received."

The two men gazed at each other. Anton lifted his hands. "So?" he said, with exaggerated calm. "About the redhead? You were saying?"

"Yeah, her. She had a personal message for you."

"Don't they all."

Nate's face stayed impassive. "She says her name is Fiona Garrett. And that she's in trouble. Ring a bell?"

Anton stood there, mind wiped blank. Shocked stupid.

Fiona.

The heavy beat from downstairs made the building throb dully, like a wound when the painkillers started to wear off. He couldn't seem to breathe.

Nat's eyes narrowed. "I guess that answers my question. Is everything okay?"

"Fiona?" The name stuck in Anton's throat like a rock. "You're sure she said Fiona Garrett?"

"Yeah, I'm sure. What's up with her? She pregnant? Do you owe her money? Does she want to break your kneecaps? Does she intend to sue you or shoot you or castrate you?"

Anton shook his head. "No. I haven't seen her in years."

Nate's puzzled frown deepened. "Dude. Is there something I need to know about this girl?"

Anton shook his head. "Old stuff," he said. "Ancient history. We grew up together. In the mountains."

"Wait. You mean she's from GodsAcre?" Nate's eyes widened. "Holy shit!"

"Yeah." His friend had gotten a crash course on Anton's whacked-out GodsAcre childhood last week when he'd accompanied Anton back to Shaw's Crossing after Eric and Demi's wild adventure. Anton still wasn't used to having anybody know so much about his ugly history. The revelations had made him feel uncomfortably exposed.

He turned to the security monitors on the wall. "Where is she now?"

Nate pointed at one of the screens. "That's her. Waiting by the staircase near the back bar."

Anton studied the camera feed Nate had indicated. Yeah, it was the girl they had pointed out before. The hot one who'd asked for a private meeting with him earlier.

Which he had regretfully declined. He hadn't recognized that girl as Fiona. Not in this bizarre context. Certainly not in those clothes.

In fact, he still wasn't convinced that woman could possibly be her.

Women reached out to him all the time. As his celebrity had grown, he'd gotten accustomed to the sex that was continually on offer to him. It got boring sometimes, but it was convenient. Whenever he felt the urge, he barely had to reach out his hand. And with a bare minimum of mental acrobatics, he managed not to feel guilty about it. They came to him begging to be used, and sometimes he obliged them.

Two things he made sure of. First, any woman he fucked clearly understood that it started and ended there. Second, any woman he fucked walked out of his presence weak-kneed with sexual satisfaction. He made it absolutely worth their while. A point of pride.

When he saw the redhead, he hadn't even seen her face. He'd been tempted by the long legs, the high-riding breasts with tight nipples poking out the stretchy fabric of her dress. In those spike-heeled boots, she'd only be an inch or two shorter than his six-foot-three frame. He had a weakness for long red hair and the freckles that usually came with it.

He'd thought about having her brought to him. Imagined fingering her into whimpering readiness. Making her come repeatedly before he bent her over the big desk in his soundproofed lair, her pussy hot and slick and utterly primed.

He'd have her keep those silver boots on while he put it to her from behind. Deep and hard.

But no. Shaw's Crossing, Otis's funeral and the vicious attack on Eric had left a bitter taste in his mouth. Murderous rage seethed inside him, looking for an outlet.

No sex for now. Not until he managed to chill...the fuck...out.

The redhead's back was to him in the camera, offering an amazing view of a world-class ass. Her back was straight and upright. The long, wild mane of fiery hair looked right, but he couldn't see her face.

"Who's closest to her?" he asked.

Nate muttered into his Bluetooth. "Wong is close," he said, after a moment.

"Have him ask her to look up at the camera. I need to see if it's really her."

Nate's eyes widened, but he relayed the message without comment. Jim Wong, one of his security experts, entered the camera's view, a hulking Asian man, immensely tall and broad, with a thick neck, a goatee and a long ponytail hanging down the back of his leather jacket. Wong approached the redhead, spoke into her ear and politely gestured toward the video camera mounted on the wall.

The girl's long hair swung out around her like a cape as she turned to look at him. Her big, bright eyes were painted up with smudgy black, blazing and intense. He couldn't make out the color in the camera, but he remembered it perfectly. Stormy slate-gray on the outside of the iris, fading to light gray and then a sunburst of amber gold right around the pupil. Amber that matched her hair and her freckles. Fi had been covered with freckles.

The brightness in her eyes sparked a restless, uneasy stirring inside him. Lust, fear, all mixed together, way down deep.

Yeah, that was Fi. There was no mistaking that defensive, screw-you-too look in her eyes. The sexy shape of her full mouth. Those high, sharp cheekbones. She was no longer the skinny waif with the thick red braid. She was taller now, still lean and slender, but filled out. She looked lithe and strong. Her lips were painted hot red.

She faced the camera head on, with an aggressive, wide-legged stance like a comic book gunslinger. A glittering belt of crystal studded links hung low on her hips. She stuck out her chest, hands on her hips, elbows out. Staring him down.

After a minute or two, she lifted her hand, fluttered her fingers at him, and blew him a kiss. Her dark eyebrows were arched up high. As if she could see right through the camera, all the way to where he stood, frozen and dithering.

What are you waiting for? You scared? Of me? Awww.

What the *fuck* was she doing here? Tonight of all

nights? He was still all wound up about what had happened to Eric back in Shaw's Crossing. Dealing with Fiona would put him right over the top.

Besides Anton and his two brothers, Fiona was the only other survivor of the lethal shit-storm that was their childhood. Everyone developed his or her own fucked up coping mechanisms for dealing with massive trauma. Evidently Fiona's had been to morph into a drop-dead gorgeous, man-killing femme fatale.

Damn. There were worse strategies.

"Tell Wong to bring her up," Anton said.

He turned to the viewing window, checking his own reflection before he could stop himself. He'd changed a lot in the thirteen years that had gone by. The last time Fiona saw him, he'd been almost eighteen. No tats. His hair a long, shaggy, dark blond mane. He'd looked very different.

His current bad boy DJ vibe was edgy and hard. Hair buzzed off tight on the sides, longer on top, gelled up into an artful, spiky mess. A bespoke designer jacket hung open, flaunting his eight-pack abs and putting the tattoo art that covered his shirtless chest on full display. A garish, jewel-studded pendant dangled over his heart. His professional look was carefully cultivated, and definitely not for everyone.

Nate didn't miss a trick, goddamn the man. He caught Anton checking his reflection and snorted under his breath as he turned to the door.

"Smile, lover boy," he said. "I'll tell you if you have spinach in your teeth."

"Fuck you, man." Anton slammed the door after him, cutting off Nate's laughter.

2

*F*ake it till you make it, Fi. That's what we all do. Don't think
you're so damn special. Imagine they're all naked. Everyone
feels scared and awkward. Not just you.

That was her cousin Patti's standard lecture from the
old days, when she was teaching Fiona how to navigate the
"normal" world. The post-GodsAcre world.

She'd tried to practice Patti's advice, but it hadn't been
much comfort to her then.

Nor was it now. Every thought of what happened to
Patti caused intense pain.

Focus, damn it. Fiona followed the burly Asian guy up
the stairs to the lofted space above, grimly intent on keeping
her ankles from wobbling in her ridiculous boots. She'd
chosen them for the girls-gone-wild sex-bot vibe, but they
practically crippled her. If she needed to fight or run, she'd be
meat. And she was intensely conscious of the deadly threat
hanging over her. Every second of every day.

And damn. If just staring into a video camera that

might or might not have Anton Trask at the other end made her knees turn to jelly, what would the real, flesh-and-blood Anton do to her?

Hoo, boy. Her mind could keep itself happily entertained for hours with that idea.

It took all the nerve she had to get all glammed up and slutty like this. It wasn't something she did often. Or ever. Not for years, anyway, and she'd only ever made the effort on Patti's insistence. Patti's pet project had always been Fiona's beautification.

Though 'domestication' might actually be a better word.

Fiona had done her best to play along. Patti was only trying to help. But she had to fight conflicting inhibitions to do it, and it had not been easy.

Jeremiah Paley, the leader of the survivalist cult where she'd grown up, had insisted that women and girls dress in modest, feminine clothing. Fiona had dressed according to his dictates, but modesty hadn't done her a damn bit of good when Redd Kimball arrived at GodsAcre. His hot stare had felt like spiders crawling over her skin.

She'd tried to fade away and evade his notice. It hadn't worked.

A deep hesitation to invite male attention had stuck with her ever since. When she tried to push back against those deep-rooted fears, she ended up overcompensating, egregiously. She overdid it and went all-out sexpot. Put out confusing messages. Got into all kinds of embarrassing trouble.

The whole thing was more hassle than it was worth.

Patti had despaired of her. She'd tried so hard to teach her awkward, tongue-tied country mouse cousin to pass for a normal California girl. The hair, the make-up, the clothes, the laughter, the lightness. Hah.

Fiona gently pushed away her memories of bouncy, friendly, giggling Patti. Later for that. The pain would wait for her. Pain was endlessly patient.

Today's goal was to face Anton Trask and ask for his help. Enough shivering and sighing. The guy's only sin was in being gorgeous, talented and charismatic.

He was her hero. Quite literally. But for Anton, she'd have been married off to that sleaze-bag Kimball when she was fifteen. Which would have killed her.

'No' had not been an option at GodsAcre. What Jeremiah said was law.

The bouncer was pushing open a heavy door and gesturing for her to enter. The time for frantic second-guessing was done.

Fiona walked into a large, wood-paneled room. It had sleek, essential furniture in black leather and steel. Banks of monitors and electronic equipment were smoothly incorporated into the walls, like the bridge of a luxury intergalactic space yacht.

"Ms. Garrett?"

She jerked around, startled, but the guy who had spoken wasn't Anton. He was very tall, striking in his own right, his lean, muscular body dressed in a tailored white shirt and black dress pants. Black hair. A big, hooked nose, a strong jaw, scruffy, dark beard shadow. His keen, deep-set eyes looked her over with great interest.

"Nate Murphy," he said, extending his hand. "Anton's head of security."

She shook his hand. "Did Anton ask you to check me out for deadly weapons? I do tend to inspire terror in the hearts of men."

"Not exactly." His eyes flicked over her body. "I don't know where you'd keep deadly weapons if you had them. I won't search you. Anton said you guys go way back?"

"That's right." She just waited, offering no more details.

"So do we," Murphy offered. "I met him in Vegas a long time ago. He got me a job as a bouncer at a club he worked at on the Strip after I got out of the Marines. I can't even imagine Anton Trask as a kid."

She made a noncommittal sound. Of course not. That was because Anton had never been a kid. Neither had she. But that was nobody else's business.

When she made no further comment, Murphy opened the door behind him and beckoned her in. "He's waiting," he said. "Go on in."

Fiona took a long, deep breath and jacked up her attitude-o-meter to its maximum setting. The more nervous and scared she was, the more invincible she had to act.

Shoulders back, chest out, chin up. Proud, regal and unafraid. She strutted past Nate Murphy in a hip-swaying, take-no-prisoners saunter.

The room was dim and long, a black leather living room set at the far end in front of a bar. Low black couches and armchairs, a wide, low wooden coffee table, a dimly lit geometrically designed hanging lamp over the furniture that was a modern art piece in itself. A floor-to-ceiling window overlooking the dance club dominated the first half of the room. Pulsing lights from the club flickered against the far wall. She glimpsed the gyrating throng on the dance floor below as she walked in.

The pounding music was barely audible. It seemed a physical impossibility to insulate a room from music that loud and that close, but somehow, they'd done it.

"Fi." She froze at the sound of his voice. Even deeper and richer than she remembered. Anton had always been slow to talk and soft-spoken, but everyone always leaned in and listened to every word.

She forced herself to turn. Her heart thudded heavily in her chest.

Anton sat at a huge desk set into a niche in the back of the room. The dim light from the hanging lamp painted his starkly sculpted face with shadows. His shadowed eyes gleamed, unreadable. She tried to speak, but he beat her to it.

"It really is you," he said.

You doubted it? Who else even knows I ever existed? They're all dead. Words whirled in her head, but she couldn't pick out what to say and what to discard.

Keep it simple, like Patti always said. Keep it light. *Hi, Anton. Long time no see. Looking good. How's life treating you. Nice place you got here.*

But no. She couldn't. She had fuck-all to say to him. Mind blank.

She coughed to shake her voice loose. "Hey," she croaked. "Anton."

She'd been afraid of this. That she'd freeze, tongue-tied. Just her own frantically beating heart deafening her from the inside. She'd hoped that adulthood would help.

No such luck.

Memories rolled over her. Memories she'd buried deep and then ignored, just to keep herself sane. And Anton was splashed all over them.

How he'd broken her out of GodsAcre just in time. Led her through the woods on steep, tortuous paths where no one could follow them through the mountains, down to the town

14

of Shaw's Crossing. In the end, she'd been in such a daze of pain from the flogging, he'd carried her on his back. He got her to the bus station. Bought her a ticket to California, God knows where he got the cash. Guided her to the right bus.

And before she climbed on, he had kissed her goodbye.

That kiss was burned into her mind for all time.

She still remembered looking down through the tinted window of the bus. Anton's long, dark blond hair blowing back in the wind as the bus pulled away. Those beautiful, muscular arms, tanned to deep gold. His intense, deep-set eyes, locked onto hers. Willing her to be strong, tough. Like him. Silently telling her to never give up.

He was just as gorgeous now, despite all the changes. She missed the long hair, but the dark shadow of stubble on his chin cast his chiseled male beauty in sharp relief.

She'd been following his career since he burst on the scene years back as an up-and-coming DJ. His rise to fame had been swift, at least to outside viewers. He'd graced the covers of *Billboard*. He'd been featured in articles in *BPM, URB, Vogue, GQ*. He was splashed all over any publication, online or print, where people talked about music, fashion, celebrity, or pop culture in general.

She had read all of it. Every word of everything that had ever been published about him. He'd kept the lurid story of his childhood out of the press, God alone knew how, but he'd become even more infamous last summer after his highly publicized fling with a red-headed Hollywood starlet. The latest It Girl.

The affair ended badly. The starlet had complained bitterly. He was emotionally unavailable, she bitched. He was elusive, detached, remote. She'd felt lonely and used.

Bad Boyfriend, the tabloids blared. Fiona had read every

word, avid for more.

And there were all his videos online. Shows, festival clips, interviews. And the ads. Commercials for athletic shoes, whiskey, champagne, luxury cars, men's cologne, high-end sports watches. She watched them all obsessively, sucked into his hypnotic, complex rhythms of his dance mixes. She had her favorites saved on the desktop of her computer for quick and easy reference. Her secret addiction. He was wickedly talented.

Anton leaned back in the chair, his gaze inscrutable. As was his custom, according to the magazine articles, he was bare-chested beneath his jacket. His smooth, heavily muscled chest was densely covered with tattoos. The black satin jacket was cut perfectly for his broad shoulders.

Jeremiah Paley had hated tattoo art with a fiery, unreasonable passion. Interesting.

Anton opened a desk drawer and took out a remote, pointing it at the glass viewing area overlooking the club. She heard the muted hum of a motor, and hanging vertical blinds marched across the window, sliding into place to cover it completely.

The colored flickering light vanished. The room felt suddenly smaller. Breathlessly intimate. Another gesture with the remote, and a pool of light flicked into being all around her. A recessed bulb in the ceiling, right above her head.

Like a spotlight. As if she was the floor show, performing for an audience of one.

Patti's advice flashed through her head again. How to talk naturally to men. How to combat being shy and tongue-tied.

Just pretend he's naked.

Oh, man. Oh, no, no, no. In this case, Patti's classic

advice was a terrible idea. Once she thought it, she couldn't unthink it. And her brain just went apeshit with it.

"What's with the outfit, Fi?" he asked. "It's over the top."

Fiona glanced down at her ensemble. He was absolutely right, but she would die before she'd admit it. "It's a dance club," she said. "My general uniform is jeans and a tee-shirt. That would've stuck out like a sore thumb in here. I wanted to blend in."

His mouth twitched in an ironic smile. "You overshot the mark."

She shrugged. "What if I did? I don't consider other people's opinions when I dress myself. I got plenty of that crap back at GodsAcre. Enough to last a lifetime."

"So this is rebellion? A fuck-you to the Prophet's tight-ass memory?"

She was silent for a moment, trying to put it into words. Her trashy sexbot look was like a force field. A bizarre, counterintuitive sort of armor. She couldn't look vulnerable. She couldn't afford to show doubt. She had to look fearless, shameless, in-everyone's-face, to jack up the nerve to come here and ask for Anton's help.

But there was no way to explain it that wouldn't sound silly. Or worse, crazy.

"I don't make decisions based on the past," she said. "My choices are not a reaction to what happened to me. That would grant them power over me even after they're dead. I refuse to give it to them again."

He nodded. "But you're not comfortable in it."

She couldn't in all good conscience deny that, but goddamn him for noticing. She resisted the urge to tug the skirt further down over her thighs. Since there was nothing to tug.

"It doesn't matter," she muttered. "I'm never comfortable anyway."

His eyes turned her inside out. No one looked at her that way. She was used to being checked out, but guys mostly looked at her ass, her lips, her chest. She had her standard force field for that. Shields up, and whiz-bang, it bounced right off her.

Her shield didn't work on Anton. His eyes sliced through her defenses and penetrated straight into her soul. Anton knew all the things she couldn't bear to let herself remember. She could hardly look him in the eyes.

"I'm sorry," Anton said.

"About what?"

His eyebrow tilted up. "That you're never comfortable."

Crap. She didn't want him feeling sorry for her. She wanted to have this interchange from a position of strength. And standing in front of him under the spotlight like merchandise on sale at a brothel did not help. "Could we go sit down?"

"I'm good here," he said.

Hmm. So much for common courtesy. "Well, I'm not." She threw her shoulders back and refreshed the attitude, ratcheting it up a few notches as she strolled around his desk. "I'll just sit down right here." She perched her butt on the desk in front of him.

Anton shifted back, one leg crossed over the other. Black lace-up boots. Faded jeans clung to his strong muscled legs. Bigger and harder than the boy she had known years ago. The boy who had saved her sanity. Probably her life.

At this range, his male presence was overwhelming.

She could smell his cologne. Feel his body heat warming her skin. He exuded an aura of things about to happen. Combat readiness. Raw, seething vital energy, buzzing against her senses.

Exactly the qualities she needed on her side, since her world had gone to shit.

If she could make him believe her. If he even wanted to help her again, after all these years. That was a lot of ifs.

Maybe he wouldn't want to be bothered. He'd done his part to save her bacon years ago, and his life looked pretty sweet just as it was. If she were him, she wouldn't willingly trade in fame, fortune and luxury for a crusade into the nightmarish hellscape that was Fiona Garrett's miserable life. Why the hell would he? He wasn't stupid.

She was spellbound by the sensual shape of his unsmiling lips. His bearded scruff glinted, a mix of brown and dark gold. His keen, wary dark eyes studied her intently. The thick, dark slash of his eyebrows. That strong jaw. Everything she remembered about him, just bigger, stronger, bolder, hotter. Too much for her senses to process.

"Hello, you," he murmured.

His silky tone made her shiver. She braced her hands on the edge of his desk, fishing desperately for a logical, coherent entry point into the story she had to tell him.

"I was hoping to catch one of your sets tonight," she said. "They say you do at least one set at one of your own clubs every week. I read that in *Billboard*."

"Not this week," he said. "I took time for personal business."

She just waited for a moment, but after a moment, to her surprise, he actually answered her unspoken question. "I was in Shaw's Crossing for a couple days. With Mace and

Eric."

That startled her. "For real? God, why on earth would you go back to that place?"

"A funeral," he said. "My foster father, Otis Trask. He's the one who took me and Mace and Eric in after the fire. He died last week. A stroke." He paused. "So they say."

Her gaze dropped. "I'm so sorry to hear that," she said. "My condolences."

"Thanks. In any case, I'm scaling down the performances. I do a set once or twice a week at my own clubs. And some festivals. Hand-picked, though. I prefer to focus on my production work now. I'm sick of all the traveling, the crowds and the bullshit."

"I've heard you have clubs in Portland, Seattle and San Francisco," she said. "Plus the booming production company and all the advertising work. You must be busy all the time. It's really something, what you've built for yourself."

"I'm diversifying," he said. "I'm opening clubs in Las Vegas and Chicago next year."

"You know, I saw you at Coachella once," she told him.

"Really?" His eyes widened. "Why didn't you come backstage to see me?"

She laughed. "Hah. Do you have any idea the quantity of screaming, desperate girls who were waiting to come see you after that set? The whole world wanted a piece of you that night."

"You would have jumped right to the head of the line if you said the word."

"That's gratifying to hear," she said. "Thanks for receiving me tonight, by the way. I wasn't sure you would, after everything that happened. I thought you might want to just, you know. Shut the door on the past."

He frowned. "Because I never got in touch with you after you left?"

She shrugged, and waited.

"We stayed away on purpose, at first," he said finally. "We didn't want you to have to deal with all the bullshit after the fire. The police, the social workers. The press were like fucking buzzards. We wanted you well clear of that. We didn't tell anyone about you. It's like you were never there."

"Thanks for sparing me that," she said.

"I thought about contacting you," he went on. "Many times. I almost followed through on it, but I always pulled back at the last minute. I was afraid that you might prefer to just leave it all behind you. Close the door on it. Like you said."

"I tried to," she said. "I didn't approach you either, for more or less the same reasons. But I did follow your career. It would be hard not to. You're really famous."

His eyebrow tilted up. "You like this kind of music? I wouldn't have thought electronic music would be your thing. You don't strike me as the clubbing type."

If you're the one making the music, then hell yeah I follow it. "I'm a big fan," she said. "I don't like big crowds, as a rule, so I don't do clubs or dance floors much. But I listen to your sets all the time. I listened to last year's Tomorrowland set all last summer whenever I jogged on the beach. It was awesome."

"Thanks." He gestured toward the hidden viewing window. "You heard that kid downstairs. The one doing the opening set. What do you think?"

She considered that for moment. "Not bad. He's high energy, and he's got them dancing, but there's room for the sound to grow when the headliner comes on. The crowd will be primed for the peak set. It's good work. Disciplined. He's very switched on."

He nodded. "My conclusion exactly. He's playing his cards well."

"You're giving him his first break?"

"I believe in giving space to new talent," he said. "Let them struggle and sweat. It's their turn. I've already paid my dues."

"That's really good of you," she said.

"Just good business," he said. "An investment in the future."

"Of course. Excuse me for implying that you have a heart."

He let out a noncommittal grunt and declined to answer that.

Fiona ran her finger up the gleaming length of a fountain pen that adorned his desk. "Pretty," she said. "Solid gold, I assume."

"Of course."

"Ever written anything with this?" she asked. "A love note, a contract?"

"No."

"Just for show, then." Her mind kept racing, too rattled to settle on an intro to her crazy tale of woe. Her eyes landed on a bronze statue in the corner, lit with a dedicated beam of carefully angled light. Some tormented looking nude. "That looks expensive."

"It was," he agreed.

"So you're into art appreciation now? Classy. Goes with your glossy image."

A perplexed line appeared between his dark brows. "What glossy image is that?"

"Inscrutable bad boy genius. Pop stars and Hollywood

A-list actresses love to fling themselves against you and dash themselves to pieces."

"I'm an artist, businessman and producer," he said. "The rumors are bullshit."

"Hmm. Remember Jeremiah's sermons? As I recall, his favorite theme was 'vanity, vanity, all is vanity.' Then I read in *GQ* about your fleet of luxury cars—"

"It's not a fleet. You actually believe that gossipy bullshit?"

Hmmm, she'd gotten under his skin. "Where there's smoke…"

"There's always smoke," he said. "All those people do is blow smoke. Make your point, Fi."

She was working up to it. Verbalizing this was going to take every last bit of courage that she had. Next to the fountain pen there was a perfect, palm-sized pink rock with veins of green, tumbled to a smooth matte sheen. She hefted it. It felt good in her hand. "What's this?" she asked. "Kryptonite?"

"Just a river rock. It's from Kettle River, right below the Upper Falls."

"Oh." She set the rock back down carefully. "Why do you keep that?"

"To remember where I came from."

"Really? You need a reminder?"

"Not really. But it serves a dual purpose. I could also cave in somebody's head with it if I needed to."

"Ah. Now you're talking my language." She looked around at every detail of the luxurious room. "Fancy art. Gold pens, fancy lighting, sleek black leather…what does this man cave represent? You're too young for a mid-life crisis. Thirty-two, right?"

"Almost. Mid-life crises are for people who spend their whole lives not getting what they want. Then they wake up to it and panic. That's not me. I take what I want, when I want it. No delay of gratification. No panic buildup."

"Sweet," she murmured.

A brief smile curved his lips. "If you say so."

"But you are rebelling," she told him. "Jeremiah hated, oh, let's count the line items. Ostentatious wealth, loud music, alcohol, drugs, dancing, sexy outfits, frivolous use of vital resources. Tattoos. Even that designer jacket. What is that, Armani? You would have caught a thundering load of scorn from him about that jacket. I can already hear the rant about the decline of modern manhood into decadence and irrelevance."

"Yes, it is Armani," he confirmed. "Good eye. Glad you like it. Good thing he's dead, right? We don't have to listen to it anymore."

"Damn right we don't," she said.

There was a brief, charged silence before he spoke again. "How about you?"

Fiona looked at him blankly. "What about me?"

"Do you get what you want, Fi? Do you even know what you want?"

She bristled. "What kind of question is that?"

He took so long to reply, she started to fidget. "I haven't seen you since you were fifteen," he said finally. "Then, out of nowhere, you show up wearing a cock-teasing costume that makes you nervous as a cat in a bathtub. You seem nervous. You're twitchy and scared. Something is bugging you, which doesn't surprise me. Any GodsAcre survivor is fucked up by definition. You're not here for fun. What do you want from me?"

So much for the smooth lead-in. Fiona clutched the edge of the desk, trying to bring up the intro of her carefully scripted speech, but it was gone from her head, poof.

"This is going to sound crazy," she said.

"I'm good with crazy," Anton said. "Lots of practice. It doesn't faze me. Out with it."

"Okay." She cleared her throat. "It's about Redd Kimball."

Anton's eyes narrowed. "What about him? The bastard is dead. And I'm glad."

"Well, that's the thing," she said. "He didn't die in the GodsAcre fire. He's still out there. And now he's trying to kill me."

3

edd Kimball. Alive.

It rang in his head like a big iron bell. Anton didn't breathe. He just stood there, like he was still waiting or hoping for her to take her words back so that he wouldn't have to process that information.

It sparked a flare of killing rage that he wasn't sure he could control.

The muffled thumping of the heavy electronic beat from the nightclub below swelled in their ears in the tense silence.

There was a very simple reason why he hadn't invited Fiona to sit down on one of the couches. Or gotten up to offer her a drink, as courtesy demanded.

He didn't dare move. His dick was too hard.

He was intensely aware of every detail of her. Her lips, her eyes, her hair. The sinuous shape of her body. Her scent and heat worked on him like an aphrodisiac drug.

So far, he'd masked it from her, or hoped that he had. If

he didn't stir an inch. If he kept his leg crossed and kept his elbow angled over it and didn't move a goddamn muscle. But no fucking way was he standing up and letting her see his erection. Fiona had endured enough from Kimball. She'd been groped and grabbed and perved on and slavered over, and he wasn't putting himself into Kimball's category minutes after seeing her for the first time in thirteen years.

Hey, girl. Been a while. Say hi to my high hard one. He's glad to see you, too.

"You don't believe me." Fiona sounded unsurprised.

She'd misread his startled silence. "Fi, I didn't say that I—"

"I don't blame you. Believe me, I know how crazy it sounds. But it has to be Kimball. It's the only explanation for the things that have been happening to me."

Anton closed his eyes for a moment, breathing down the red fog of rage and confusion that Kimball's name had invoked.

Concentrate, dickhead. Listen to what she has to say. This is about her. Not you.

He opened his eyes, and looked up at her. The light above her head lit up the edges of her red hair like a burning halo. "Tell me why you think it's him," he said, keeping his voice rigidly calm.

She nodded. "Okay. So after you and your brothers broke me out of GodsAcre, I went to my Aunt Michelle in California. As you know."

"I remember," he said. "I bought the bus ticket."

"Right. So, I turned up unannounced on the doorstep of my Aunt Michelle and my cousin Patti. My cousin was a few years younger than me, but she seemed older. And younger, too, at the same time. If that makes any sense."

"It does." Memories of those that bizarre year of high school in Shaw's Crossing after the fire that destroyed GodsAcre flashed through his mind, and his body.

At almost eighteen, he'd felt like a total alien in that suffocating little town on the lake. Shaw's Crossing was like another planet, after Jeremiah's remote doomsday prepper enclave in the mountains. And that was entirely apart from the nightmare story of the fire.

Anton and his brothers were lethally trained commando warriors who could kill in countless different ways, but they'd never played a video game, or seen Friday night football, or gone to a movie theater, or walked through a shopping mall. They'd never even watched a fucking TV show. He and Eric and Mace had felt like time travelers from a long-past century, adrift in a noisy, senseless world filled with unspecified dangers against which they had no clue how to defend themselves.

They'd learned, though. Fast. The bullies had learned to keep their distance in a hurry. The fact that the three of them had managed not to kill anyone during that surreal period of adjustment was a miracle in itself, in retrospect. It had probably been a closer shave than anyone ever needed to know. Otis himself might not have guessed the mortal danger that some of those teenaged assholes at Shaw's Crossing High School had been in during the Trask brothers' first, critical phase of culture shock.

Somehow, they got through it without breaking any necks or slitting any throats.

"Patti tried so hard to help me," Fiona went on. "You know, in trying to act like a normal girl, whatever the hell that meant. I was such a freak in high school."

"Yeah, us, too," he agreed. "Everything was different

than how we'd been taught."

"Exactly. So there I was, parked with Patti and Michelle. My aunt was just hoping that Mom would show up and take some responsibility for me. Then we heard the news about the fire. And Aunt Michelle stepped up for me. Became my legal guardian." She paused for a moment. "Thank God. I would have been so screwed without them."

"Your mom would have gotten there eventually, if it hadn't been for the fire," Anton said. "She wanted to follow you. She wanted out of that godawful place so bad. Everyone did in the end."

Fiona looked perplexed. "How do you know what my mom wanted?"

"She told me," Anton said. "When she came to thank me for helping you escape."

He remembered Bridget Garrett's brief, surreptitious visit vividly. He'd been in the infirmary at the time, in agonizing pain after Kimball had flogged him for the crime of spiriting Fiona away from the marriage bed.

Fiona's mouth tightened. "Oh. You mean, doing her job for her?"

Fair enough. Fiona had a right to be angry. Bridget should have protected her daughter. Someone else, preferably a grown-ass adult, should have tried harder to oppose the toxic craziness of that place. But by that time, things had taken on runaway train momentum. Jeremiah had lost his shit, everyone else was confused, cowed and scared. Jeremiah's mind had been completely disordered at the end, and that sadistic prick Kimball was running GodsAcre himself, gleefully administering draconian punishments left and right. Kimball had flogged Anton personally, having discovered that he had a natural talent for it. Anton was lucky to have

29

survived.

He hadn't felt lucky at the time.

"She should have protected you," he agreed. "She knew that. She felt guilty."

Fiona turned away. "Well," she said, her voice low. "She failed, and then she died. So it means essentially nothing."

"If you say so," Anton said. "Let's get back to why you think Kimball's alive."

Fiona nodded, and cleared her throat. "So anyhow, my cousin Patti tried to help me pass for normal, as best she could. I got through high school. Went to college, studied programming, coding, web design, internet marketing. I started a website service that matches students to career programs in art and graphic design, and I was expanding to do the same for music schools. The schools pay a fee for anyone I match to them who enrolls. I was doing okay. I had eight people working for me full-time, all remotely. I bought myself a cottage on the beach in Highettsville."

"If you can afford a house on the beach anywhere in Southern California, then you were doing better than okay," Anton said.

She shrugged. "I didn't have money problems, if that's what you mean. Until recently, anyway. Um...this is really hard to talk about. Please don't interrupt again."

"Got it. Sorry."

She paused for a moment, gathering her thoughts. "So, a few weeks ago, I went to a professional conference. I don't go to many, because I'm a kind of a hermit, but it was a good networking opportunity, and some of the people who work for me were going. So I gritted my teeth and went. Patti asked me if she could come down from San Francisco and stay at my cottage while I was gone. She'd just gotten dumped by some no-good boyfriend and she wanted some soothing beach time. I said yes, of course. I was gone for a little over a week. And when I came home…"

Her voice choked off as if a hand had squeezed her throat. She rubbed the front of her neck, mouth tight. Eyes shut. She clearly didn't want to let herself cry in front of him.

"Are you okay?" he asked carefully.

"They'd killed her." It burst out of her, fast and high-pitched as if the words were under pressure. "I found her lying face-down in the kitchen. Her throat had been cut. Blood was everywhere. The floor, the walls. They tore off her shirt. Cut up her back."

Anton's hands closed to fists. He let out a long, slow breath, trying to calm down the freaked-out stress response happening in his body as he pictured her, all alone, coming home to a scene of horrific butchery.

Goddamn. He had to keep cool, lucid, logical. To help her. *Chill out, bonehead.*

"Fi," he said. "I'm so sorry." The phrase felt stiff in his mouth. Flat, threadbare, useless, trite. There should be something better to say, but he didn't know it.

"It hadn't been very long," Fiona said. "She was still…" She coughed to clear her throat. "It had been ten to twelve hours. That was what the crime scene techs said."

"It's fucking awful, Fi," he said. "I hate that this happened to her, and you. But I don't see the connection."

"I haven't finished yet," Fiona said.

"By all means, then." He gestured for her to go on. "Tell me the rest."

Fiona twisted her fingers together. "Do you remember when I got flogged? After I tried to run away from Kimball the first time?"

Yeah, he fucking remembered that. In vivid detail. That was the night that he'd decided that GodsAcre needed to end. And that Redd Kimball urgently needed to die.

He'd fully intended to kill that bastard himself. He didn't give rat's ass about consequences, even if they killed him for it. Fuck them all. It would have been worth it.

But the catastrophic GodsAcre fire had beaten him to it. While simultaneously destroying everything else in his world.

"I had scarring afterward," she went on. "A few of the cuts were really deep. One scar in particular was always sore and red. I took it for nerve damage. Figured I should just suck it up. Sometimes stuff just hurts for no good reason, right? You know how you can just get used to pain? Until it doesn't even occur to you that you could ease it?"

He nodded.

"Well, it was like that. Then five years ago, I was riding my bike downtown, and some guy opened his street side car door. I was thrown from the bike—"

"Oh, ouch," he said, wincing. "Fuck, Fi."

She waved that away with a dismissive flap of her hand, and straightened up from her perch, pacing around to the other side of the desk. "I promise this is relevant to my story," she assured him. "It's not just a list of all my random cuts and bruises since I last saw you. So anyhow, I broke my arm and some ribs in that accident, no big deal. But when they X-rayed me, they found a sub-dermal capsule in my back. Embedded in the scar tissue. Of that scar that never quite healed. The one that always hurt."

Anton sat bolt upright in his chair. "The *fuck*?"

"Yeah, I know. It grossed me out, too. Someone stuck that thing into my wound before they stitched it up. The capsule was hidden inside in the deepest scar."

"What was on it?" he asked.

"A computer chip was inside the capsule," she said. "All that I found on the chip was a link to a password-protected portal. But I never managed to get through the portal. It's a mystery. Probably always will be."

"Where's that chip now?"

Fiona pointed at her right earring, a gleaming teardrop bead of white gold. "Right here."

"You wear it?" He was taken aback. "On your body?"

"Day and night." Fiona unfastened the earring and carefully unscrewed the hanging bead. She held it up, and he saw a plastic protective capsule protruding from a hollow cavity inside the bead. "I had the earring designed for it. It's always with me."

She came forward and handed it to him. He held it gingerly, as if it were alive.

Then he looked up into her eyes. "Jesus, Fi," he said quietly.

"It's my river rock," she told him. "To remind me of where I came from. But I can't cave in anyone's head with it, unfortunately."

"It's messed up," he told her. "Take it off, flush it down the toilet and move on. Kimball's dead and gone. Stop dragging him around with you. That thing is poisonous."

"I know, but I can't. Believe me, I've tried. But it's got its hooks into me. It's like a compulsion." Fiona fingered the teardrop bead. "I felt so violated. On top of all the other slime he flung at me, he'd put something inside of my body for safekeeping. I carried that chip around for him without even knowing it for eight years. I will never stop wondering why. I can't let it go, Anton. I need to know. So…there it is. That's

33

why I'm here. Someone killed Patti, taking her for me. They looked for something in her back, with a knife. The only person who knew about that chip would be Kimball. So...I thought you'd want to know that bastard is still alive. If I were you, I'd want to know."

He tried to breathe out the tension building inside him, but with all his relentless practice at controlling his own mind, it wasn't working today.

"Why are you so sure it was Kimball who put it there?" he asked. "Or that it was Kimball who killed Patti? Do you have any proof of that?"

She gave him an incredulous look. "No, but who else would? He had the opportunity. He was running GodsAcre at the end. Everyone else was running scared. Besides, it just has his stamp on it. The gross factor, you know? He got off on using people, humiliating them, making them feel small. What could be more humiliating than using my body as a goddamn envelope?" She paused for a moment. "Other than the obvious, of course," she added grimly. "And that would have been next for me if you hadn't busted me out of there."

Anton was swift to change the subject back to the computer chip. "You don't actually remember him putting that capsule into you, right?"

Fiona hesitated. "No," she admitted. "I must have been unconscious. Like I said, I didn't even know it was there. And now there's no one left to ask. Everyone else who might possibly have known something about it is dead."

"So is Kimball, Fi." It came out harsher than he meant for it to sound. A flat statement of fact. "He's one of the twenty-three GodsAcre adults who had dental records on file that the techs could use for comparison. He is definitely dead. There are pictures of his charred skull in the police files."

"Hear me out, Anton," she said. "I'm not finished yet."

Anton settled back into his chair, his jaw aching with tension. "Go on."

"I found Patti face-down in my kitchen. Her back was covered in slashes, and the deepest cuts were right where the doctor had found that capsule on me five years ago. There were other slashes, but they looked more random. Like someone hadn't found what they wanted and had a tantrum with the knife." She stopped, calming the shaking in her throat by swallowing over and over. "The evidence techs told me those cuts in her back were post-mortem," she finished.

"You think someone wanted this chip, mistook Patti for you and killed her to get the chip out of her back," he said flatly.

"Is there any other logical explanation? Given the circumstances?"

"None of this is logical, Fi," he said.

"It's the plain facts," she insisted. "How else can I interpret them?"

He let out a slow breath. "Was Patti similar to you in looks?" he asked.

"Very much so. Two peas in a pod, my Aunt Michelle used to say." Fiona reached into her evening bag and pulled out her phone, tapping at it. "My mother and my aunt both had the Garrett look. Tall, redheaded, freckled, big mouth, big eyebrows. And we both looked like our moms. Here, take a look. This is a picture of the two of us just last year."

He loved Fi's eyebrows. They were thick and dark and bold, winging across her face at a dramatic angle. With her sharp cheekbones and her full, sexy mouth, she had that striking bone structure and stunning eyes that made heavy eyebrows look good.

But instinct warned him against making personal comments about her looks. Not in the context of this conversation.

In the photo she showed him, Fiona stood by a smiling girl, their arms around each other's shoulders. Superficially, they were similar. Both were tall and slim, with long, thick red hair. Both would attract attention wherever they went, the kind of rubbernecking that caused car accidents. But beyond the superficially obvious, they weren't alike at all. Patti's red hair was layered, blown out and styled into loose, fashionable ringlets while Fi's kinked wildly around her shoulders, untamed. The younger girl's face was softer, rounder. Her laughing blue eyes flirted with the camera while Fiona's gray eyes sliced into the viewer's gaze like twin knives. Fi's body was tighter, sculpted and toned. Patti's frame was slighter, with narrower shoulders. Fragile looking.

There was nothing fragile about Fi. Her strength was on full display at all times. It worked on his hormones like gasoline on a bonfire. The way she looked in that silver mini dress, God. It made him want to leap at her like a starving predator. *Gimme that.*

Chill. Down, boy. She was bereaved, afraid. She'd come to him for help.

Dressed for seduction.

He cleared his throat self-consciously. "It looks like you worked out a lot more than she did." The only comment he dared to offer.

"Martial arts," Fiona said. "But you can see how someone could have taken her for me, right? Especially if they hadn't seen me recently."

He studied the women in the photo, trying to make himself see the similarities rather than the yawning abyss of differences. Maybe they were differences that only a veteran of GodsAcre could sense.

"I see how, I guess," he admitted. "What I don't see is why."

"They attacked her in my house, Anton! They searched for the chip in her back! With a knife!"

"The wounds in her back could be a coincidence," he said.

She gave him an incredulous look. "They tried again, Anton. Three days later, after they read the news and figured out that they killed the wrong woman. They attacked me again, outside the hotel where I was staying in downtown Highettsville."

Anton's body contracted, imagining it. "Did they hurt you?"

She shook her head. "No, just a couple of bruises. They weren't expecting me to fight back as hard as I did. I stunned one of them by bashing his head into the car door. Kicked the other one in the head and ran like hell, screaming at the top of my lungs. Too many people were around, so they backed off. For now."

He was taken aback. "You fought them off all by yourself? For real?"

"Don't look so surprised," she said. "It's the one thing Jeremiah's training was useful for. I've never had to eat bugs to survive, or stitch up my own bullet wounds, or skin my own squirrels. But I can kick ass if I need to. Hard enough to give myself an opening to run, at least."

"Wish I could have seen it," he said. "Must have been a hell of a show."

"Hardly." Fiona's voice was grim. "If those pricks were the same ones who killed Patti, I should have broken every bone in their bodies except for their jaws, so they could have been interrogated. But they took me by surprise, and I panicked. I ran like a rabbit and let those bastards get away. I was so pissed at myself."

"Don't be," he said. "It's amazing that you could fight off two killers singlehandedly and get clear of them. I would have done the same myself."

"Oh, please," she said. "What bullshit. Not Jeremiah's shining star. The Anton I knew would have beaten them to a pulp and tied them up with a freaking bow."

Anton rolled his eyes. "Please. Don't even start with that. That was old and tired even back when we were kids."

"Sorry, but it's the simple truth," Fiona said. "You can't get away from it. Jeremiah always held you, Eric and Mace up as examples for the rest of us. His star pupils."

"Yeah, and Jeremiah was a huge pain in the ass. I did not appreciate it at the time," he said. "Neither did Eric or Mace. And this is exactly why."

"Especially you, the oldest," Fiona continued, relentless. "The cream of the crop. The vanguard of the army of the righteous. But the rest of us lowly foot soldier grunts picked up a few useful skills, too, here and there."

"I'm glad those skills served you," Anton said. "I'm glad at least some of the crazy shit we learned at GodsAcre was useful for something. What do the police think?"

Fiona's mouth tightened. "The police don't know what to think. They definitely suspect that my life is more complicated than I let on, but they can't find any proof, and that's because there isn't any. I wasn't supposed to leave town after what happened, but to be honest, Highettsville is much safer without me in it. I'm sure the cops there would be glad to see the last of me, after all my troubles."

Eric and Demi's near-deadly misadventures up at GodsAcre last week flashed through Anton's mind. But how the fuck could there be any connection to that? How was that even remotely possible?

It wasn't. It couldn't be. They were all dead. Dead in that fire. Everyone but Fiona, himself, and his two brothers. He'd said the same thing to Demi and Eric. Whoever was gunning for Fiona, it couldn't be Kimball, or anyone else from their past.

He was hesitant to mention Demi's and Eric's troubles to Fi, though. In her grieving, paranoid state, she could seize on that and build it up in her mind into something that it wasn't. She might draw connections that didn't exist.

Best not to conflate those two separate disasters. Kimball was dead. GodsAcre was a moldering ruin. He would do Fiona no favors by getting her all worked up about Eric and Demi's misadventures.

But he wasn't going to let her wander around unprotected until he knew who the fuck was attacking her. And then destroyed that filthy bastard with his bare hands.

He laid the capsule containing the computer chip in the middle of the desk.

"So," he said, very cautiously. "Nothing is happening in your current life that could have possibly triggered all this. You're absolutely sure of that?"

Her brows snapped together. "Seriously, Anton? You think I lead a secret life as a criminal, or a drug dealer, or a mafia mistress?"

"I wouldn't judge you if you did," he said. "I know where you came from. I saw what was done to you. People get complicated under pressure. A GodsAcre escapee will always win the first prize in a most-fucked-up-childhood competition."

She laughed out loud. "Sorry to disappoint you, but I'm actually not that complicated," she said. "I'm squeaky clean. Like I said, I'm a hermit. I live alone, I work alone. My business activity is all virtual, my employees live all over the country. I shop online, I get my groceries delivered and left in a big wooden box at the end of the driveway so I won't have to deal with the delivery person. The only place I go regularly is a martial arts dojo three times a week to train. I bother absolutely no one. It would not be possible to be more reclusive and boring than I am."

He looked her up and down. Boring, his ass. "Hard to believe."

"Believe it," she told him.

"So they haven't tried attacking you again?"

"Not yet, but probably just because they haven't caught up with me yet. I've been moving constantly, and using only my cash. Paranoid, maybe, but what can you do."

"Me, too," he admitted. "Paranoia comes with the territory for us Prophet's spawn."

"Prophet's spawn?"

Anton was embarrassed to have let that slip. "That's just a random insult we got back in high school," he told her. "Me, Mace and Eric started calling each other that as a joke when we were living in Shaw's Crossing. It wasn't a good joke, but it stuck."

"Prophet's spawn," she repeated slowly. "Yeah, that sounds right. And it's why I'm here. Only another Prophet's spawn could understand what I'm talking about."

"You think they're still out there looking for you?" Anton asked.

"Of course they are," she said. "They want their chip

SHANNON McKENNA

back. They're happy to kill for it. But they won't get it. Bastards."

They gazed at each other. She seemed to be waiting for something from him. He was afraid to guess what it was. She was wound up so tight. He didn't want to get this wrong. "So what exactly are you asking from me, Fi?" he asked.

"I was hoping…" She stopped, bit her lip. Then she took a deep, slow breath and tried again. "No one gets it," she said. "And I can't really blame them. It all sounds crazy when I tell my story. Like one of Jeremiah's paranoid rants. But I thought…maybe you would get it. You were there. You knew Kimball. How evil he was."

"Yes, I did." Anton refreshed the picture on the smartphone screen with a tap and held it up to her. "But aside from him being officially dead, there's another thing. You and Patti definitely have a family resemblance, but no one who knows you would mistake you two. I wouldn't, and Kimball wouldn't, either, if he were alive. Not even after thirteen years."

"He could have used hired muscle, like the guys who attacked me at the hotel," Fiona argued. "He could have just given them an address and a description and a photo. Patti could absolutely be mistaken for me in a photo."

Anton braced himself. "Fi, face it," he said. "It can't be Kimball. You have to let that go."

Fiona's face stiffened. "You're so sure. After the story I just told you."

"I saw the fire myself," Anton said. "Kimball was in the Great Hall with all the others. No one got out of there. No one could have survived that place. It was a fucking inferno. They were all trapped inside. Someone had put big padlocks on the inside of every exit. They found them afterward, still locked.

41

The whole thing happened really fast."

Fiona picked up the capsule and screwed the bead of her earring back together, fastening it back into her ear. "I know," she said. "But someone put this thing into my body thirteen years ago, and now someone wants it back bad enough to kill for it. Who else knew it was in there?"

"I understand, but—"

"They killed my Patti." Her voice began to shake. "She was a good person. Sweet. She never hurt anyone in her life. They tried to kill me, too, and they'll keep on trying until I'm sliced into ribbons. Who would do that but Kimball? Who else would hate me that much?"

He held her gaze without flinching. "Kimball's charred body was fused to his mattress springs," he said. "His teeth matched the dental X-rays. It was a positive match. The forensics experts had no doubts."

"I know this, Anton! But I still—"

"There's a lot we don't know about the GodsAcre fire. How it started. Who put those padlocks on the doors. Why he did it. We'll never know the answers to those questions. I had to move on or go fucking crazy wondering. So do you, Fi. Let's not dispute those few verifiable facts that we actually have. Please. That way lies chaos."

"Chaos. Yeah. That pretty much describes my life recently." Fiona picked her phone and slid it into her bag. "So you think I'm crazy." Her voice shook. "Someone is after me, trying to kill me. And you don't believe me."

"I did not say that, and by no means do I think you're crazy," Anton said. "I think you're amazing. A survivor. A powerhouse. I admire the living hell out of you. You're not crazy, Fi. You were forged in fire."

She waved that away. "Never mind the sweet nothings.

Patti's death is real. So is the attack on me at the hotel. Those incidents were both reported in the local newspapers. They're a matter of public record. Read about them online. Go on, look them up on your phone. Everything I said is independently verifiable."

"There's no need for that," Anton said. "I never said I thought you were lying, and I never said you weren't attacked. I'm sorry about your cousin being killed. I don't dispute that you're in danger, and I'll protect you from—"

"That's gallant of you, but it's not about that." Fiona's voice was tight. "I wanted to bounce ideas off one of the few people in the world who might actually believe me. So much for that hope."

"Fi, I didn't mean to—"

"Patti was on a very short list of people on this earth that I give a shit about. I'm going to find her killers and crush them. If it kills me, which it very well might. I understand if you'd rather continue to believe that scumbag is still dead. I'd do it myself if I could. But I don't have that luxury. So never mind. Forget I came. I'll take it from here."

"Stop, Fi," he said forcefully. "Listen. The world is filled with bad shit. No arguments there. You're just hitting a fresh patch. You think it's Kimball out of habit, but it can't be him. I'm not saying that your bad guys doesn't exist. I'm just saying that they're new bad guys. Same evil, new packaging. Just as bad. Just as dangerous. So let's put aside the issue of Kimball, and concentrate on—"

"What about the way they cut up Patti's back? How do you account for that?"

"I can't account for anything," he said. "I don't have the answer, Fi. I'm sorry."

Fiona's lip shook, but she sucked it sternly into her

mouth. Tears were a luxury she clearly did not permit herself. "I should have said this sooner," she said, her tone suddenly formal. "But I owe you my life. You got me out of that place just in time. Being married to Kimball would have been the death of me, literally. So, um, thanks. Come to think of it, I probably should have led with that as soon as I walked in."

"I don't need any thanks," Anton said. "I'm glad I got you out in time. And I'm really glad you were safe and gone when the fire happened. I just hope that your aunt's place in California was a better life for you."

"It could hardly have been worse than GodsAcre," she said. "But yeah, it was an okay place for me to land. I was lucky to have my aunt, until she died last year. And I had Patti." Her face contracted. "Um...anyhow. I'll go now. Sorry I bothered you."

"Fi. Don't." His hand shot out and caught her wrist.

The contact was pure energy. It blazed through then, making him stiffen and gasp.

Fiona looked down at his hand clamped around her wrist. His big, thick-knuckled fingers, covered with tattoo art, dark against her freckled skin. "I have to go, Anton."

"Where?" he demanded. "To some economy hotel on a strip mall somewhere? Nothing but a door lock and a flimsy chain between you and your problem?"

"Not your problem," she said. "Don't worry about it. I'm managing."

"The hell I won't," he said. "You can't walk away after what you just told me."

"It's not up to you." She tugged at her arm. "Let go, Anton."

His fingers tightened. "Stop playing games with me. You've been up in my face and flaunting yourself since you showed up at the door, Fi. Starting with that dress."

"Oh, please," she snapped. "Give me a break."

"That wasn't calculated? You strike those red-hot sexpot poses with every man you talk to?"

"I'm dressed for a nightclub. Don't take it personally."

"So you're the only one who gets to take things personally, then? Strutting around this shit neighborhood in the middle of the night dressed like a call girl?"

"That's Jeremiah talking, and I don't have to listen to that crap anymore. I was fine coming here, and I'll be fine leaving. God help the fool who tries to mess with me."

He stood up, towering over her. No longer any reason to hide his hard-on. "Stay with me," he urged. "You'll be safe with me. Whenever I'm not personally with you, I'll have highly-trained security agents covering you twenty-four seven."

That look in her eyes pulled at him. Anger, defiance, fear. He felt it with his secret senses, forged in the crucible of GodsAcre. They'd grown up in a hothouse of pathological fear. Anton recognized fear when he saw it, no matter how it masked itself.

Even fearful, her wild, beautiful energy pulled him like a tow chain.

She shifted backward, but the desk blocked her retreat. Anton waited for a cue. She moistened her lips until they gleamed, her breath hitching shaky and fast.

She could step to the side if she wanted to. He wouldn't stop her.

She didn't. She just reached down with both hands, and clutched the edge of the desk. Anchoring herself, as if he were a high wind she had to brace against.

She didn't flinch when he lifted her up and set her on

his desk. Leaning closer, into her heat, her scent. Falling into each other's gravitational field. It felt inevitable, like the pull of a star. She seized his upper arms, steadying herself.

He inhaled her sweet, hot scent, lost in her huge, varicolored eyes. Her warmth, the smooth, tender texture of her soft skin. New leaves, flower petals.

And then he was kissing her. Helplessly, desperately. Like he was miles underwater.

Like he'd been holding his breath for thirteen fucking years.

Like she was his only source of air.

4

Fiona wound her arms around his big shoulders. She craved his heat, his energy.

This was so sweet. She was going to pay for this in blood. And she didn't care.

His kisses were a revelation. A wordless truth she'd never grasped, finally made plain. His strength and tenderness enveloped her, his warm lips moved over hers. The kiss was deep and sweet and searching. His flavor intoxicated her. He was the taste of wildness and magic, freedom and power. Wind in her hair and ocean waves crashing on the shore, huge and hypnotic and endless. The milky glitter of stars splashed over a midnight sky. The melding of mouths, the sensual dance of their tongues.

It was the lure and promise of the unknown—and a glimpse of the glories beyond.

She finally understood the fluid language of kissing. It slid into place in her mind, no more faking or guesswork. She knew what they were saying to each other, and she would never be done saying it. It was infinite. Endless.

And she was falling to pieces. She felt unspeakably vulnerable. Helpless with yearning. That hot, restless ache, so deep in her body was like nothing she'd ever felt.

A spell had been lifted, and some previously unknown part of her was running wild and frenzied. Driven wild by this sudden release. No reasoning with it, no controlling it.

Anton had defined her taste in men. Men were only attractive insofar as they resembled him, and even after thirteen years she still had dreams about him and woke up with her heart pumping like she'd been sprinting.

But her girlish dreams were tame in comparison to the real Anton's rock-hard, solid manhood. His seething heat, the muscles in his thighs as unyielding as steel cables.

She hung on for dear life. Gasping for a mouthful of air so she could to get back to kissing, tasting, exploring. She ran her fingertips over the hot, supple skin of his face, feeling his high cheekbones, the rasp of stubble on his jaw.

She felt so moved. This feeling, welling up and overflowing. The warmth. The softness. The wanting. It was too much. She just…couldn't. She didn't dare.

She pulled away, and hid her face against his jacket. This was uncharted territory. This was not part of the plan. This could destroy her.

"So hot," he whispered. "So sweet."

"I'm not sweet," she muttered, her voice muffled against his shoulder.

"I just tasted you. I say you are." He nuzzled her hair. "Come home with me."

God, what a fabulous prospect. But she knew what would happen if she accepted it. She already felt naked, unraveled. She had to stay strong.

She pushed him away, and he went still, eyes wary. "What is it, Fi?"

"I'm sorry," she said, her voice small. "I don't mean to jerk you around. And I don't want to be a bitch. But I didn't come here just to get nailed."

His gaze narrowed. "I'll back off if you want. Just be clear."

The subtle reproach in his words put her on the defensive. "I didn't mean for that to happen," she said. "That…came out of nowhere."

Anton shrugged. "I don't think so," he said. "It was a long time coming."

"I just wanted someone to believe me," she said. "If I can't get that here, I can't get it anywhere. So it's time to move on."

"I never said your problem wasn't real. Just that it's unlikely that it's Kimball. It doesn't matter who's after you. I'll still help. We'll pin down whoever's messing with you together, and I'll help you make him pay for hurting your cousin. You have my word."

"And the sex would just be a bonus?"

Anton's eyes sharpened. "What does sex have to do with anything? If it happens, it happens. And only if you want it. I won't pressure you. No strings."

She slid out from between him and the desk, cursing the wobbling heels. It was hard to balance when her knees were shaking. "There's no such thing as no-strings sex."

Anton's eyes burned with controlled anger. "You're being unreasonable."

"Yeah, I get that a lot," she told him, backing away. "It's the reason I work alone. Look, this shouldn't have happened. I have to go hunt whoever hurt Patti. I'm sorry, because you are super-hot, and I'd love to indulge, I really would. But I just don't have the bandwidth to be your red-hot sex kitten right now."

"Fi, calm down."

Her back hit the hanging blinds that covered the viewing window, rattling them.

Fiona became conscious of the pulsing vibration of the music below. Anton's intense masculine energy had dominated her senses so completely, she'd forgotten the dance floor was there, despite the thumping beat that shook the building.

"I'm sorry." She lurched toward the door. "I shouldn't have bothered you. I'll take it from here. Bye."

"Aw, fuck. Fi!"

She burst through the door, and was confronted with Nate Murphy and the big Asian bouncer, identical startled looks on their faces. She must look like a woman who'd just been kissed senseless by the ultimate dreamy sex god, Anton Trask.

Surely she wasn't the first, and she certainly wouldn't be the last.

She wiped her eyes, and her hand came away streaked with mascara. The psycho girl look. Wet-eyed, feral, mascara-smudged raccoon mask. Hair out to here. Face hot. Mouth swollen and tingling from his kisses. Scared half to death by freaking everything. Including the way Anton made her feel. Such a dumb thing to be wound up about now.

She felt like she was running for her life as she bolted for the door.

Icy-hearted killers she could maybe outwit, or even overcome, if she was fast, and took them by surprise. And fought like a screeching hag from hell. Maybe.

But not if she felt like this. Exposed, naked, shivering. Vulnerable.

She couldn't do battle in this condition.

5

nton burst into the connecting room to find both Nate and Jim Wong frowning at him. He stopped his headlong charge with enormous effort. He couldn't physically detain her, not in her current state of mind. But he had to protect her.

"Follow her," Anton directed Nate. "I can't lose sight of her. I'll get the car and catch up. I need to know the hotel where she's staying."

Nate looked bemused. "Seriously? That's my job description now? Stalking your disgruntled girlfriends for you? Jesus, Anton."

"This isn't a lover's quarrel," he snarled. "She's in danger and I have to watch her back." He turned to the security screens. "Where is she now?"

"Malik?" Nate growled into his headset. "Eyes on the knockout redhead with the silver thigh-high boots coming down the stairs...yeah, that's the one. Tail her until I get down there to take over. Boss's orders, that's why...none of your business. Just do it." He gave Anton a martyred look. "I'll go catch up with Malik. Hurry up with the car, man. I don't want to spend my night tailing your flame. That is not a good use of my time."

Anton ignored that. "Hang way back," he warned. "She knows your face. Don't let her see you, or she'll rip your head off. She's a skilled martial artist." He turned to Wong. "You come with me in the car. And get the gun safe open."

"Jesus. The things we do to get by," Nate muttered under his breath as he left.

Wong and Anton loaded up with the stash he had in the safe. A Beretta 93, two H&K MP5K machine pistols, a couple of Glock 19s, several loaded magazines. Anton kept his armory in tiptop working order, cleaning and testing and practicing regularly. Jeremiah's training, pounded into him at a tender age. Old habits never died. Not this one, anyhow. Not for his brothers, either.

The elevator in his office that took them down to his dedicated garage had never been so fucking slow. Anton set the garage door to grind open as he and Wong got into the black Porsche Cayenne and revved the engine as he waited. He accelerated through the door the instant it rose high enough. "Call Nate," he directed.

Wong put the call through. "Hey, dude. Update?" He listened, and looked at Anton. "Walking north," he relayed. "Headed toward the warehouse parking lot."

"Stay on the line," Anton directed.

"You got it, boss."

Anton didn't blame Fiona for panicking. The trauma she'd been through changed a person on a chemical level. He'd learned that firsthand after the GodsAcre disaster. His stress flashbacks had gotten less severe with time, but his hyper-vigilance had never really subsided. It was a constant, low-level buzz in the back of his mind, keeping him always combat-ready. Just like Fi. Skittish and wary. Ready to bolt, or else fight like hell.

Seeing Fiona had jacked him way up into the red zone, which was right where he was going to stay until he was sure she was safe in an armed fortress. With him.

This whole thing felt like the Prophet's curse. The Trask brothers' catch-all phrase for the shit luck that dogged them whenever they were in Shaw's Crossing.

It seemed to be spreading. Like cancer.

Kimball's face floated through his mind. That taunting, self-satisfied glint in that asshole's eyes, when he had something on you and got off on the power it gave him. The memory made Anton's skin prickle and crawl.

Couldn't be Kimball, he reminded himself again. Let that go. The teeth on that charred skull had matched the dental records. Kimball was done. Dust in the wind.

But there were those fucking death clusters. Groups of people in Shaw's Crossing who had all died of apparently natural causes at suspiciously close intervals. More than once. No sign of foul play. The only suspicious element being the timing.

The latest death cluster had been last week. It had started with Otis.

Otis Trask, the ex-police chief, had taken in Anton and his brothers after the GodsAcre fire. He'd kicked their rebellious asses through high school and out into the world. A hard, stern, uncompromising man, but he truly cared about them.

Anton still hadn't processed Otis's death yet. It was still sinking in, drip by drip.

And Eric was convinced that Otis's death, apparently a stroke, had been murder.

Three people made up last week's death cluster. After Otis, there was Terry Cattrall, the real estate agent who had gone up to do an appraisal of GodsAcre. Demi's father, Benedict Vaughan, was the third victim. Vaughan had been involved with the thugs that had attacked Eric and Demi. No one knew how, but no one was all that surprised. Ben Vaughan had always been an asshole. Anton would shed no tears for that guy. Not many would.

And Otis had gone up to GodsAcre the night before he'd died . He'd found the place full of cars, trucks, earth-moving equipment, and a huge hole in the ground near where the caverns used to be before Mace and Eric blew them up the night of the fire.

Otis had tried to tell them more. He'd left messages on their phones, urging them to call and hinting at important info that he wanted to deliver in person.

They hadn't gotten back to him in time. He died that same night.

They were stopped at a fucking interminable red light, cars in front of him, cars behind. He sat there, fingers drumming the wheel, on the verge of exploding. He shouldn't have let Fiona leave the club. At the cost of zip-tying her and locking her in a room. *Fuck.*

"Give me that phone." He took the phone from Wong's hand and held it to his ear. "Status report?"

"Don't micromanage," Nate growled. "I've got her covered. And you better find some other asshole to sit outside her hotel, because I do not feel like doing that tonight."

Anton ignored that. "You've got eyeballs on her right now?"

"Yes. In my direct line of sight. In those boots she'd be visible from space. She's walking through the parking lot by Malheur Imports, and she…oh *fuck* me!"

"What?" Anton yelled. "What just happened?"

"Black Dodge Ram. Four big guys. They just threw her inside, and they're on the move. Doubling back onto Hastings, northbound. Haul ass and pick me up!"

Tires squealed as Anton darted and weaved through the traffic, horns all around him blatting in angry protest.

6

Fiona kicked out blindly, landing a blow on somebody's fleshy thigh. A grunt, a curse. *Crack*, everything went black…

…and then pain and noise roared back again in a massive, sickening wave.

Someone punched her lower back. She tried not to cry out as the blow landed. She'd be peeing blood for a while. If she ever got the chance to do anything so mundane as pee again.

Don't. No space in your head for that. Not helpful.

The Jeremiah litany in her head kicked into action. *Pain is all in your head. Just a story you tell yourself.* That last had been one of the Prophet's favorites. *Pain can only hurt you if you believe in it.* Same rule went for fear.

Hah. Say it until your throat cracked, but pain still hurt. And she was still scared.

Someone had duct-taped her wrists behind her back. Her shoulder sockets burned. The SUV swerved from lane to lane. There were several men in the car, and even through the burlap sack, they stank. She smelled their sour armpits, their foul breath, their feet.

Someone put a clammy hand on her bare thigh and pinched. She kicked out explosively, unable to stop herself.

Whack, right to the head. Her punishment.

Don't vomit in the bag, she begged her heaving stomach. *Just don't.*

She was grimly resolved to stay conscious. This was no bad dream. The monsters had gotten the better of her. She was fucked. But she had to at least try to fight.

It couldn't have been longer than twenty minutes, if her time sense was to be trusted, when the vehicle slowed to a crawl. The front passenger side door popped open. She heard a clang, the groan of a rusty gate. Cooler air rushed in, giving her goose-bumps.

Something horrible was going happen here. Soon. *Go down spitting nails.*

That persistent hand insinuated itself under her skirt again, fondling her hip. She clenched her teeth and did not allow herself to react. She didn't need another punch to the head. Her stomach was already heaving. Bile burned in the back of her throat.

She had to look as limp and beaten and helpless as possible. Wait like a patient predator for her best chance to do the most possible damage.

It might not be significant damage, bound hand and foot. But she had knees, teeth and her own hard head, and absolutely nothing to lose.

Chains rattled. Bolts were drawn back. The vehicle moved…then stopped.

She stayed limp as she was pulled out, hoisted up. One

man took her by the armpits, another by her legs. They hauled her from some place with very little light to a place with no light at all, at least not through the bag. She smelled motor oil, cement dust, mold. Sounds echoed, like a big warehouse. An animal had died nearby some time ago and decomposed. She caught a dank whiff of bat shit.

An abandoned, forgotten place, far from help. No one would hear her scream.

They flung her down and she hit a cold, damp concrete floor, *whump*. A bone-rattling, full-body slap. Their voices faded in and out as waves of pain swelled and broke.

"…big waste, if you ask me. I say, have some fun first and then cut it out. She'll be a fucking bloody mess afterward."

"The boss said get the capsule and don't get distracted. He wants her for himself."

"The boss ain't here! Who's gonna know? We don't want all that blood on us, right?"

Fiona's gorge rose. Her heartbeat swelled in her ears.

Play dead. Helpless. Harmless. Beaten. No threat. Just a vulnerable girl.

"…heard how she fought off the guys in California, right? Did you miss that detail, genius? This one's tricky. A real bad bitch. Leave her the fuck alone."

Crap. So much for the harmless damsel act.

"Gimme a fucking break," the first voice complained. "There are five of us. One for each arm and leg, and we take turns."

"Wilson told me what happened after that clusterfuck up at the Hole," the other guy said. "The squad leader was the only survivor and the boss shot that fucker right in the face for screwing up. Wilson spent the rest of the day cleaning up the mess. We get the goods, and we take her straight to him. Boss gets first crack. Maybe you'll get lucky after he's done. If there's anything left."

Dread swamped her, making her mind go dark. She fought to stay conscious.

God, what was it with her? From heaven to hell in a blink. That moment with Anton had been sweet beyond her wildest dreams. Typical, that she took a nosedive into the shredder right afterward.

For something that good, there had to be a reckoning.

And that was the Prophet talking. She had to get that guy out of her head.

The bag was whipped off her head. Fiona coughed out dust and gulped air, spitting out mouthfuls of hair from her dry mouth. She blinked in the thin light of a naked bulb that was dangling on a cord from above. The weak pool of light didn't penetrate far.

The place was what she expected. Empty, echoing. Endless shadows as far as she could see. Shelving units, machines, dust and grime and garbage.

The guy who took off her hood was big, with a face as wide as a dinner plate, pitted with old acne scars. His balding scalp was shiny with oil. He held a long, wicked looking notched knife in his hand. No fussy scalpel for this guy. He meant business.

She cleared her throat. "What do you want from me?"

He backhanded her. "Shut the fuck up, cunt."

She started to mouth off, just on principle, and thought better of it. There was going to be so much pain tonight. No need to beg for more.

"Hold her up," the plate-faced guy growled. "Pull down that dress."

"Now you're talking." It was the first guy she'd heard, the one who had been lobbying to get his raping in before the cutting started. A horse-faced guy with sunken cheeks, wet, purplish lips and bushy eyebrows. He smelled like meat gone bad.

Horse-face wrenched her dress down to the belt around her hips and let out a growl of lascivious approval.

"Stop that shit," the top guy growled. "Hold her still. Move that hair over to the side and get the fuck out of my light."

The other men milled around. One gathered up all her hair in his fist, twisting it into a thick rope and wrenching her head to the side.

"At least we know it's the right girl this time," Horse-face said. "She's got a fuckin' diagram on her back." He pinched her nipple. His hot breath made her gorge rise.

Pop. The sound was big but dull, like loud clap. The chortling and muttering suddenly stopped. No one moved, or breathed.

Fiona saw it first. One of Horse-face's eyes was a dark, gaping hole. Dark blood trickled down his face like tears. The other eye was still looking at her, blinking.

Then the crushing grip of his enormous hands eased. He toppled backward like a chopped tree.

"Fuck!" someone bawled. "Rafe's shot!"

Pop. Another man lurched forward, falling to his knees. Someone was out there in the dark, shooting with a silenced gun. *How...?*

The room erupted into gunfire and Fiona hit the ground. She opened her eyes, and found her face just inches from Rafe's one staring eye. Blood was pooled below his head, spreading toward her. She didn't dare move. Gunshots stuttered over her.

Rough hands grabbed her and hauled her up against a man's chest. Plate-face was using her as a shield. His thick, sweaty arm crushed her throat. She couldn't move her neck. All she could see was the swaying light bulb, but Horse-face and at least one other guy were down, leaving three. She heard more shots. A screech from across the room.

Couldn't breathe. Couldn't see. Passing out. *Air.*

A gun barrel was shoved against her scalp, hot as a brand from being discharged in quick succession. She tried to flinch away, but her head was clamped against his chest, immobilized against the burning metal. *Fuck,* that hurt.

"Stop shooting, or I blow off her head!" Plate-face bellowed.

SHANNON McKENNA

7

Fiona struggled in the moon-faced guy's grip. Every detail of her half-naked body was crystal sharp. She looked like she was lit from the inside in the light cast by that watery, dangling light bulb. Even smeared with blood, she glowed like a star.

Anton stared through the scope of the MP5K, crouched behind a stack of crates. Precision shooting required detachment. He sought the necessary calm. Utter stillness.

The smothering arm of the moonfaced guy had forced Fiona's chin way up. His gun barrel was still buried in the tangled mass of her fiery hair as he backed away, keeping Fiona between them. "I'll blow her fucking head off, prick!" he bellowed.

Anton barely heard him. All he saw were crosshairs wavering over the explosive tangle of Fiona's blood-drenched hair and her assailant's wild eyes, half hidden behind it.

The SUV parked inside the structure fired up. Headlights sliced through darkness as the engine roared to life.

Boom. The sound of glass shattering. Nate had shot out the Dodge's windshield. The headlights slewed away toward the big open door. The guy holding Fiona twisted to look, opening his mouth to yell. Fiona wrenched her jaw free and bit down on his arm.

He shrieked, yanking at his arm. Fiona sagged in his arms, sliding down—

Anton squeezed the trigger. *Boom.*

The man jerked and toppled, taking Fiona down with him.

Anton bolted toward her. He heard the fleeing SUV rev its engine and *thud-thud* loudly over something. Muzzle flashes and gunshots came from the open back door, and then the Dodge accelerated out the open garage door and was gone.

Anton skidded to his knees in a pool of blood. "Fi?" His voice sounded faraway to his own ears after the gun blasts. "You all right? Hurt?"

"I'm good. Just trying to get this beast off me. I can't breathe."

He heaved her attacker's bulk off her and helped her sit up. Her arms were wrenched back behind her. She was covered with blood. Not only blood. The back half of her attacker's head was gone. The former contents of his skull were everywhere.

"Are you shot?" he asked. "You're bleeding."

"Theirs, not mine." She wheezed and coughed. "I was lying in a puddle of it."

"Oh. Fuck. Fi." His hands were shaking. "You're not hurt?"

"Nope. Um, Anton…my hands? Got a knife?"

"Uh...yeah. Sorry." He rummaged for his pocket-knife, cursing at how clumsy he was. Since when did his hands shake? What the fuck was that about?

He got the knife out and open, and sawed through the duct tape. Fiona let out a gasp of pain as her hyper-extended shoulders released.

"Anything broken? Or cut?" he asked again. "You're sure?"

"I'm fine, just cold." She struggled to tug the dress over her blood-spattered breasts. "I'd like my legs free, though. Can I use your knife?"

Get with the fucking program, Trask. "I'll do it." He got to work on the plastic ratchet cuffs that bound her ankles.

Nate emerged into the light, and made a startled sound when he saw the state she was in. "Holy shit! I'll call an ambulance."

"Not her blood," Anton said. "But call one anyway."

"No!" Fiona sounded panicked. "I don't need an ambulance!"

"Call it," Anton reiterated grimly, as the cuff snapped and her legs came free.

Fiona rubbed her legs and tried to get them back beneath herself, but kept thudding back down onto her ass. Anton felt like he'd been disassembled and then put back together backward with all the bolts loose.

"Fi," he said. "You scared me out of my goddamn mind."

"Tell me about it," she said fervently. "I had a few bad moments myself. How many were in the car that got away?"

"Two, I think. Both wounded." It was Wong walking into the pool of light, his rifle slung across his shoulder. "We took down three."

Nate turned back, putting his phone into his pocket. "Ambulance on the way," he said. "Cops, too."

"Oh God, no," Fiona said, dismayed. "I don't need medical attention. Or cops. They'll just slow me down. What I need is to disappear."

"You're not disappearing until you see a doctor," Anton told her. "Which means you have to talk to the cops, too. So prepare your thoughts."

She made a distressed sound. "Great. That'll be about as much fun as it was in Highettsville. Are any of them alive to interrogate?"

"I shot one in the knee on purpose," Nate offered. "But his own people ran over him on their way out. I'll check on him just in case, but I'm pretty sure he's done for."

Her ankle wobbled. The boot heel had broken. "Shit," she muttered. "Of all times to break a heel."

"I'll call someone and have them bring you fresh stuff," Anton said. "What's your shoe size?"

She shot him a look. "Anton. I have my own stuff. Don't stress yourself."

"What did those pricks want from you?" Wong asked.

Fiona's bloodied hand drifted up to touch her earring, reassuring herself that it was still there. "This," she told him. "They wanted this."

"Your jewelry?" Nate looked dubious. "This was no robbery. These guys had a plan, and they weren't after earrings."

"There's a microchip inside," Anton said. "But we don't know why they want it."

Nate and Wong looked each other and then at Fiona. "Sounds like quite a story," Nate said. "Whenever anybody wants to tell it."

"It wasn't my story to tell," Anton said.

Nate gave him a level stare. "It is now. And I'm entitled to hear it."

"We'll talk later," Anton told him. "I'll tell you everything."

"Just tell me this," Wong asked Fiona. "If you had what they wanted, why didn't you just give it to them?"

Fiona gave Wong a blank look. "Are you kidding? They would have killed me anyway. Why make it easy for them? Fuck those guys."

The three men exchanged eloquent looks.

"That's one way to look at it," Nate murmured. "Damn. This girl is lethal."

"As lethal as she needs to be," Anton said. "She's still alive, right?"

"Guess you have a point."

The amusement in Nate's voice bothered him, and Fi was swaying on her feet, so Anton swept her up into his arms and carried her outside toward his Porsche, ignoring her confused murmurs of protest. They could wait for the ambulance out there. It was sheltered and private, not soaked in blood or littered with corpses.

He set her on her feet by the SUV and opened the back door. Fiona almost fell inside as she got in. Her movements were stiff and halting, but she scooted over to make room for him.

Anton took off his coat and slid in after her, wrapping it around her. She was trembling violently, and her teeth had started to chatter.

"You saved my ass again," she said. "But I'm not thanking you this time, buddy. I can't encourage you. Don't get in the habit. I'll go soft, and we can't have that."

"Making you go soft sounds like fun," he told her.

She let out a jerky laugh, pulling the jacket tightly around herself. "As lethal as she needs to be, hah. You know what, Anton? That might just be the sweetest thing anyone's ever said about me."

He slid his arm around her shoulder, squeezing gently. "You're a sad case, Fi."

"Don't I know it," she said, and promptly passed out.

8

Fiona drifted in and out. She was dimly aware of flashing lights, concerned faces. Lights shined into her eyes. Hands, palpating her skull and spine. She heard voices, felt the sting of needles, and sank into a fragmented jumble of nightmares.

When she floated back up to consciousness, she had an IV rack beside her and a needle taped to her arm. She was lying in a bed in a hospital room.

It was very quiet. The lights were low. She wore a hospital gown, and someone had swabbed the worst of the dried blood off her but it was still matted in her hair. She put her hand to her ear to ascertain that she was still wearing her earring. *Yes.* Thank God.

She sat up, wincing. Everything ached and stung, and she felt fuzzy and out-of-focus. Must be whatever meds they had given her. She struggled to concentrate.

Then she noted the shopping bags and shoeboxes piled

against the wall near the bed. She swung her legs over the edge of the bed and leaned over, hissing with pain, to peek inside them. Wow, look at that. Jeans, a sweater, underwear, socks. The other bag had a warm winter coat. Slate-blue Gore-Tex. That Anton. What a guy.

Fiona sat a minute listening to the hospitals sounds. It was so quiet. It was very late, or else very early. Her first thought was to check her phone for the time, but smiled at herself. As if her bag could have made it through the evening's adventures. It must still be in her abductors' van, along with her car keys, driver's license and cash. God, even her hotel room key, too, which sucked, since the hotel where she was staying printed the hotel name on their key cards. Unfortunate, given that all her stuff was in that room. Her cash and all her credit cards were in the safe, such as it was. She hadn't used her credit cards since she ran away from Highettsville.

Cash-only had narrowed her choices of lodging, but she didn't dare use the credit cards. They would leave a bright red arrow for her enemies to follow if they were tech-savvy, which she had to assume they were. They wanted that microchip, after all.

She'd been lucky that she had a stash of cash in her house. Another holdover from her GodsAcre mindset—to have her emergency go-bag always packed in case of…well, whatever she could imagine, and she could imagine quite a bit. A few thick wads of banknotes was part of that go-bag. But she'd run through most of it, by this point.

She had no choice but to risk going back to the hotel. If she survived, she would retrieve her stuff, then go to a bank machine and take out the biggest cash advance she could get from each of her credit cards to replenish her money stash.

Then she'd run like hell again. Dive back into hiding while she pondered her next move.

A shitty, no-future kind of plan, but the best she could do with her limited resources.

Fiona pressed her bare feet against the cold floor and lurched to her feet. She hated to hurt Anton's feelings after he'd fought for her so valiantly, but she didn't have any bullet wounds or broken bones. She wasn't at death's door. A few bruises, a sore spot on her head. No biggie. She could walk. Run, too, if she had to. And she most definitely had to, with no cash for cab fare. Or even a city bus.

Boo-hoo. Too bad.

Waiting around passively for other people to make decisions for her was not a long-term or even a short-term strategy. She was immensely grateful to Anton and his men for coming to her rescue, but if he didn't believe her story, she had to keep moving.

The truth was, she didn't have the energy to oppose that overwhelming alpha-wolf vibe that Anton had going on. She wouldn't be able to keep him from playing the macho hero, just like he'd done tonight. He'd get himself killed, and it would be all her fault.

She didn't want to live in a world that didn't have Anton Trask in it. How flat and dull and stupid that would be.

Such a shame, the way things had gone down tonight. To think she could have chosen Door Number One, and be sipping fine champagne in a big, comfy bed in some luxury stronghold with Anton Trask stretched out before her. Stark naked. Dick in hand. Smoldering at her dangerously with those beautiful bedroom eyes of his.

But no. True to her nature, she'd opted for Door Number Two. Blood, guts, violence and death, her standard

71

default setting. For fuck's sake.

But enough with the regrets. A fresh squad of Kimball's thugs were probably already moving in her direction. Everyone concerned would be safer if she left this place right now. Except for her, of course.

But that was just how she rolled.

She plucked the needle out of her arm and got to her feet, steadying herself with the IV rack. Whoa, whatever they had given her was unpleasantly potent. Fiona shuffled barefoot into the bathroom and switched on the light.

She winced at what she saw in the mirror. Her eyes were doing that reflecting-back-the-fiery-pits-of-hell thing, and her face was ash-gray under the smeary remains of blood and makeup. And to top it off, she sported horror movie blood-dreads.

She scrubbed her hands and forearms in the sink. The water ran pink. Then she did what she could about mascara smears with the stinky anti-microbial hospital soap. No time to wash blood out of her hair. Vanity could wait. She had no extra energy for it.

The clothes Anton had left fit perfectly. Warm and comfy. Good quality hiking socks, yay. The two shoeboxes held hiking boots, one pair in a size six and a half, one in size seven. The sevens slipped on like they were made for her. The coat fit her perfectly.

There was a pack of hair ties, a toothbrush, toothpaste and a comb. She made use of all of them. The blood-encrusted hair was too big a job to tackle right now, so she divided it into three rough, sticky bundles and braided it into a stiff rope. Her fingers were so cold and shaking, it took her several tries to get it right.

A look out at the corridor showed her that no one was

moving around out there. It also showed that this place wasn't a public hospital at all, but a posh private clinic. That Anton. Throwing money around like he was made of it. Which he probably was, come to think of it.

She spotted an exit sign and made for it, taking the stairs down to the ground floor. She stole through the quiet lobby area, drifting like a shadow past the administrative spaces where the night shift people lurked. No one noticed her. Not that they would have stopped her, but it was just as well not to engage.

She walked out the front door unchallenged, put up her hood and hunched her shoulders against the dawn chill. She picked up the pace to get away from security cameras.

"Fi! What the fuck?"

She spun around, heart thudding wildly. "Shit, Anton! You startled me!"

Anton strode toward her. Wow. He was more crazy gorgeous than ever. A long, black wool coat billowed out in the chilly wind, which ruffled his shock of tawny hair.

"Going somewhere?" His voice was mild, but his dark eyes burned hot.

She stuck her hands into the pockets of her coat. "Um. Thanks for the heroic rescue. And the medical attention, and the clothes. I'll pay you back when I—"

"Please. Don't even start with that."

She backed away from the intense emotion radiating off him. "What are you doing loitering out here? It's cold and damp. You should be resting somewhere."

"I just got here," he said. "I've been at the police station for hours, going over what happened tonight with the detectives. I called one of my security guys to watch this entrance until I got here, in case they decided to come back for you. Wong's covering the parking garage entrance. Nate's still down at the station. But nobody gets into this place without us knowing who they are and why they came. Not while you're in residence here."

"Oh." She was startled by the vehemence in his voice. "I see. Well…thanks. But it's no longer necessary. Since I'm, ah…leaving."

"You thought I'd leave you here unguarded?"

"It never occurred to me that anyone would guard me in the first place. I'm accustomed to looking after myself. Your concern is appreciated, but I'm good now."

"Fi." His voice was rough. "Please. Don't."

"I have to keep moving," she told him. "Don't you understand? They caught up to me at your club tonight, and you saw what happened. I can't relax for one second."

"Did you see what else happened?" he demanded. "Did you see us come after those bastards and cut them down? Did you see us bust you loose and send them running? Did that detail escape your notice?"

"No, it did not," she said stiffly. "And I think I thanked you already, but in case I didn't sufficiently — "

"I don't need a fucking pat on the head, Fi! That's not the point!"

"Don't take this personally," she soothed. "Those guys were going to chop me into chunks. You expect me to loll around in a fancy private clinic, taking it easy, and waiting for them to get themselves organized again?"

"I agree, and I'm glad you're ready to leave, because this place is not easy to secure. Let's go to my place."

"You are not listening me," she said wearily.

"No, you're the one who's not listening," Anton said. "I believe you about Kimball, Fi. That he's alive."

She gaped at him, flummoxed. "Ah...but...but—you do?"

"Yes. I'm convinced. It's either Kimball, or some asshole who actively partnered with him back in the day. And whatever they want, I think it's connected to GodsAcre. God knows how, but somehow it is."

She swayed on her feet. It was almost dizzying to have someone actually believe her. She couldn't quite take it in. "Well, ah. That's great," she said haltingly. "It's nice to have my theory validated."

"Stay with me," Anton said. "My home is secure. And I mean, super-paranoid-Prophet's-spawn-level secure. I've got kick-ass security experts on call. One of them is already in place at my apartment. I called him to watch our backs and keep his eyes on the security monitors while we rest. Come to my place now. Take a deep breath. Clean up, rest up, heal up, chill out. We'll figure out what the fuck is going on together."

Together. Well, hell and damn. The wind ruffled the shock of dark blond hair that stuck up like a brush on top of his head. The intensity of his beautiful dark eyes made her shake. He was so gorgeous, it would be hard to think straight even if she weren't exhausted and traumatized.

It was so tempting. But one did not make life-or-death decisions based upon a man's sex appeal.

"Why the change of heart?" she asked, playing for time.

"Five armed assholes prepping to slice you open was pretty fucking convincing," he said. "But even if I hadn't seen that, weird stuff has been happening to Eric and Demi back in Shaw's Crossing. I wouldn't accept the idea that your problem was connected to theirs, but now I see that is has to be. I'm sorry it took me so long."

"It's okay," she said. "No sane person would have

swallowed it."

"I should have," he said grimly. "I didn't want to have to think about that fucking place again. I wanted so bad to be done with it, I almost got you killed."

"Ah, not really, Anton," she murmured. "I did that all by myself, thanks very much. Who's Demi?"

"A woman that Eric met in high school, when the three of us were living in Shaw's Crossing, after the fire. I didn't know her myself except by sight. I left Shaw's Crossing before she and Eric got involved. Eric was crazy in love with her, but Demi's dad hated his guts, and it all went to hell. Then last week, after Otis's funeral, they hooked up again, but some goons tried to kill them, up at the ruins of GodsAcre. And Eric thinks that they're the same people who killed Otis."

Her mind reeled at the implications. "Killed Otis? Your foster father? You think that he was killed?"

"Eric is sure of it. Deadly trouble on two fronts, both involving people from GodsAcre. Maybe it's the same problem. So? Let's face it together. Pool our resources."

She let out a bitter laugh. "I don't have any resources, Anton," she told him. "I got nothing. No clues, no insights, I don't even have any fucking cab fare. All I've got are a bunch of stinking assassins riding my ass, and they're not going to help you very much."

"They won't get near you if you're with me," Anton said. "Besides, you've got more than nothing. You have the ultimate thing. Why else would they be hunting you?"

"The microchip? Sure, I have it, but that doesn't mean it's any good to us. I can't get into the portal, so it's not a resource at all. It's just an enigma to torture me."

He shrugged. "Yeah, but it's also bait. Leverage. A bargaining chip. Someone wants it bad. Who knows? That

SHANNON McKENNA

someone might be willing to start a conversation with us."

She shrank back. "You want to *converse* with the asshole who did this to me?"

"Sure," Anton said. "Until I can lure him close enough to tear him limb from fucking limb."

Their eyes locked, and Fiona let out a long, unsteady breath. "Now you're talking."

"And you're finally listening?"

She nodded.

"Those guys who took you tonight should never have gotten near you," he told her. "That's on me. I should never have doubted you."

She rolled her eyes. "Stop. It's not your fault, Anton."

He waved that away. "My place has state of the art security, an armed guard, soft beds, hot showers, good food, strong coffee, a powerful computer system. If you come with me, nobody will beat down a flimsy hotel room door and drag you off. I would see them coming from a mile away, and I would destroy them."

She stood there, contemplating it. It sounded amazing. But her natural instinct was to assume that anything that tempting had to be a trap of some kind.

Then again, this was Anton. He'd come through for her before in her time of need, when no one else had the nerve.

She closed her eyes for a moment, let out a shuddering breath, and gave in to sweet temptation. "Okay," she said softly. "Thank you. I accept. I would love a shower and a few hours of uninterrupted sleep."

Anton smiled at her, and that assault upon her sensibilities took whatever starch was left right out of her knees. "I'll tell Wong to bring the car around for us."

"What about the cops? Don't they need to talk to me?"

"They were going to come here tomorrow, but I'll call the detective and tell him you're at my place now. He can talk to you there, after you've rested."

Rest. What a concept. She hadn't actually slept since she found Patti's body. She didn't feel safe enough anywhere to let herself relax. And she had never been a great sleeper to begin with.

The SUV pulled up. The big Asian bouncer who had been at the club and with Anton at the warehouse was driving the car. His window hummed down.

He gave her a toothy grin. "Nice to see you on your feet."

"Fiona, this is Jim Wong, one of my security specialists," Anton said.

She gave Wong a wobbly smile and climbed into the back seat. "Thanks for your help earlier," she said.

"My pleasure," Wong replied.

Anton got into the back seat right next to her, to her surprise. He scooted over and sat much closer than he needed to. Arm to arm. Thigh to thigh.

He generated so much heat. It felt good, but it made it hard to breathe.

It took a while to make their way through the city. Seattle was already starting to wake up and go busily about its normal weekday, while she cruised along in her own strange parallel dimension of doom and blood. Trying to fake it.

Like she'd essentially been doing ever since she'd escaped from GodsAcre. Thirteen years she'd been pretending to be a normal person who inhabited the normal world. Never quite sure if she was convincing anyone. Or if there was any point in trying.

She didn't have to fake it with Anton. It was a

wonderful feeling, on top of all the other intense and inconvenient emotions she had about him. Finally, someone could see the darkness and blood that stalked her for what it truly was. He saw it, acknowledged it, and best of all, he didn't even seem all that intimidated by it.

That didn't make it any less a problem, but oh, sweet, sweet relief, not to be completely alone with it all.

She gasped, jerking up when she felt him shake her arm. "Huh? What?"

"Wake up," he said. "We're here."

She looked around herself, nerves jangling. "Where? What? Where am I?"

"It's okay," he soothed. "You're safe. You just dozed off, that's all. We're home."

Holy crap. Since when had she ever dozed off? In the best of circumstances, sleep was a challenge for her. She did not doze. She was hyper-aware of her surroundings.

She must be wrecked, to nod off in somebody else's car after all the shit that had come down that night. Maybe it was the drugs they'd pumped into her at the clinic.

She followed Anton out of the car on a street full of what must have once been old brick warehouses, but these buildings were aggressively gentrified. Sleek, clean, with huge, sparkling clean windows and leafy rooftop garden terraces.

There was a sign above the nearest door. *Hellbound Productions.* Wong waited until Anton got the gray metal armored door open before he pulled away.

She followed into an entryway, and waited as he unlocked yet another door and then led her into a deluxe wood-paneled recording studio. There were big soundproof booths, banks of recording and mixing equipment, a drum set, walls hung with guitars. Shelves covered with awards and honors, statues and plaques.

"You live in here?" she asked him.

"My apartment is upstairs. The ground floor is all Hellbound Productions."

A beefy guy tattooed up to his neck with lots of facial piercing came to greet them.

"Fi, this is Mitch," Anton said. "He'll watch our backs while we get some sleep."

Fiona shook Mitch's enormous hand. His thick fingers were tattooed with letters, but she was too tired to read the words they formed. "Glad you're here," she told him.

"You betcha. Rest easy," Mitch called, as Anton herded her into a freight elevator.

"I'll try," she called, as the mesh cage started to rise.

The apartment that the elevator opened onto was astonishing. Huge, open spaces, a lofty ceiling with skylights in addition to huge arched windows that marched along both sides of the building. Gleaming oak plank floors. Strings of lights on black cables stretched out high across the vaulted open spaces. The second floor was lofted, with a staircase leading up to the walkway. A big kitchen at the far end, a dining room table in front of it. A Persian rug dominated the living room area, defined by low plushy couches and chairs. There was art everywhere, the walls were covered, but she didn't have the juice to take it in. In the far corner was a nook with more couches and chairs and a huge TV screen. Or rather, it looked like a nook in comparison to the vastness of the rest of the space. The nook alone had more square footage than the first floor of her beach house.

Fiona stood in the middle, turning around to take it all in. "Wow, Anton. Looks like you didn't absorb Jeremiah's loathing for wealth and ostentation."

"This isn't ostentatious."

She tried not to smile at the edge in his voice. "Sorry about that. I'm not being a bitch on purpose. It's just my default mode. Believe me, I like money just fine. I'm not bad at making it myself, at least when people aren't actively trying to kill me. And I liked my funky little beach cottage with my ocean view. But it's nothing like this place."

"I'd like to see your beach house."

Something clenched inside her. "I don't think I can ever live there again," she said. "I'd see Patti every time I walk in. I see her every time I close my eyes already."

"I hear you." He took off his long coat and held out his hand for her new Gore-Tex jacket, hanging them both up in a closet hidden in the paneled wall. "Tell me what you need to get settled in. Breakfast and coffee? Some food? Or a glass of whiskey and a bed with the shades drawn?"

"Some food might be good. It's been a while. If it's not too much trouble." She swayed, steadying herself on the banister of the stairway that led up to the loft. "And a shower, definitely. Shower first of all. I can't stand having this blood in my hair."

"I'll get food going. Bedrooms and bathrooms are upstairs. Let me carry you up."

"Hell, no." She backed away, holding up a warning hand. "You will do no such thing." Her voice cracked with exhaustion, but she gave him her sternest look. "It was bad enough when you did it back at the warehouse. I can walk."

His arms dropped. "Just this once?"

"No. Lead the way. Eyes facing front. I can drag my own tired ass up the stairs."

Anton started up the stairs in front of her. As

requested, he did not turn to watch her stumbling progress in his wake, nor did he look back when he led her down the long lofted walkway overlooking the huge space below. Various doors opened off it. The slanted ceiling above them had big skylights inset at regular intervals.

Anton led her into a room that was large and beautiful, and sparsely furnished. A king-sized bed with a comforter, many soft pillows. Reading chair, table and lamp. A push of a button angled the hanging blinds to instantly block out the morning light from the enormous windows. He snapped his finger, and a reading light flicked on from the bedside. A rosy, welcoming glow warmed the shaded room.

"The bed's made up. I told my housekeeper to get the bathroom ready," he said.

She smiled at him. "Figured I was a sure thing, did you?"

"I hoped for the best," he said. "There are towels, toiletries, whatever you need. Clothes in the drawers and the closet."

"Clothes?"

He gave her a speaking look. "Of course, clothes."

"I'm not destitute," she reminded him. "I have clothes at my hotel."

"And a team of my armed security staff can retrieve them for you as soon as possible. In the meantime, until we get around to it, you have something to wear. Anything else you need, just let me know."

They stared at each other. Awkwardness was in the air. After all the drama and violence, she felt almost shy. The images were right in the forefront of her mind. That world-shaking kiss at his club. That long-ago kiss at the bus station in Shaw's Crossing.

"I'm sorry I didn't believe you," he said again. "About Kimball."

She waved her hand. "Don't be. I know how crazy it sounded. How crazy it still sounds. Besides, it's not like you threw me to the wolves. You told me you'd be glad to help. I still flounced out with my panties in a wad just because my feelings were hurt. It was childish of me, and you are not responsible for what happened after that."

"They almost killed you," he said.

"But they didn't. Don't apologize again. Relax. Please."

He grunted. "Relaxing is not one of my shining talents."

"Mine, either," she admitted. "But we have to try. And this place seems like a good place to do it. The best place I can imagine."

"I'm glad you feel that way. I'll head on downstairs and get some food going." He stopped with his hand on the door handle, looking oddly unsure of himself. "I'm glad to have you here safe," he added, looking a little embarrassed. "I'll let you get cleaned up."

She gazed at the empty door frame after he left, considering what he said.

Safe. A word she couldn't quite grasp. A concept she had no framework for. The world was savage, and safety was an illusion. That was a truth she knew in her bones.

Except for Anton himself. In her head, he was exempt from that harsh rule.

That fantasy of safety and protection he held out to her was a shining, seductive promise. She just wanted to fall into it and never come out.

It couldn't possibly be real, but she almost didn't care. She just wanted to let the lovely, beautiful lie go on for as long possible. Spin it out. Make it last.

She'd deal with the ugly truth when it crashed down on her. Not before.

9

Anton's ears strained to hear the hiss of water in the pipes from Fiona's shower upstairs as he got busy in the kitchen. Ten minutes…twenty…thirty. She was in there for a full forty-eight minutes before the rush of water finally went still, and he'd already grilled and rested the steak for the sandwiches, prepared the bread, sliced the tomatoes, washed the lettuce, gathered the fixings, set the table. He tried not to monitor her with his imagination the whole time. Picture her wet, gleaming. Soapsuds sliding down her strong, sexy body. He tried, but he failed and gave into the fantasy.

Lather, rinse, repeat. Had to be tough to get all that dried blood out of her hair.

Then the water stopped running and she started in with the blow drier. His fantasy shifted seamlessly to a naked Fiona in front of the bathroom mirror, that mass of red hair fanning out behind her stunning body, fluffed up into a wild halo by jets of hot air.

It wasn't right to be on fire with lust tonight. He'd

promised he would keep her safe. She'd just been freshly traumatized, on top of her other trauma.

This was no time to fantasize.

Noises from upstairs finally ceased. No more audible waypoints for what Fiona was doing in there, so he grabbed his phone and went out onto the kitchen terrace to call Eric. It was still early, but both of his brothers slept about as well as he did. He called them whenever the urge took him, and they returned the favor.

Eric picked right up. "Took you long enough to call me back, for fuck's sake," he bitched, in the hushed voice of a man trying not to wake up the person in bed with him. "You just getting home from the club now? Jesus."

"I didn't call to hear a lecture," Anton told his brother. "Sorry to interrupt you while you're lolling in bed with a woman, but it's been a long, weird night."

"I'm not lolling in bed with 'a woman,'" Eric said. "I'm lolling in bed with 'the woman.' The only one for me. Big difference, man. Get your terminology straight."

"I meant no disrespect to her," Anton said. "But I didn't mean to open that can of worms right now. We've got other stuff to talk about. And isn't this mating intensity of yours a little premature?"

"No. It's years overdue. Seven years, to be exact. That's a long time to pine. I'm not waiting another goddamn second. Fuck the curse, man. It's taken enough from us already. No more. You and Mace can be my best men, and we'll get married as soon as we can organize—"

"Whoa, whoa, whoa! Take a breath. You guys almost got killed just a few days ago. Can we get back to that before we start with flower arrangements and seating charts?"

Eric made an impatient sound. "Just be happy for me,

man. I know it feels strange and you're not in the habit, but just try. Isn't it good that I come up on the winning side for once?"

"It's awesome," Anton said, hoping to God it was true. "Just hold off on the victory dance, because Fiona almost got herself killed tonight, and she thinks that Redd Kimball is behind it. She thinks he's still alive. And she's starting to convince me."

That news cut right through Eric's giddy euphoria. "Fiona's there?" he finally said. "With you? In your house?"

"Yeah, she came to the club tonight."

"Kimball, alive? How the fuck can Kimball be alive? They found his charred body. They had the dental records. The cops crossed him off the list."

"Yeah, they did." Anton swiftly recounted the tale of the subdermal capsule in Fi's back, and the murdered lookalike cousin. "They took another shot at her, just a few hours ago," he finished. "Same deal. Tried to slice open her back. They want that chip. Nate and Jim and I got there just in time. We killed three of them and sent the rest running."

"Fiona's okay?"

"Yeah. Bruised and tired, but okay. She's in one of my guest rooms. She's tough."

"Why am I not surprised?" Eric said. "I'm glad she's okay. And with you. I never thought we'd see her again. Crazy, about that microchip. Damn. Kimball, huh? What are the odds that this happens to Fiona at the same time Demi and I get in trouble?"

Eric had been quicker to make that mental adjustment than he himself had, Anton reflected grimly. "Exactly," he said. "About your text. You said that you were researching, what? Biological weapons?"

"Don't sound so skeptical. Demi and I heard them talk about it. One asked the other if she was in the database, and the guy said yes, that she was in Shaw's Crossing during that period of time and yes, she was definitely exposed. What else could he be referring to but a pathogen? I'm thinking, it must be something that makes the exposed person vulnerable to the death-pen. You saw the security footage from Demi's dad's house."

"Yes, I did." The video from Benedict Vaughan's security system had left him in a state of flesh-crawling confusion. The same men who had attacked Eric and Demi up at GodsAcre had made an earlier visit to Ben Vaughan's house that same morning, and the security camera had recorded them pulling out a device, like a silver pen, or a small flashlight. They'd pointed it at a locked door, without even opening it...and Demi's father had dropped dead on the other side. On the spot. Heart attack. Door still locked.

It could be a coincidence, of course. Natural causes. That was the usual refrain. In Shaw's Crossing, coincidences and natural causes were way too thick on the ground.

Otis's death being one of them.

"You think they used that thing to cause the death clusters," Anton said.

"Yes," Eric said. "It's the only thing that makes sense. It works on people who were exposed to the pathogen within that specified time window. It didn't work on me, but it worked on Demi's dad, and her mom, too. They taunted Demi about her mom. And me about Otis."

The thought of those pricks hurting Otis made Anton's hands clench into shaking fists. He shoved the seething rage down deep. "But what the fuck could they possibly want?" he said. "There's nothing up there. And if there was, it would be ruined by now."

"That's what I thought, but they'll kill for whatever it is. I'll never forgive myself for sending Terry Cattrall up to GodsAcre. I convinced myself that the Prophet's Curse was mythical bullshit, and Terry paid the price."

"That's not on you," Anton said, knowing it was useless. "You couldn't have known. You weren't the one who hurt him. That's on them."

Eric didn't even reply. As usual, he took full responsibility for that disaster. As if he could somehow have seen into the future and predicted what would happen to Terry.

Eric had sent Terry Cattrall, the real estate agent, up to GodsAcre to appraise the property on the day after Otis's funeral. The plan had been to sell that place as fast as possible, for any price they could get for it, and get it off their backs forever.

But Terry had not come back down, and his wife had called Eric in a panic. Eric drove up to discover that Terry's Jeep had gone off a cliff and was smashed at the bottom of Kettle Creek Canyon. There had been no indication that Terry's car had slipped in the mud, or tried to brake on the muddy, unpaved road. His tire tracks led straight off the cliff.

Eric had called the cops, and hiked down to see if Terry was alive. Eric had been the one to tell Terry's wife that her husband was dead.

He'd been doing all the heavy lifting by himself up to now, and he was sick of it.

Anton let out a slow breath in the heavy silence. "I'm sorry," he said, not for the first time. "We shouldn't have left you there alone."

"Nope, you shouldn't have," Eric agreed swiftly. "So

come back. Terry's funeral is Friday. Demi's dad's funeral is the day after. We could use the company."

"Tell Demi I'm sorry she lost her dad," Anton said. "Even though she's way better off without that dirtbag sleaze in her life."

"Tell her yourself when you come. I won't miss that lying piece of shit one bit. I still can't believe he set his own daughter up to be kidnapped. It was pure dumb luck that I was with her when they came for her."

Anton grunted. "I can't believe I'm saying this, but that town is even more fucked up than I thought."

"Yeah, tell me about it. I could use some backup. Soon. Now would be good."

"I'll send Nate back up as soon as he's gotten a few hours of sleep," Anton said.

"How about you? You coming?"

Like Eric's tone gave him a choice. "Of course I'm coming. Fi has to talk to the detective about last night's attack, and then we'll get on the road. I haven't talked to her about it yet, but she wants a fight, so I'm sure she'll want in. Did you talk to Mace?"

"We've been messaging. He's on his way back, but it'll take him a couple days. He's driving to the airport in Nairobi right now and catching the first plane out."

"I'll text you as soon as we set out."

"Demi says to tell you she has room here. There's a bedroom and bath upstairs."

"I'll find another place for us to crash," Anton said. "Wouldn't want to cramp the lovebirds' style. Try to be dressed when Nate gets there tomorrow, okay?"

"Fuck you, man." There was laughter in Eric's voice, something Anton had seldom heard, if ever. None of the Trask brothers had ever been particularly playful. Jeremiah had pounded that out of them. Training to be the vanguard of the righteous was no laugh riot, and the Prophet had made damn sure that they never lost sight of that fact.

Eric sounded transformed.

"Ah, there you are. Nice view you've got out here."

Anton turned, startled. Fiona leaned in the doorway, dressed in the clothes his housekeeper had found for her. A clingy dove gray jersey sleep shirt and loose matching pants, and a long, soft charcoal colored sweater wrap that hung past her knees. Her hair was a glossy cape of dark red rippling waves. "I didn't hear you coming," he said.

Her lips curved. "Jeremiah taught me not to make any unnecessary noise, just like he taught you."

"True enough," he said. "Feeling any better?"

"Yes, much. It's great to have clean hair." She crossed her arms over her chest, glancing back over her shoulder. "Smells amazing in there."

That reminded him abruptly of the food that he'd prepared. "Oh, yeah. I'll put our sandwiches together. Do you want me to heat up the steak?"

She stepped back to let him through the door and trailed him back into the kitchen. "Not on my account," she said. "It looks great just as it is."

She watched him swiftly assemble two sandwiches, piled with slices of steak. He presented one of them to her. "Steak on sourdough," he said. "Fixings and veggies are on the table. Hope medium rare works for you."

"Perfect. But you didn't have to go to all this effort. Toast or a yogurt would have been fine."

"Like hell it would. After what you went through? Wine or beer?"

"No, I'll just grab myself a glass of water."

Anton hadn't realized how ravenous he was until the first bite. Conversation flagged while they devoured their sandwiches.

After Fiona finished hers, she sipped her water and looked around, taking note of what was on his walls. Then she set the glass down and got up to stare at the huge collection of antique historic weapons displayed there.

"Good God, Anton." She leaned closer to peer at piece at the center of the nearest array, an ancient bronze shield decorated with swirling circular patterns and studded with cabochon garnets and amethysts. "You've got your own personal medieval armory."

"Some are older than that," he told her. "That shield is dated at 200 BCE. Celtic."

"Wow," she whispered, moving on to a heavy broadsword, its ancient blade pitted with rust, the letters engraved on the blade just barely visible. "And this one?"

"Tenth century," he said. "Scotland."

She took a step back to get the whole effect. The weapons were arranged on the wall in a sunburst pattern, the shield in the center. Swords from various periods, of various styles, in various states of decay, along with axes, billhooks, crossbows. Halberds and flails and maces.

"These aren't reproductions." Her quiet statement wasn't a question.

"No, they're the real deal," he confirmed. "Each one with its own history."

"They look like they belong in a museum."

"Pretty much," he said. "I outbid museums for a lot of these pieces."

"And I'm guessing your modern weapons collection is

just as extensive?"

"More so," he admitted. "But I don't display those. Not in my living area, anyhow. They have a dedicated room. They're not for show. They're for real. Like last night."

She harrumphed. "And here I thought you were Mr. Mellow."

He snorted. "Hardly. Jeremiah's legacy. Mellow isn't really a menu option for the Prophet's spawn."

Anton felt strangely self-conscious as she studied his collections. Almost no one ever saw the décor in his private living space other than occasionally his brothers, and a few select employees from his clubs, like Nate, Mitch and Wong. He was unused to revealing his secret obsession, or feeling like he needed to justify it to anyone. He'd never considered how weird and over-the-top it might seem to an outsider.

"It's just a hobby," he said, to fill the uncomfortable silence. "An expensive one."

"Hobby?" She harrumphed. "I don't think so. Hobby is too lightweight a word for something this dark. Quilting is a hobby. Baking is a hobby. This is something else entirely."

"I trained intensively at warcraft until I was almost eighteen," he said. "I could have gone pro, like Mace. Eric, too, for a while. It was the obvious choice for all of us. But I had to push back. The entertainment industry felt like the opposite of all that. I can hear Jeremiah's tirade about cultural rot and moral degradation in my head. But the warcraft is still inside me. It didn't go anywhere. It has to come out somewhere." He gestured at the wall. "I guess it comes out here." He looked up the weapons. Better not to shine such a bright light into this part of himself if this was how it felt. "Welcome to my dungeon," he said under his breath. "Guess that's why I don't do much entertaining."

Fiona's eyes were thoughtful. "Do they make you feel safer?"

He considered it, and shook his head. "Not really," he said. "But I still keep trying."

"Tell me about it. I carry a weapon on me all the time whenever I don't have to go through airport security," she told him. "Even if I'm just putting gas in the car. You?"

"Always. Standard Prophet's spawn behavior. I feel naked without a weapon."

"Same," Fiona told him. "I was unarmed tonight just because my bad girl dress was so tiny. There was nowhere to put anything. What have you got on you right now?"

"When I'm dressed for the club, I can't wear the shoulder holster for my Glock," he said. "It doesn't fit under the designer dress jackets. But I always have a mini-revolver on my ankle, and a boot sheath for a knife and another one in my belt buckle. And the sole of my right boot has an insert that's wirelessly connected to this ring." He held up his hand to show her the ring, a heavy tangle of gold and silver bands and studs. "Depress this ring here, and see? Look at my foot." There was a click, and a short, wicked looking blade snapped out of the toe of his boot.

Fiona let out a startled laugh. "Sneaky. I want one of those."

"I'll show you the designer's online catalog on the dark web. Deadly Beauty, it's called. This woman lives up on the Washington coast. Her stuff is amazing. High-end jewelry design, merged with high-end weapons design. Every piece is an original."

"She sounds like my soul sister," Fiona said.

Anton held up his pendant. "This is one of hers."

"I noticed that before." She moved closer to look at it.

"It's beautiful. What is it, white gold and…?"

"Diamonds," he said. "White and yellow diamonds."

"Super-deluxe. What's the trick? Does a blade pop out of that one, too?"

"Nope," he said. "It's a flash grenade."

Fiona had been about to touch it, but she rocked back. "You're kidding me!"

"No. It'll flash seven million candela and bang at a hundred and seventy decibels. The light activates all photo receptors in the eyes of your enemies for a few seconds, blinding them. The sound will deafen them for a little while, and hopefully disturb the fluids in their inner ear, impairing their balance. Yours, too, incidentally, but tough shit. Life's full of tradeoffs."

She gazed at it with fascination. "I can see it, now that you told me. It looks stylized to resemble a miniature grenade, but I would never have thought it was real. And covered with white gold and diamonds? That's wildly extravagant and wasteful. Like a solid gold toilet."

"I guess, but it's part of the designer's philosophy. They're secret stealth weapons. You'd only use one as a last resort. A last resort is the only time when you truly understand how worthless and meaningless gold and diamonds and money actually are. That's what she told me, anyway. Made sense at the time."

Fiona blew out a breath. "Wow," she murmured. "And I thought I had issues."

Anton lifted the chain off his head and placed it over Fiona's head. "Take it."

She shrank back. "Oh, no. No way. I can't possibly."

"Please." He lifted her hair clear of the chain and let it settle around her shoulders, enjoying the silky brush of it against the backs of his hands. "Take it. I got this necklace for you, Fi. I just didn't know it until this moment."

"But...come on, Anton!" she protested. "It's covered with diamonds!"

"It looks fucking perfect on you. Beautiful. Dangerous. Mysterious." He paused for a moment. "Explosive."

She snorted. "You big flatterer." She looked down at the heavy pendant dangling below her breasts, and cupped it in her palm. "I'm sorry, but I can't accept this."

"Humor me," Anton wheedled. "It looks right on you. It feels right."

"But I don't feel—"

"Just for now," he coaxed. "Just while we're working together to fight Kimball. Wear it all the time, until we solve this. It'll make me feel safer. Please."

She held it up, dangling it before fascinated eyes. "I won't accidently set it off, will I?"

"No, you have to work at it. The pull ring is tucked into this niche here," he said, showing her the trick. "Pry it loose with your nail, and then yank it hard to pull the pin. That releases the spoon and lets the cap fire, which ignites the fuse. Two, maybe three seconds, and then bang."

"Got it."

Anton took a step back to admire the effect. The pendant swayed just below the soft jut of her breasts. It glowed. Like her eyes. That look they had. Lit up, switched on.

So fucking hot.

"Does it make you feel safer?" he asked.

Fiona waited for a moment to reply.

"No," she said softly. "But you do."

10

Fiona turned away from him, the second the words came out of her mouth.

Damn. That had sounded so clingy. Needy. *Grow up, girl.*

She clutched the pendant in her hand. It was still warm from Anton's body. She kept her hot face averted and strolled along the wall, staring at his collection. Swords switched gradually to spears, and then to a sunburst of Japanese samurai swords.

Anton followed behind. "How about you?" he asked. "You said that you do online marketing, you work for yourself, and live like a hermit. Have you got any hobbies?"

"The dojo, I guess," she offered. "I go there three times a week. I practice my fighting forms on my terrace. I jog on the beach. I devour books. Oh, and I garden. Believe it or not. Flowers and herbs, mostly."

"Your mom was a gardener," he said. "I remember that."

"Yeah. She planted all the flowers around the Great Hall. I resisted for a while, because I didn't want to be reminded of her. It made me too sad. Then someone gave me a cactus as a business gift. It bloomed one night, on my terrace, like magic, and I was hooked."

By now she'd reached the entertainment nook, with several deep, plushy couches angled toward a huge television screen. "Check this out," she said. "A homebody's video fantasyland. Netflix and chill—but on steroids."

"You're welcome to indulge. Anytime. Do you like movies?"

"Love them," she said. "I don't go out much, so I tend to binge TV series, too."

"What's your poison?" he asked. "I'm guessing, thrillers? Horror? True crime? Mystery cop shows? Dystopian post-apocalyptic fantasy?"

"God, no," she said, with a shudder. "I avoid that stuff at all costs."

"So what, then?"

For some reason, she was reluctant to tell him. She was blushing, for God's sake.

"Historical stuff," she said defensively. "Period pieces. Comedies of manners. A really good adaptation to a Jane Austen novel is my idea of the perfect TV show."

He looked startled. "Really?"

"Yep. An aristocratic, good-looking gentleman of the ton falls in love with a genteel young lady with no fortune. I can't get enough of that stuff. It's my thing."

"Huh," he murmured, looking fascinated. "I'll be damned. Who'd have thought."

"Yeah, I know. The big drama of the story is getting an invitation to the ball. The deadly danger is that she'll tarnish her reputation. The big action scene is a quadrille with the hero on the assembly dance floor, or a run-in at the milliner's shop with the bitchy mean girl. The love scene is when the gentlemen bows over her gloved hand in the garden and vows his eternal devotion. It's silly, I know. But it makes me feel..." Her voice trailed off.

"Safe," Anton finished softly.

Fiona opened her mouth to tell him that was not true. That was ridiculous, in fact. But her voice wouldn't work. Her throat shook too hard.

Anton reached out, and took her hand. He bowed over it, slowly and deliberately, and pressed the gentlest whisper of a kiss against her knuckles. His lips were so warm and soft. That brief touch was deliberate, and seductive.

"My lady," he whispered.

She swallowed, hard. "Are you making fun of me?" she asked shakily.

"Never." His voice was solemn.

That inner earthquake got stronger. It would fracture her into pieces. Her eyes fogged up, and her throat hot, tight and quivering.

She must be having a stress reaction. Adrenaline crash. Only explanation.

She pulled her hand away, backing away. "Ah...well. I'm wrecked," she babbled. "Time to get some rest. Thanks for making dinner. Or breakfast. Or whatever that was."

"No problem." Anton straightened up. "Sleep well. Call me if you need anything. My room's right next to yours."

"Will do. Goodnight. Or good morning, I guess I should say. Um...bye."

She hurried up the stairs.

"Fi," he called.

She turned around. "Yes?"

"I'll leave my bedroom door open," he said. "Leave yours open, too. And if you need me, just call. Really."

"I'm sure I'll be fine," she assured him.

That smile. God help her. She was going to carry with her into her dreams.

Anton felt incredibly restless. Even with Mitch standing guard, his battle readiness would not stand down even slightly. He sprawled on the bed, staring at the ceiling fan that the decorator had chosen for his room. His ears straining to hear Fiona breathing in the bed next door.

He was so grateful that she was breathing at all.

After a while, he got up and wandered past her open door to make sure that she was curled up in the bed, safe and protected. She was there, a slight lump beneath the covers. Her presence gave him a warm glow of satisfaction, way down deep. He knew better than to examine the feeling too closely.

He'd fucked up. Letting her run out the door and into harm's way. Fate had given him a free one, but he wouldn't be so lucky a second time. He had to step up his game.

He focused on his breathing, like he was doing long-range target practice. Going to the empty, no-mind place. Slowing onto the spaces between breaths, between heartbeats—

A wrenching scream tore the air, and suddenly he was airborne, gun in hand, heart banging as he bolted across the hall, ready to tear her attacker apart—

No attacker. It was just Fiona, sitting up in bed, her

eyes wide and unseeing. Her tousled, fiery mop of hair hung over her face. She was locked in a nightmare inside her mind.

"Fi?" he said gently. "Wake up. You're safe."

She shuddered convulsively, and buried her face in her hands. When she looked up again, she could see him. She rubbed her wet eyes. "Did I scream?" Her voice was hoarse.

"Like a tin whistle."

"Shit," she murmured. "Sorry I woke you."

"I wasn't asleep," he told her. "I don't really sleep much."

She smoothed her hair back, twisting in into a thick rope over her shoulder. "Me neither," she admitted. "I have big sleep disturbances. Patti was a good sport about it, but eventually my aunt put me in a room above the garage just so they could get some sleep."

"I'm sorry," he said.

"Oh, it was okay. Kind of a relief to have some privacy. College was a problem, though. Dorms and apartments didn't work. I had to rent a detached house off-campus."

"I see." He leaned against the door frame, wondering if she was ready to have him inside the room with her yet. "What was the dream?"

"Just a dumb old recurring nightmare." She hid her face, sounding exhausted. "Always the same damn thing. I swear to God, I am so sick of it."

"Tell me," he said.

She shot him a rueful glance. "Trust me. You don't want to hear it."

"I do, actually," he told her.

Fiona looked dubious. "Come on, Anton. Other people's dreams are boring."

"Fi, there is fucking nothing about you that could be

boring to me," he admitted.

She laughed. "That's such bullshit, but I appreciate where it came from."

Her laughter broke the tension. He dared to step inside the room, and she kept on smiling. So far, so good. "It's true," he said. "Speaking for myself, of course."

Instantly the air between them took on that thick, charged feeling. Fiona's eyes slid away from his.

"So?" he prompted, laying the gun on the dresser. "The dream. Let's hear it."

Fiona sighed, and gave in, drawing her knees up to her chest and wrapping her arms around them. "It's about Titus. Remember him?"

"Of course." Titus had arrived at GodsAcre along with Kimball, in a wheelchair. He had stayed the entire last year with the community before the fire ended everything. He had been mentally disabled in some way that Kimball had never fully explained. Some kind of brain injury. He could walk a few steps, in a shambling shuffle when pulled or pushed, but he couldn't walk on his own steam, or talk, or communicate in any way. He just sat in his cheap wheelchair, wherever he was put, drool hanging off his chin.

But Anton remembered the look in Titus's eyes, which wasn't clouded at all. His eyes had been lucid, and desperate. Looking into them had been like listening to a person who was constantly screaming for help, while never being able to save him.

Kind of like the fire itself. The GodsAcre Great Hall, full of trapped people, screaming in terror and agony. No way to get them out.

The story of his fucking life.

Anton pushed that memory way down before it

hijacked his brain and walked in and sat down on the foot of Fiona's bed cross-legged, facing her. He caught a couple of appraising glances she sneaked at his naked torso. That was promising.

"So?" he asked her. "What about Titus? What happens in your dream?"

"You remember that I spent that whole last year taking care of him, right?"

"Fourteen months," he said.

She looked impressed. "Huh. You were paying attention."

Fuck yeah, he had. He'd paid minute attention to everything involving Fiona Garrett. "I remember when Kimball got there," he said. "And Jeremiah told Kimball to pick out someone to help him take care of Titus.

"Yeah," Fiona said. "And he picked out me."

Her eyes were haunted. She'd spent that entire year working twenty-hour days, all alone with Titus. Spoon-feeding him, wiping his mouth, helping him to the bathroom, keeping him clean. No breaks, no days off. No more school, no more combat training. No more hiking or swimming in the summer, no more sledding or skiing in the winter. Just lonely drudgery, attending the silent, desperate, trapped Titus, day in and day out. It would have driven anyone nuts, even if that had been the worst of it.

But it hadn't been. The worst had been when Kimball decided that Fiona was more than old enough to serve him in other ways, too.

Jeremiah had actually consented to Kimball's whim, and before Anton knew it, wedding plans were underway. They were going to force her to marry that prick.

Several people had disapproved loudly, Anton and his

brothers among them. But by that time, Jeremiah was too far gone from sanity to be reasoned with. They just got a wild, screaming rant about kids gone soft, unwilling to face adulthood, unwilling to do an honest day's work, and if they wanted to see unfair, just wait until the Crash. They'd see what unfair looked like, oh yeah, they surely would when the world exploded into violence and chaos with death at every turn, etc., etc.

No, there had been no help from Jeremiah. It had been up to Anton and his brothers to bust Fiona out of that hellhole. At any cost.

"Tell me your dream," he urged her again.

Fiona's hair swung forward, hiding her face. "Remember how Titus used to call me 'Kitty?'"

"It was the only word I ever heard him say," Anton said.

"Well, in my dream, he can talk, and he's calling me that. He says, 'Kitty, where are you? Kitty, help me. Kitty, get me out of here.' There are flames closing in all around us and no way out. They get closer and closer. And that's it. Then I wake up." She looked up at him, her eyes wet. "That was how Titus died, right? In the fire?"

Anton nodded. "Like all the rest of them."

"And my mom."

Anton placed his hand on her foot, underneath the comforter. He wrapped his fingers around her toes and squeezed gently. Hardly daring to breathe.

She didn't pull away, so he left his hand there. "She wanted to follow you."

"You told me that before," Fiona said. "I just wish she'd wanted it more."

"She was too scared of Jeremiah and Kimball to run,"

he said. "It got so fucking weird up there at the end. As you know."

Bridget Garrett had stolen painkillers for him from the GodsAcre pharmacy, after Anton was flogged. She'd smuggled them in to him. He'd been out of his mind with pain but Kimball had forbidden the medics to give him anything to dull it.

He still remembered Kimball's sneering voice. *Medicating him would defeat the purpose of the punishment, now, wouldn't it? Let him feel it. Maybe he'll learn something.*

But there was no need to tell Fiona any of that.

"She felt bad about letting you down," he said finally. "Things went bad so fast at the end. She didn't adjust in time."

Fiona made a derisive sound. "Things had been bad for me for a long while before that. But never mind. I have to let it go. She's gone, and there's no one left to be mad at."

"I get you." Anton had been furious at Kimball for years for dying in that fucking fire. He'd wanted so badly to strike that bastard down. See the light in his eyes go out.

He let the silence deepen, keeping his hand wrapped around her foot. "I could take you to her grave," he offered.

Her head jerked up. "Huh? Whose?"

"Your mom's," he said. "She's in the cemetery at Shaw's Crossing with all the others. There's a single monument out there with all their names on it."

Her eyes sharpened. "Not Kimball's name, I hope?"

"Fuck, no. We told them to keep his ashes the hell out of there. But all the rest of them are on the monument. Titus's name is there, too, even though he couldn't be positively identified. He doesn't have a last name on the headstone. I don't think anybody ever knew it. I saw that headstone when I was back for Otis's funeral."

"Otis," she said. "That's the name of the man who took you in after the fire? I'm glad someone stood up for you guys. You deserved it. All of you."

"He adopted us legally," Anton said. "Gave us the Trask name so we wouldn't be stuck with Paley for our whole lives. That was a real gift. Dragging around Jeremiah's name would have been like a ball and chain. So we're all in mourning. You've got Patti, we've got Otis."

"Yes, we do have that in common," she said, staring down at his hand, slowly massaging her foot.

"I made my own memorial for them," he told her.

"Yeah? Where?"

He held up his arm, indicating the tattoo that covered his shoulder and upper arm. "Right here," he said. "They're always with me."

Fiona looked down at his Celtic cross tattoo, perplexed. "You mean, the cross?"

"Look more closely," he told her.

She did so. He felt the warmth of her breath blooming rhythmically against his skin. The effect it had on him was predictable. "Can you see them now?" he asked.

"Yes," she whispered, laying her forefinger against his arm.

The shape of the cross was made up of the names of all of the victims of the GodsAcre fire. Fiona studied it for several minutes, moving her fingertip over each name, reading them aloud like a litany. "Jeremiah Paley," she whispered, when she reached him.

"Yeah, he's there," Anton said. "I was really angry at him for failing us, but he still belongs there. What happened wasn't his fault, whatever the cops decided in the end. He was mentally ill, but he wasn't a stone cold killer. And he taught

106

us solid skills along with all the wacko stuff. I mourned him, too."

Fiona kept on moving her finger down the cross made of names, and stopped for a moment when she got to Bridget Garrett. She moved on without comment, but when she reached the base of the cross, her breath caught. "Timothy Paley, Jonathan Paley, Annika Paley, Bonnie Paley," she whispered. "The littlest ones. I remember them."

"Timmy would have been sixteen years old a couple months ago, if he'd lived," he said. "We had his third birthday party just a few weeks before the fire."

"I remember." Her voice was thick. "I tried to feed Titus some of Timmy's birthday cake. He wouldn't even try to swallow it. It just fell out of his mouth."

After a moment, her finger moved down to the strip of text that crowned the rounded top of the Celtic cross. "He trains my hands for war so that my arms can bend a bow of bronze," she read aloud. "Jeremiah's favorite take-no-prisoners psalm."

"We put it on the gravestone in the cemetery, too."

"That seems appropriate." She turned away for a moment, and then seemed to give herself a little shake. "So, Anton," she said, her tone suddenly businesslike "You said earlier that Eric is convinced that Otis was murdered."

He tightened his grip on her foot. "That's right."

Fiona scooted closer, arranging herself cross-legged in front of him. "There seems to be a lot going on with Eric and Demi," she said. "So tell me more."

So he told her the whole tale of his younger brother's wild adventures with his new girlfriend. Eric's run-in with the mysterious could-it-be-a-bioweapon. Thing led to thing, and finally he ended up telling her all the bad shit that had happened in Shaw's Crossing, before the fire and after. The violence, the death clusters, the panic. The paranoia.

He kept his hand wrapped around her foot as his words petered out. There wasn't much left to say, except how after the fire, there had been nothing left of GodsAcre or the Prophet for the people of Shaw's Crossing to hate except for him, Mace and Eric. The Prophet's spawn. Convenient and available for quick-and-easy vindication.

It had been a bad scene, but there was no point dwelling on it now.

"Anyhow," he finished. "Eric wants us to go back to Shaw's Crossing. I don't know how we're going to start figuring all this shit out, but whatever's going on, chances are it started there, and I promised Eric I'd help. Come with me if you want. I'd understand if you'd rather stay away. I can make sure you're safe and comfortable here."

Fi just looked at him. She grabbed his hand and squeezed it.

The gesture wasn't sexual, but the contact triggered an intense cascade of physical awareness. He was hyperconscious of her strength, the hard, bright look in her eyes, her indomitable nerve.

It blazed right through him. The energy went straight to his dick.

"I'm in," Fiona said. "Let's go right now. I'll get dressed."

"First, rest up," he said. "We eat, we coffee up, we talk with the detective, and then we go."

"I can't help the cops, Anton. Not while we're operating in parallel realities. In their reality, Kimball is dead. So what can I do for them, and what can they do for me? It's a waste of everyone's time until I can prove that bastard's still alive."

"Let's just try not to piss them off, just for starters," he suggested. "Start by being polite and jumping through their hoops. Besides, there are cops and there are cops. You might get lucky. The guy I talked to last night seems smart. He grilled me left, right and sideways. He really wants to get to the bottom of this."

"Fine," she said, resigned. "I'll talk to him, and I'll try not to piss him off. Then we go to Shaw's Crossing. On the warpath."

"That's my Fi," he said. "As lethal as she needs to be."

Her eyebrow tilted high. "My Fi?'"

A guy can hope. It was way too soon to say the words.

But he didn't let go of her hand.

11

His fingers tightened around hers. The intimacy made her shiver. The heat of his dark eyes. That velvety, soothing sorcerer's voice. The innocent, utterly panty-melting toe-massage. And that was supposed to calm her down? Hah.

She was anything but calm. He made her frantic, just sitting there, breathing.

Anton felt the heat crackle in the air and his eyes flashed. Their hands clenched.

"Not a good idea," Anton said.

She didn't bother pretending to misunderstand. "Am I too lethal for you?"

"Fuck no. But you were just abducted and attacked a few short hours ago. It's not a good idea, right after a traumatic event. Emotions running hot."

She dismissed that with a wave of her hand. "Screw trauma," she said. "If I let trauma stop me, I would have tapped out a long time ago."

"You should be resting," he said.

"I did rest, actually. Quite a bit of rest, by my standards. I'm not a great sleeper." She took his other hand and twined her fingers through it, too, contrasting her freckled fingers with his golden ones. "You said that the sex would be its own thing, remember? Separate from protection, the past, the killers. Just its own crazy, magic thing."

Anton closed his eyes. "Don't mess with my head," he muttered.

"I can't help that," she told him. "Sorry, buddy. I've only got one setting, and that's messing-with-your-head-at-maximum-intensity. But I have tell you something first. Something really embarrassing. In the spirit of full disclosure."

He looked cautiously intrigued. "I'm listening."

She took a breath to calm the queasiness. "I haven't been with anyone for a long time," she said. "Years, actually. Because the last time I tried to be intimate with someone, it, ah…it didn't end well. And I mean, it really, *really* did not end well. I cannot overstate that enough."

He shook his head. "Context," he said. "Details."

"The guy ended up in the hospital." She dragged the words out reluctantly. "Shattered jaw, sprained neck. Lucky to be alive. He ate through a straw for three weeks."

His face went cold, his dark eyes taking on a deadly glow. "What did he do to you?"

"Nothing," she said swiftly. "Really. That's what was so awful about it. The poor guy did absolutely nothing to deserve that, and I felt like such shit for hurting him."

Anton's expression did not change. "What happened?"

She couldn't hold his gaze while talking about this. "A stress flashback, I guess," she said. "That's the best I can figure because I don't remember a damn thing. The way he tells it, I just freaked out and attacked him. I have no reason to think that he's lying."

"Damn, Fi," he said. "That sucks."

"Yeah, it did. So anyhow. Needless to say, that relationship ended before it even began. And well…that was it for me, sex-wise. Never had the nerve to try it again. Besides, word got around, which pretty much torpedoed my dating prospects. You know, stay away from Fiona-the-psycho-hell-bitch if you value your life, not to mention your balls. I figured I'd just be a do-it-yourselfer. Simplify my life, save money on makeup and waxing and all that crap." She paused. "Until just now, I mean."

"I see," Anton said. "What exactly do you mean by telling me this?"

"It's not obvious?" she said impatiently. "I have this problem. And it's not a small problem. You should be aware of it, if you get intimate with me. You should be on your guard. Hell, you should probably sign a fucking waiver, if we come right down to it."

"I get it, Fi. You're terrifying. You're lethal. I knew that already. Relax."

She frowned at him. "Now you're making fun of me. You absolutely needed to know this before we did anything. Unless this is a total buzz-kill for you, of course. In which case, no hard feelings. I wouldn't blame you."

A furtive glance downward was all it took to confirm that his buzz had absolutely not been killed. The loose black sweat pants he wore did nothing to hide his unflagging erection. That was an encouraging sight, though his face looked grim.

Still. From what little she understood of men, one thing

was clear. In any sort of dispute between a normal guy's head and his dick, the dick usually won. Who knew, she might still get lucky. Then again, this was Anton. He was anything but normal.

Of course, he'd caught that swift, surreptitious glance at his lap. "Yeah, I'm hard as granite," he admitted. "Every time I look at you."

"Well, good," she said. "That's good, right?"

He'd turned her hands palm side up and massaged them. The sensation was marvelously confusing. Warmth pulsed through her body in response to his touch.

"This is the thing, Fi," he said thoughtfully. "You would never get the drop on me, not even if you had another fugue episode. On that count, put your mind at ease. That said, I still wouldn't want to find myself playing the bad guy in your one of your stress flashbacks."

She closed her eyes as tingling warmth spread all through her. "I can't make any guarantees," she told him. "It's not a conscious thing."

"I understand." He massaged the balls of her thumbs. "Do you want to be tied?"

The question came as a surprise to her, but his tone was so calmly matter-of-fact, she forced herself to consider the idea in the same dispassionate way he'd presented it.

After reflecting for a moment, she shook her head. "Not my style," she said. "It would make me panic. I'm a control freak. I just want..." Her voice trailed off.

"What? Tell me."

"Oh, hell, I don't know," she said, rebellious. "To be normal. To want something good, and just take it. Without running huge risks, having it be this huge fucking production with all these huge fucking issues. Is that so goddamn much to ask?"

A hint of a smile flashed over his face. "Forget normal. I'm a GodsAcre survivor like you. We're a mess. On the bright side, whenever I get involved sexually, the big complaint that I always get is that I never let down my guard. In your case, that's actually a plus, right?"

She was surprised into a smile. "Ah...I guess so. In a way."

"So? There you go. I'm paranoid, uptight, hyper-vigilant, have excellent reflexes, and I'm fully warned and ready for total mayhem. We've ticked all the boxes. I'm the perfect candidate for you, Fi. So, green light. You want me, you got me."

Delicious anticipation made her hands shake. "So, ah...you'll be careful?"

"I'll be fine," he assured her. "I'm like boot leather. You can't hurt me."

"You better deliver on that promise, big guy. Or I'll kick your ass so hard."

That set them both laughing, which she sensed was probably as rare an event for him as it was for her.

Wow, who knew about those crazy gorgeous dimples he had. She'd almost never seen him smile, not even as a teenager. Nor in all his DJ performance clips or videos.

"So, ah." She dragged her gaze away and cleared her throat. After her big Mata Hari come-on, now she was absurdly shy. The blushing maiden routine. It felt ridiculous, but her face was dangerously hot. "So how do we, um, go about this?"

"Slowly," Anton said softly. "No sudden moves."

An odd sound was coming out of her. She was faintly horrified to realize that she was giggling. The fuck? She coughed, choking it down. "You have condoms, I take it?"

"There's a full box in the drawer in the bedside table. I picked them up tonight, just in case. But it's early for that. No hurry. We won't be needing those for a while yet."

"I want to get on with it," she confessed. "Before I fall to pieces."

"Fall to pieces?" He lifted one hand, then the other, kissing them. "You say that like it's a bad thing. But that's my ultimate goal. To melt you down. Make you forget absolutely everything except how good you feel." His low voice caressed her ears.

Hurry. Before I fuck it up. Before it's yanked away from me. Before I crash and burn.

That's what she really meant, but she held it back. She'd already presented herself as the girl with the big hairy mental health issues. No need to hammer that nail still harder.

She wanted this so badly, and it looked like she might actually get some. She would not cheat herself out of her prize with stupid, nervous babble. Her life could be over at any moment, for fuck's sake. And she'd been dreaming about getting it on with this guy ever since she figured out what getting it on actually was.

This was her chance. She was goddamn well taking it.

Fiona rose up onto her knees in front of him. She slid the pajama pants down and wiggled them off. Then she seized the hem of the soft gray jersey nightshirt, whipped it off over her head and gave it a playful, stripperish twirl before she sent it flying.

That left her clad in nothing but the black lace boy shorts she'd selected from the assortment of lingerie she'd found in the drawer. There had been something for all tastes. Tonight, her taste had run to something that would display her ass to its very best advantage. Just in case.

The boy shorts were evidently doing their appointed job. He just looked at her, his throat working. He couldn't get the words out.

Then he finally did. "Fi," he said thickly. "You're so fucking beautiful."

Yes. That was how this needed to be. That was how she wanted him. Mind blown, with that dazzled look on his face. It lit her up inside. Her chest felt glowing and hot inside.

She swayed forward, swung her leg over his, and seated herself on his lap. Legs around his waist.

"Fearless," he whispered, lifting his arms to embrace her.

She smacked his hands down before she realized what she was doing.

"Oh, crap," she hissed, mortified. "Sorry. I'm enthusiastic, but...I'm twitchy."

"Sorry if I rushed you."

"No, no. I just got ahead of myself. Damn. So much for fearless."

"Have you changed your mind?" he asked. "We could wait."

"Hell, no! Not at all. I don't want to wait. I came on to you, remember?"

A lazy smile spread across his face. He took her hand, pressed it against his chest and sank backward, sprawled out over the tangled sheets. "Go for it," he said. "Have your wicked way with me." His voice was velvety. "You could knock me over with a feather."

Oh, what an angle. She feasted her eyes on all the details of his powerful chest and belly, stretched out before her. The smooth heat of his skin. Taut, sinewy muscles beneath. His heart thudded hard against her hand. His erection strained against the sweat pants.

Her own hunger had to be written all over her face. She was panting, face hot, lips parted. Undone by that sweet, yearning ache for more, more, more.

Anton put one hand over her hand, pressing it harder against his heart. Then he reached up slowly, and placed his hand in the same place on her chest. Over her heart.

She started to swat it down and found her hand clamped in his big fist. She yanked it away by reflex, but his grip was somehow both gentle and implacable.

"You have to let me touch you, Fi," he said.

"I do want to be touched." Her voice shook dangerously. "That's the crazy thing. I really do. But that just…happens."

Anton took both her hands in his and pulled them to his lips.

He started kissing her fingertips. One by one. Hot, slow, deliberate kisses. Each separate one meant something incredibly specific that only her body could understand. He spoke directly to her hands, bypassing her confused, messed up head. Using a language she had to be slower, calmer, less jacked-up to understand. Demanding that she relax.

It was driving her crazy. Tense as she was, his slowness was excruciating.

"Anton," she said. "For God's sake. Get on with it before I start screaming. I didn't go skidding up to the brink of death tonight to get my pinkies smooched."

"Too bad," he said. "Scream if you need to scream. I'm making this up as I go along. But I'm not going to be an easy lay."

"What do you mean by that?"

Now he was kissing her knuckles, with the same languorous pace. "I'm not going to run with you headfirst into a brick wall," he said. "I want to go deep inside, where the good stuff is. For that, you have to slow down, and be brave. And trust me."

Her chest hitched. "I don't know how," she admitted.

"Me neither," he said. "I'm improvising. But rushing it, being sloppy and careless, that's not the way. That much I'm sure of."

"Anton," she whispered. "You're making me nuts."

"Relax," he urged. "But keep on squeezing me with your thighs, exactly like that. Drives me crazy."

She laughed. "Didn't even know I was doing it."

He caught his breath as she wiggled and swayed over him, pulsing with her thigh muscles. "Oh, yeah," he groaned. "You feel so good against my cock. So hot. Slow down a little. Dance on me. Just let yourself feel it."

She could hardly help it. His voice had a soothing, hypnotic power. So did his seductive kisses.

She swayed over him, stroking herself against his stiff cock. He pulsed his hips, rubbing the unyielding bulge of his erection right exactly where she needed to feel it. Her hands had magically transformed into wildly erogenous zones. Every kiss to them had a direct line to her face, her breasts, her pussy. The center of her chest.

Their gazes locked. Beyond words. A shuddering groan of need vibrated in his big chest, she felt it under her hand, but he stayed the course, continuing with his slow, sensual grind as the energy rose up again. Rising, cresting. Impossibly high. She couldn't survive that much pleasure. She would drown in it.

He sucked her fingertips into his mouth, a tender pull,

demanding that she let go and let it take her away. The wave lifted her…and broke, crashing through and over her.

She wiped out. Pure, wild pleasure blanked out everything in the world.

When her eyes opened, she was collapsed against his chest as if she'd melted there, panting for breath. She found herself rolled over and pinned on her back. His throbbing cock pressed against her tingling, sensitized clit. Her legs twined around his thighs.

She wiggled beneath him, not to get away but just to feel that perfect pressure right where she wanted it. Pulling him closer with her legs. Straining, twining. Pulsing.

No words. He was kissing her, hungrily with breath-stealing intensity. But she wanted to feel his bare chest against hers. She fought to free her hands, turning her face away. "Anton," she gasped. "My hands."

"You want me to let go of them?"

"No. I like to have you hold them, but put them up over my head. I want to feel your chest."

"You got it."

He pinned both her wrists to the pillow right over her head and got back to madly kissing her again.

Fiona bucked and arched beneath his steely weight. So good. Something big, strong and hard to hang onto, to shove back against. She craved it. The pulsing grind of his erection against her drove her mad. So was the teasing friction of nipples against his hot, hard chest, the rasp of his chest hair, his demanding kiss. Winding her up again, to sensations that were wild, uncontrollable.

Shattering her again.

It took even longer to drift back this time. He had a dazed, wondering look on his face when she focused on it.

"Fi," he whispered. "You're incredible. So responsive."

You're doing all the work, big boy. I'm just lying here, coming like crazy. She would have said it if she was capable of speech, but she was utterly liquid. So soft. All she could manage was a dreamy smile.

He wrapped her fingers around the wrought iron curlicues of the bed's header. "Grab onto these," he said. "Hang on."

He slid down her body, stopping when he sensed her sudden panic. "It's okay," he coaxed. "I'll make you feel so good. I'm desperate to taste you. Tell me if I can."

She bit her lip, breathing raggedly. "You can," she forced out, unsteadily.

Anton shifted his weight and deftly tugged the black lace boy shorts down and plucking them off her ankles. He tossed them behind himself, then pushed her legs open and settled himself between them.

He studied her body with absorbed fascination, stroking the shape of the neatly-trimmed triangle of auburn hair that decorated her mound. Tracing it with his fingertips. "Wildest dreams gorgeous," he said. "Fi. We're good, right? You're still okay?"

"So far, yeah," she whispered. "Not much longer, though, you tease."

"It'll be worth it. I'm going for the big payoff." He pressed hot kisses against the hollow of her thigh and pushed her legs still wider, teasing her pussy lips open. "So wet and pink and hot. I can't get enough of that beautiful thing."

She gasped as he pressed his lips to her mound and stroked his tongue tenderly along the divide of her pussy lips. Pressed his mouth to her clit, gave it a long, tender pull before expertly fluttering the tip of his tongue across it. Kissing, sucking, licking. He thrust his finger deep into that slick well, spreading her juice around. Lapping it up, calling forth more. Making her so soft and open.

Making sure he would fit. The thought gave her a trembling rush of anticipation.

It felt so good. Even better than it had in the club, with all her barriers down. Stark naked, wide open and vulnerable. Gasping at each luscious stroke.

Better than excellent. So hot. So exciting. Getting busy with a guy who wasn't afraid of her. Oh God, she could get used to this. In a heartbeat.

Watch yourself, girl. Don't get needy. You'll kill it.

She shoved the thought angrily away and slid her fingers through the stiff brush of his thick hair. Trying to trap him there forever. He laughed under his breath.

"Hang on," he urged her. "Almost there."

"Anton," she gasped out as the pleasure overflowed its bounds, again.

She felt the mistake she'd made as soon as her eyes fluttered open this time. She was shivering, limp. Damp with sweat. Her soul as naked as her body. The earthquake inside her again. But bigger.

She pushed it away, tried to breathe down the panic. Get a grip, girl. Anton had saved her ass. From Kimball, years ago. From the kidnappers. Twice now and counting.

For that reason alone, she shouldn't freak out on the guy. His only crime was in making her feel too good for her comfort zone. She would not push him away tonight.

She had to stay in the moment. Let herself feel it. Kimball would not rob her of this, too.

Anton shifted over her, reaching to the bedside table for a condom.

He'd already kicked off his pants. He sat on his knees between her legs, smoothing latex deftly over his cock. And what a cock it was. Wide and thick and flushed hot and red with eagerness. Jutting high. Ready to serve.

He stroked her thighs, tenderly pushing them open. Took himself in hand and petted her pussy lips with his shaft. Slow...up...down. Sliding tenderly. Oh yes.

She let go of the textured iron bars of the bedframe and pressed her hands against his chest. Not pushing him away, just admiring him with her fingers. The fast throb of his heart, the supple heat of his skin, the sheen of sweat, the hard muscle moving beneath. He nudged his cockhead into place at her opening, pushing against the snug opening.

He covered the hand on her chest with his. "Say yes if you want me inside you," he said. "Give me a signal."

Aw, screw it. She was already destroyed. What was a little more devastation? She'd go stark screaming crazy if he didn't get that thing inside her right...fucking...*now*.

"Yes," she said.

12

Anton fought for control on that slow, incredible push into her body. Eyes locked. Souls and bodies fused. A breath from exploding. Fiona was so strong and lithe, shifting beneath him, canting her hips to take him deeper. He clutched her hands. His own hands shook. He forced his fingers to relax.

Fi dug her nails into his chest, shivering. Her eyes were dilated with emotion. She was slick and soft, but very tight. He tried to be careful, to go slow, but Fiona reached to grip his ass with her nails with a gasp of pleasure. Pulling him in. Getting him going.

He needed no more encouragement. He drove inside, feeling the small, strong muscles inside her tighten, squeezing him. His cock shone with her slick balm.

Not too fast. Not too fast, damn it. Her strong, lithe body took him so deep. Each thrust a long, suckling, perfect pull that just made him more desperate for the next.

He wanted to come right now, and he wanted it to last

forever. He wanted it all.

Her hand was splayed on his chest, stoking a ferocious blaze of light inside him. He felt lit up like a star. Both of them, celestial bodies on fire. After all his tough talk about never letting down his guard. It was bullshit. He was at her mercy as they madly fucked their way to a frenzied supernova.

The climax seized her first. She clutched him as her pussy gripped his cock, stiffening beneath him with a low cry. The rippling pulses around his cock dragged him right along with her.

He came harder than he ever knew he could. Depth charges, underground. Blasting through level after level of hidden barriers inside him. Stuff he'd buried. Stuff best left lost and forgotten. There it all was, in his face. A big pile of smoking rubble.

He went to insane lengths to avoid feeling like this. Helpless, vulnerable, wide open.

Fiona had turned her face away. Not a good sign.

He eased his cock out of her, sliding to one side so she could breathe. As soon as he lifted his weight, she promptly rolled over and sat up on the edge of the bed with her back to him. Curling corkscrew wisps of her long hair swung over the dimples at the top of her ass. So damn beautiful.

Anton tried looping his arm around her waist and pulling her back toward him, but she stiffened.

He let his arm fall, dismayed. Pretty fucking tense, after an orgasm like that.

"Hey," he said carefully. "Ah...you still good?"

"I'm great." Her voice sounded cool and remote. "You were excellent."

He waited for a moment to reply, choosing his words

with great care. "I wasn't talking about my sexual performance. I was talking about how you feel."

She cast a bright smile over her shoulder. "Fine. And so are you, thank God. You're not unconscious with a shattered jaw or a broken neck, so I'll call that a win."

"If you say so. But not needing urgent medical care after sex strikes me as a pretty low bar."

"Not for me." Still that detached tone. "It means everything to me. You broke my spell. Yay, Anton. My hero. Now I know that I'm capable of having sex with a man without mortally injuring him. Whether I can repeat the experience with another person is anyone's guess, of course, but it's still good news. So thanks. I owe you. As usual."

He jerked up onto his elbow, stung. "What the fuck is the matter with you?"

"Nothing," she replied. "You were excellent. The sex was great. No complaints."

"So why do I feel like you just slammed a door in my face?"

She slid off the bed and picked her nightshirt up off the floor. "I didn't get the impression that you were all that hungry for intimacy."

"Based on what?"

She snorted as she wrestled the garment over her head. "Don't play dumb," she said. "You're a big celebrity. Even more since you had the scandalous affair with the girl from the robot movie. The press goes nuts for the red-hot muscle-bound DJ genius tattooed stud-muffin."

He was appalled. "You're talking about fucking tabloid gossip?"

"It's hard to look away when I see you in the supermarket check-out line. Bad Boy DJ Stud Bangs Naughty

Starlet."

"You know that shit is made up, right? I could sue them, but who gives a fuck?"

"I don't dwell on your public persona," she informed him. "But your standard routine is common knowledge. When it comes to sex, you keep things super-light. You're in high demand, and you have a lot of turnover. You've never deviated from this playlist. I'm doing us both a favor by adjusting my expectations accordingly, right?"

"You're panicking," Anton said.

"No, Anton, this is the opposite of panicking. This is facing reality. Being a grown-up." She twisted her hair into a braid and wound the tail of it around her finger, refusing to meet his eyes. "I thought you'd be glad I'm not getting any big ideas. I won't get big ideas about you, and you don't get any about me. Simple. Deal?"

"Fi, damn it—"

"Let me finish." She held up her hand. "It's tricky, because we have this big dramatic past, and you saved my ass, not once, but twice. Plus, you're a total god in bed. Even so, I'm not confused, okay? It was wonderful. I loved every second of it. We clear?"

Anton got up and grabbed his sweat pants. So angry he didn't dare to speak for a moment. It wasn't right to lay that on her right now. She had enough to deal with.

He'd suck it up for now. But he wasn't going anywhere.

"We're clear," he said evenly. "But you don't need to be so fucking defensive."

"I'm sorry if I hurt your feelings. On the bright side, I didn't break any of your bones, right? Baby steps for me."

He gazed at her, considering a long list of angry

responses, and discarding them all, one by one. He saw the fear behind her words. Fear couldn't hide from him, no matter how it masked itself.

"Thanks," he said finally. "I'm grateful to have been left alive and in one piece. Real generous of you. Try to get some sleep. I'll be right nearby if you need me."

It was all he could trust himself to say.

Miserable as she was, Fiona couldn't help but admire the stunning naked back view of his body as he stalked out the door, anger radiating off his back. A miracle of nature. An ass that perfect should be illegal.

She was being a bitch, but she had to establish the rules upfront. She had enough problems. She did not need to dig for more. She couldn't get mushy for a single second. Because that guy could wreck her without lifting a finger.

All he had to do was get bored. As was his pattern.

She washed up in the bathroom, still weak in the knees and slightly sore in her lady parts. She curled up in the bed again, tossing and squirming. All stirred up. She could hear the muffled roar of traffic in the streets. The bright glow of daylight outlined the slats of the blinds as she tried, in vain, to power down. She curled into a ball and pulled the cover over her head, leaving just a small hole near her nose to let in the air.

The restless half-sleep she achieved turned into a parade of gruesome images. The face of the man named Rafe, with a hole where his eye should be, staring at her. Gunshots battering her ears. Flashlight beams slicing the darkness, dancing crazily around the warehouse walls. The sound of that van, thudding heavily over a man's fallen body.

The smell of blood, brains. The awful, hot stickiness of it. All over her.

It made her want to wash, though she'd washed for the better part of an hour.

Then older memories floated up. Things she hadn't thought about in years. Teenaged Anton jumping off the cliffs into the pool of the falls. Climbing out triumphant, flinging off water, shaking it out of his hair. A shower of diamond drops flashing in the sun, his taut, muscled body gleaming. Water caught in his dark eyebrows and lashes.

Uglier stuff rose up, too. Redd Kimball, trapping her in corners. Putting his hand between her legs, his hot, sour breath in her face as he told her what he wanted to do to her. What he would teach her to do to him. How much he was going to love it.

That made her wake up, stomach lurching. God, she wanted those memories out of her head. But his filth was stuck in there like tar. She couldn't wash it away. She couldn't even keep it hidden anymore.

She got up, pacing around the room. She found herself out in the walkway that overlooked his apartment. She leaned over the railing and looked down at his palatial apartment. The Persian carpet was being hit with a patch of watery sunlight from one of the skylights, and the rich blaze of colors was an assault on her tired eyes.

She slunk back into the shadows of the walkway and peeked in the open door of the room next to hers. Anton's room. He was sprawled on the bed. Fast asleep.

She padded in, her bare feet not making a sound. Anton's room was similar to hers but even larger. It was a corner room with windows on two sides, not just one. The bed was huge, but Anton was so long, he used up a hell of a lot of it. He'd tossed the comforter halfway off the bed, but the sheet was still draped over his hips.

He was still stark naked.

She inched closer. His naked body exerted what felt like an actual gravitational force on her. She gazed at his back, admiring the breadth of it, the shape of his powerful muscles. No tattoos on the middle of his back, oddly enough.

Then she saw the marks, and stopped cold. Inched closer, leaning in.

His back was covered with scars. Like her own, but there were more of them.

Many more than she had. Deeper, too. She had only four slashes that had been severe enough to leave marks. He had twelve she could see from halfway across the room, though the way they were cross-hatched over each other made them hard to count. His whole back was a snarl of ragged scar tissue.

That hadn't happened before she left. She would have remembered that.

This had happened after her escape. And the fire had happened eight days later.

This was the price Anton had paid for getting her away from Kimball.

Her eyes fogged up, and her throat ached. Her own scars throbbed in sympathy. She thought of the doctor who found the capsule in her back. How the woman had lectured Fiona for not getting that inflamed welt checked out years earlier. 'That's just basic, elementary self-care,' the doctor had scolded.

Self-care, hah. It was the engrained GodsAcre mindset. Pain was to be endured, not alleviated. Just one more of the many ways that place had dented her.

Her face was hot. Her chest and throat felt soft and full and shaking.

Oh, God, don't. Back away. Let the man sleep. If she reached out to him, she was only going to screw it up again. Piss him off more, one way or another. Sure as sunrise.

But still, she crept around his bed to look at his sleeping face. His dreams had to be as ugly as hers, but in sleep he looked relaxed, younger, more like her memories of him from GodsAcre. His mouth was so gorgeous. Full, sexy, hot. Kissable.

She pinched his sheet between her fingers. Lifted it slightly. Peeked beneath.

Hoo, boy. He was fully erect. Look at that. What a marvel. She hadn't yet had a proper opportunity to admire his spectacular penis up till now. He'd been too busy using it to drive her wild with pleasure. It was a fabulous specimen. Thick and blunt and up for anything. Now-now-now, gimme-gimme-gimme. His whole body radiated feverish heat.

She wanted to crawl into that huge warmth and never come back out.

"See something you like?"

Anton's voice was low, but it still made her jump. His eyes were hooded, inscrutable. "Sorry," she said, flustered. "Thought you were asleep."

"You thought I could sleep through a gorgeous woman sneaking into my room to check out my dick?"

"I never got a good look at it." She climbed onto the bed. "You were too busy going all super-alpha on me. I never got a chance to play with it."

"Fi." His voice had a warning tone as she slid down alongside his body. "Hang on. Wait a second."

"Shhhh." She seized his cock. "Don't talk. Just let me..."

"Oh. Fuck. Me." His voice choked off as she explored him boldly. Every red-hot, over-the-top detail of him. She squeezed and stroked his thick, broad shaft from root to tip, tracing the pulsing veins. He was as hard as marble. She cupped his balls and pressed a slow, sensual kiss against his broad cockhead, sliding her tongue all the way around it.

"Hello, you," she murmured. "I never got properly introduced."

"God, Fi..." His voice broke off into a hiss of pleasure as she swiveled her hand along his rigid shaft, rubbing the slick, hot pre-come against her palm, feeling that rapid, throbbing pulse against her fingers as she milked him. She licked him, savoring the taste, the texture of him. Smooth, hot, hard. Salty and sweet. She squeezed out more pre-come and polished his cock with it, making it gleam. It looked fierce and enthusiastic.

Anton wound his fingers into her hair. "You're just fucking with my head right now," he said, breathless. "Then you'll freeze me out again afterward, right?"

"Oh, probably." She gripped the base of his cock and licked slowly up his length. "I'm a huge pain in the ass, I know. Let me at least try to make it worth your while."

He started to speak but gave up the attempt when she sucked him into her mouth.

What with all her various troubles, she'd never had much of a chance to practice at oral sex. Truth to tell, she hadn't seen the point in doing so. Only now had the point become manifestly clear to her. If it was Anton writhing and moaning with pleasure while she rocked his world, then yeah. It was worth the effort.

And as an unexpected bonus, it also turned her on

beyond belief. She felt superhuman. A goddess, bestowing the gift of ultimate erotic pleasure upon her chosen one.

She slid her tongue teasingly around his flushed, heart-shaped cockhead, flicking the little slit at the end tenderly. She loved the way his reaction vibrated through them both. She pulled his thick, stiff cock inside her mouth, which took some doing, and slowly found a rhythm that worked, and when she did, she clutched his ass and pulled him deeper, sucking him. Slow, sensual strokes that she felt through her whole body, as if he were fucking her mouth. Her breasts tingled, her thighs squeezed tight around her thrumming clit. Her fingers dug into his muscular ass. Long, eager sucking pulls.

His breathing got harsher. His hands tightened in her hair. Almost there.

She wrapped her hands around the base of his cock. Squeezing, pulling, sucking him deep inside once again. His body shook with agonizing tension.

He went rigid and let out a muffled shout, spurting hot jets of come into her mouth. Her thighs tightened around the pulsing glow of excitement between her legs, and her own orgasm pumped through her a moment later. Waves of pleasure, pumping down her thighs, out through her toes. Up through her chest.

They both went still, after many shivering seconds, and she pulled away and wiped her mouth.

Anton was giving her that wondering look he got, as if she'd just magically materialized in front of him. "Did you just, ah...come again?"

"You make me hot," she told him. "It made me come. Go figure."

"Come whenever," he assured her. "I love when you come. I'm just surprised."

SHANNON McKENNA

She straightened her nightshirt with a shrug. "It worked for me."

Anton rolled up onto his elbows. "Yeah, but for how long? You spit in my eye after the last time. Then you sneak in here two hours later and blow me until I explode. I don't know what to think, Fi. I'm getting fucking whiplash trying to keep up with you."

She hadn't prepared a coherent answer, so the incoherent truth just fell out. "I felt bad," she said. "Everything I said is perfectly true, and valid. But it sounded bitchy and cold and horrible. And you didn't deserve that."

"I see," he said. "So this is your idea of an apology?"

She shrugged. "I communicate better nonverbally."

"Is that a joke?" he demanded. "You think this is funny?"

"Not at all," she said. "It's just the naked truth. I'm awkward that way. I blurt out whatever's in my head, which tends to be a social disaster. And I get snarky and confrontational when I'm nervous, but you knew that already. I just came in here to see if you were awake. Lo and behold, you had this gorgeous hard-on, so I, ah…got inspired, and I went for it. End of story. Random impulse."

He sat up, frowning. "I make you nervous?"

Great. He had to choose that part of her embarrassing little speech to fixate on.

"Duh," she muttered. "You have to ask?"

"Why?" he demanded. "Why on earth would I of all people make you nervous?"

"We're not getting into it right now," she said, as the phone on the bedside table vibrated. She exhaled in relief as he leaned to grab it. Saved by the bell.

"What's up?" Anton said into the phone, and listened

133

to the reply. "Oh fuck, already?...yeah. Okay, whatever. Give us ten, and send him on up."

He put the phone down with a sigh. "Detective Marchese is here to talk to you."

She slid off the bed and headed for the door. "Better go brush my teeth."

13

Anton provided coffee and set out a plate with some of the pastries his housekeeper had left, leaving Detective Marchese, a cherubic middle-aged man with sharp brown eyes and a mustache, sitting at the dining room table with Fiona. He got busy prepping a meal in the kitchen while Fiona and the detective talked, trying not to eavesdrop and failing completely.

Marchese seemed okay to him, as he had at the station. The man had struck him as intelligent during their long interview the night before, and Anton approved of his calm, respectful manner with Fiona. She dutifully ran through all the events of last night for him, after which Marchese pressed her to talk about her troubles back in Highettsville. Fiona grimly told him the whole story, but left out the microchip in her back.

Marchese, not being stupid, sensed a hole in her narrative and pressed for more.

Fi being Fi, got nervous and testy about it. "You can

talk directly to the police in Highettsville," she told him. "Detectives Rob Marcos and Angel Zeilinski handled the case. I'm happy to provide you their direct numbers. I told them everything and gave them everything. They have my phone and computer records, GPS records on my car, my business, my website, my personal and business bank accounts. I offered all that info to them, and I offer it to you, too. Every detail of my life is an open book. I did absolutely nothing to provoke these attacks. Ever. And neither did my cousin Patti."

"I already spoke to Detective Marcos in California this morning," Marchese said. "He was surprised to hear that you were so far from home, but he didn't seem all that surprised to hear that you'd gotten into trouble again."

Fiona's shoulders hunched up defensively, and she twiddled the necklace he'd given her. "What's that supposed that mean?"

The detective sipped his coffee, working the uncomfortable silence. But Fiona was not so easily manipulated. It would take more than silence to intimidate her.

Marchese finally set down his coffee. "What you said checks out," he conceded. "You lived alone in that house on the beach cliff where your cousin was killed."

"That's right."

"And you work alone. Your entire business is online."

"Yes, exactly," she said. "I'm actually kind of a hermit."

"So what moved a quiet homebody hermit to drive all the way up to Seattle to visit an infamous nightclub?" the detective asked.

Anton snorted from the kitchen. "Infamous, hah," he murmured. "I wish."

"Infamous, definitely," Marchese repeated firmly, his

eyes still fixed on Fiona. "Why did you come all the way up here?"

"For me." Anton walked out of the kitchen. "She came up here to see me."

Detective Marchese looked him over. "And this would be, ah…why?"

"We knew each other as kids," Fiona told him. "We grew up together."

Marchese looked at him, then at her. "But you're not related by blood."

It wasn't a question. The guy didn't miss much.

"The place was like a commune," Anton said. "Me, my brothers, Fiona, a bunch of other kids. We're not related by blood, no, but we were like family."

"I see." Marchese made a note in his little book and turned back to Fiona. "So, you drove up here to call on him for moral support, after what happened at home?"

"I guess," Fiona said. "Advice. Protection. Though I didn't know how badly I needed it until he pulled my ass out of a sling last night."

"Yes, yes." Marchese studied her and then Anton, waiting hopefully for more.

When no more was forthcoming, he let out a disappointed sigh, and pulled a card out of his pocket. He put it on the table in front of Fiona. "Call me if you think of anything else, Ms. Garrett."

"Of course. Have you identified any of the bodies?"

"Only one of the three so far," Marchese said. "He has an extensive criminal record. Rafael Baher. Does that name ring a bell?"

"No," Fiona said. "Like I told you, I'd never seen any of them, and I'd never heard of them."

"They certainly seemed to be specific about you," Marchese commented. "If any insight as to why that might be so comes to mind, you'll share it with us?"

"Of course. I'll call you right away."

"It would be helpful if you'd stay in town for a while," Marchese said, pulling out his phone. "Both of you. Is there a number where you can be reached, Ms. Garrett?"

"Not at this moment," she told him. "I'm currently without a phone since the attack. I lost it last night, along with my wallet and my car keys."

"We'll get her a replacement phone right away and call you with the number," Anton told him. "We're driving up to Shaw's Crossing for a funeral later today, but we should be back soon. It's less than three hours away. And we'll be together the whole time, so if you need either one of us, just call me. You have my number."

"A funeral, you say?" Marchese perked up. "Who died?"

"My brother's fiancée's father," Anton said. "We're leaving right away."

Marchese harrumphed. "Brother's fiancée's father," he repeated slowly. "And you're going to his funeral? You must be one hell of a close-knit family."

"Yeah, we're real tight."

Marchese took his leave shortly afterward, looking unsatisfied. After he got into the elevator and the doors closed on him, Fiona turned to him.

"Anton," she said, in a warning tone. "You're doing it again."

"What?" He grabbed a cinnamon roll and took a bite. "What did I do now?"

"Rushing in to save me. It's getting to be a habit for

138

you. I appreciate the thought, but I was doing just fine. My conscience is clear."

"No one's suggesting that it's not," he replied. "Not Marchese, and certainly not me. But you're starting to look like you're hiding something. And that's because you fucking are. Why didn't you tell him about the chip in your back?"

Her chin went up. "Why didn't you, if you thought he ought to know?"

"It's not my story to tell. I was waiting for your cue, but you never gave it. You went to all this trouble to convince me that it's relevant. Why not tell Marchese, too?"

She rubbed her eyes. "I don't dare," she muttered. "I can't tell the cops. Not yet."

"Why? You'll have to spill it sometime, and if you wait, you will have squandered their good will. Why hide it?"

"Because it's evidence, and I would have to hand it over to them," she said. "And that thing is mine. I paid for it in blood. It was part of my body for eight years and I'm not giving it up to them or anyone."

He was taken aback by her vehemence. "Fi," he said. "Chill."

"Sorry." She shook her head, hard, as if she were trying to shake something out of it. "The chip has a link to a portal online. Password protected. It gave me six login attempts. I've been racking my brains for the password for five years."

Understanding dawned slowly. "I see. How many login attempts have you burned so far?"

"Five." Fi's voice was bleak.

"Ah. One more shot." Anton laid the cinnamon roll down on the plate. "And you think they'll kill your last chance to get in."

"They might." She shrugged angrily. "Yes. I have

control issues, I know this. But I'm justified this time. I just can't afford to risk it."

"The cops won't see it that way," he said. "You're not doing them any favors by withholding this info. It's pointing their investigation in the wrong direction."

She shook her head stubbornly. "I just can't risk it. Not yet."

Anton paused for a long time to find words for the thought that was slowly forming in his mind. "I think I know where this is coming from."

She shot him a wry look. "Oh, great. This should be good."

He ignored the sarcasm and went on. "It's the voice in your head. I know, because I have it, too. Jeremiah's voice. It says, watch out. Stay sharp. The Man is out to get you. No one can be trusted. Rely only upon yourself. Don't let yourself be had. Don't be a sucker. Any of that sound familiar?"

She scowled down into her coffee. "That's not what's happening."

"Maybe Jeremiah was right about where this is all ultimately going," he went on. "Who the fuck knows. But if we're going to live in this world, we have to find some sort of middle ground. We have to play by their rules, more or less. Or we will hit a wall."

"I know Jeremiah was nuts," she said. "Believe me. I know that."

"Yes, but you soaked some of it up anyway. I know you did, because I did, too."

"You don't look like you've hit any walls," she said. "You function just fine in the big bad world, you famous electronic music genius and style icon, you. Jet-setting around the globe, lolling on yachts, sipping fine champagne with topless movie stars."

He just looked at her and waited. Refusing to rise to the bait.

She let out a sharp sigh and lifted both hands in defeat. "Fine," she said. "You're right. I'll look for some middle ground. As soon as we go to Shaw's Crossing and I learn a little more, I'll call Marchese and tell him about the microchip. Will that satisfy you?"

"Yes," he said. "But what would satisfy me even more would be some food."

"Food?" Fiona looked like she'd forgotten what it was. "You mean, right now? We just ate."

"That was hours ago. It won't take long to get something on the table. I already prepped it."

"Let's make it quick," she said. "Let's go. Please. Let's go and do something, somewhere, before I go crazy or get myself killed. Whichever comes first."

"There's a suitcase in the closet upstairs," he said. "Go pack up. The going crazy part's not up to me, but I'm not going to let anybody kill you."

"Aw," she murmured, turning toward the stairs. "That's sweet."

14

Sizzling sounds and amazing smells were wafting up into the loft from Anton's kitchen by the time she finished her packing. She'd found an expensive travel bag in the closet, and she placed a travel beauty on top of the new clothing that Anton had provided and zipped it all closed.

Wasteful as hell. She had a suitcase full of perfectly good clothes in her hotel room, but she'd be insane to get near the place right now. Any fool who'd looked in her evening bag and seen that key card would know she'd been staying there. And Kimball was no fool.

By the same token, any fool could also guess where she was right now. But she wasn't there alone, and that made all the difference. Illusory though the feeling might be, she actually felt safe here in Anton's sprawling luxury fortress.

As safe as she'd ever felt, anyway. Which admittedly wasn't very.

Anton was setting a cast iron skillet full of scrambled eggs, ham, onion, peppers and cheese on the table. A pile of heated tortillas was next to it. Guacamole, sour cream and salsa adorned the table. Steam rose off the food. It smelled divine.

"Breakfast for dinner," Anton said. "Dig in."

Fiona sank down into the chair, her appetite shocked out of its coma once again. She'd never seen anything so appetizing. At least not since last night's steak sandwich.

She loaded up tortilla after tortilla. Goopy and gloppy and hopelessly messy. Salsa and sour cream and melted cheese oozed every which way. She ate a big plate of food and washed it all down with more coffee.

They squared the kitchen away together in record time, grabbed coats and bags and took the elevator down to the street level. After a few words to Mitch, Anton led her through a corridor that opened from the back of the recording studio into a big private parking garage.

Anton's collection of luxury cars could only be described as a fleet, exactly like the *GQ* piece and the fawning e-zines had described it. But she was so mellow after that fabulous meal, she just got into the big BMW X7 that he indicated without giving him any shit about it. The security cameras showed no one lying in wait on the street, so the garage door ground upward, and they were on their way.

Once out of the traffic-choked city they made good time. The miles sped by, but it had already been afternoon when they set out, and daylight faded fast. It was full dark by the time Anton got onto the smaller highway that wound through the mountains toward Shaw's Crossing.

They'd been silent for most of the almost three-hour drive, weighed down by their dark thoughts. But a question kept pressing on Fiona's mind, and as they got closer to Shaw's Crossing, she finally worked up the nerve to ask it.

"Have you been back up to GodsAcre since the fire?" she said.

Anton was silent for a while. "No," he said. "All these years, you couldn't pay me to get near that place. Not even when we found out that we owned it. Me, Eric and Mace. Twisted, huh? It shook down in the end that we were Jeremiah's legal heirs, since he legally adopted us years back when he married our mom. We didn't even know. Otis dealt with all that for us, thank God. We didn't want to touch it."

"I wouldn't, either." She took a deep breath. "Do you remember that night?"

"The night of the fire, you mean."

"Yes." Fiona followed the yellow line snaking ahead of them on the dark, curving mountain with her eyes, bracing herself. Anton took a long time to answer. She was already dreading it.

"Not as much as Eric or Mace might," he said. "They'd be able to tell you more. I was sick."

"Sick how?"

He shrugged. "Don't remember. Eric and Mace dragged me out of the infirmary. We'd already planned to blow up the caverns that night and they needed me to help with the plan, even though I was in shit shape. After we detonated the charges, we smelled smoke from up the hill and saw the light from the Great Hall. The trees around it were burning. Then we heard the screams. Someone had put those huge padlocks on the inside of the big armored doors. They found the padlocks in the ruins after, still locked. I remember that night like a bad dream. I had a fever of a hundred and four. The police decided it had to be Jeremiah who locked the doors and set the fires. That he'd just snapped."

Fiona shook her head. "That doesn't sound right. That

wasn't his brand of crazy."

"I didn't think so either," Anton said. "But it was the easiest explanation they could come up with, so they went with it. There was no one left but Eric and Mace and me to argue with them."

It was another twenty miles before she worked up the courage for another pass.

"Why were you in the infirmary?" she asked.

He made a frustrated sound. "Jesus, Fi. It was a long time ago."

"Not that long," she said. "Those scars on your back. They flogged you for helping me escape. Right?"

Anton stared grimly ahead at the road. "I don't want to talk about it."

She shut up, but the closer they got to Shaw's Crossing, the louder the buzz of panic in the back of her mind. That coppery taste in her mouth. She had a clutch in her chest, as if a huge hand were squeezing it. She couldn't get enough air.

She was walking right into a trap.

But Anton was walking into it with her, she reminded herself. He might be miserable and tense, but he believed her. And she wasn't the only one. Eric and his girlfriend were under attack, too. Which sucked for them, and she was sorry, but at least she wasn't the lonesome lightning rod, attracting all the craziness only to herself. She no longer had to doubt her own sanity. She had company in crazytown.

But at the moment, those were feelings best left unshared. The exit signs for Shaw's Crossing were a timely distraction. An avalanche of unwelcome memories coming down on her. Something fresh to feel tense and ambivalent about.

They drove through the downtown area, now

shuttered for the night. She'd never spent much time in Shaw's Crossing when she was a kid, but it looked different than she remembered. More attractive. Bigger, richer, more trendy and touristy. She passed an art cinema, a sculpture gallery, an ice cream parlor. They skirted the lake, which now sported a long and handsome boardwalk, and took the road that went up through the Heights, turning onto a road she didn't recognize.

"Where are we going?" she asked.

"I rented a vacation residence up on Shaw's Bluff, over the canyon."

"Oh. So we're not staying with Eric?"

"I barely know Demi Vaughan," he told her. "I don't want to impose on her. Plus, Eric's crazy in love, and I don't want to interrupt their big bonding moment."

This clearly wasn't the moment to expand on that loaded subject, so Fiona just kept on talking. "Where did you live when you were in high school here?"

"Otis Trask's place, way out on Vensel Road. It's ours now, too, but I'm not comfortable staying there either. Not if Otis was murdered there last week."

"Not to criticize your choices, but I doubt that a vacation cabin on the bluff will be much better, security-wise," she commented. "Not once they know we're here."

"Nate spent the afternoon wiring up the security system. We'll see anything that moves for a hundred meters around. Plus, it's on the edge of a cliff overlooking the Kettle River Canyon. Easier to defend than Otis's house."

"Wow, you think of everything. So is this a hot tryst? Or a desperate last stand?"

He hesitated. "Is this a trick question?"

She just laughed. "Feeling insecure, Anton?"

He grunted under his breath, which made her laugh. "Speaking of desperate last stands, I'm pretty good with a handgun," she told him. "I'm not much of a distance shooter, though."

"Good to know. We have a big arsenal, between what Nate brought and what I brought. You'll find something you like." He paused, and added, "And, ah…for the record, it's a hot tryst. Not a desperate last stand."

She smiled to herself in the dark. "Whatever you say."

"I picked it for the view of the Upper Falls," he said. "Saw the picture in an online brochure. You'll see in the morning."

He slowed to pull into a long driveway, and after a few minutes of switchback hairpin curves up a dark, narrow road, they pulled into a parking bay that was carved into the rocks below a house perched on a rock outcropping. A tall, chalet-style house, surrounded by towering pine and spruce trees.

Nate Murphy emerged and came down the walkway as they parked.

"Hey, Nate," Anton said as he got out. "Is the place ready?"

"It's all set. I ate with Eric and Wong down at Demi's restaurant. Wong's all settled in at Demi's house to cover them for the night, and the other two guys are headed back to Seattle. That place has awesome food, by the way. Demi sent some stuff up for you guys. The fridge is full whenever you're hungry."

"Great. Thanks. Want me to take first watch?"

"Nah, I'm good. I caught a nap before, and coffeed up at the restaurant. You guys just relax." Nate grabbed her travel bag. "Come inside. I'll show you the place."

The house was too large to be called a cabin.

Luxuriously finished, paneled in fragrant warm-tinted cedar. Wood floors, vaulted ceilings, vast windows. Comfortable understated furniture in earth-toned colors. A minimalist décor designed to soothe.

She wasn't soothable. But the place was pretty, and looked expensive. Surprise, surprise.

The front room looked out over the forest hillside, but the kitchen and bedrooms in the back opened out onto a big terrace that jutted out over the deep canyon. Nate showed her into one of the bedrooms and set down her bag.

After he left, she went over and peered out the picture window, trying to see through the darkness. If they were on the top of Shaw's Bluff, they were close enough to GodsAcre that they could almost see it across the canyon. If there was light. If you knew exactly where to look. Above the Upper Falls, and a little to the right.

Such proximity to the ashy ruins of that place gave her a ghostly chill.

Anton appeared in the doorway of her room. "There's food in the kitchen, and Demi sent up a few bottles of wine. What's your preference? White or red?"

"Seriously? We're looking GodsAcre in the face, and we have evil ghosts with an unknown agenda on our asses, and you're offering me alcohol?"

Anton's eyebrow tilted up. "Ahhhh...and this is so scandalous...why?"

"Under no circumstances would I drink something that would slow my reflexes," she told him. "I hesitate to do that even in the calmest moments of my life."

Anton shook his head. "Life goals," he said. "To make your world safe enough so you can dare to have a fucking glass of wine with your sandwich."

"You think I'm being paranoid? After the way things have been going? I thought we were on the same page now."

"Sure, but you have Nate and me keeping armed watch," he pointed out. "And you have a fuck-ton of security gear to give us ample warning if anyone approaches. You can afford to have a glass of wine."

"I don't outsource responsibility for my own safety to anyone," she told him.

"Oh man, that's spooky," Anton murmured. "I just heard Jeremiah speak right through your mouth. Cold chills."

"Don't start with that lecture again," she snapped. "It was bad enough the first time. If there's coffee in the kitchen, fine. That I'll drink."

Anton looked resigned. "There's plenty of coffee. Suit yourself."

She didn't have much of an appetite this close to GodsAcre. She nibbled a ham and cheese croissant and perched on the kitchen stool to sip her coffee while Anton devoured gigantic portions of lasagna and a plate with cold cuts and salads. His appetite showed no signs of flagging, so after a while, she left him to it and retreated to her room.

She sat on the bed watching the moon rise through the huge window, wondering how to inject some steel back into her spine. Something about this place killed her nerve.

She felt like the old Fiona here. The way she'd felt back at GodsAcre. Broken down, small, defenseless. A monster's next snack. Chained up for his convenience.

She'd been overcompensating for that ever since. All her life, she'd done everything she could think of to feel strong, armored, nobody's fool. Ready for anything.

And all her efforts were for nothing. All that energy she'd invested in shoring herself up, gone in a blink. In this place, she still felt like crawling under the bed.

She threw on her coat, shoved her feet back into the unlaced hiking boots, and slid open the picture window that opened onto the wide terrace to get some wind in her hair.

Anton was leaning on the wooden railing. She joined him, and they gazed out at the canyon together. The mountaintops were bright with moonlight, but the deep chasm where the river roared faintly below was a pool of impenetrable shadow.

It was like looking out over the edge of the world.

"Can't sleep?" he asked.

"Angry ghosts," she replied. "They make too much noise in my head."

"They shouldn't be angry at you," Anton said. "You never did anything wrong. Not a goddamn thing. Ever."

"Neither did you," she pointed out.

He grunted under his breath. "I'm no saint."

She turned to look at him. "No? Is that why your nightclubs are named Hellbound? Was that a fuck-you to Jeremiah? Another rebellion?"

He was silent for a moment, and then shook his head. "I just thought it sounded good," he said. "I wanted something loud. In-your-face. Unashamed."

They listened for a few minutes to the rush of the wind in the trees and the chatter of the creek. Then Anton spoke again.

"I didn't think I was reacting to Jeremiah at the time," he said. "But who knows what's down there. In the snake-pit of my mind."

"It's ugly down there," she said.

"True thing," he agreed.

After a moment, Fiona put out her hand, laying it on

his arm. "I'm so sorry that Kimball beat you because of me."

"It doesn't matter anymore," he said.

"It mattered to me," she said. "It meant everything to me."

"I knew what would happen to me when I did it," he said. "I knew exactly how angry he would be. I know how it would play out. Nobody forced me."

A hot pressure was building in her throat. "Kimball flogged you himself, right?"

He didn't bother to confirm it. "I don't regret helping you run away. I've done some questionable shit in my life, most of it self-serving." His eyes caught the moonlight as he faced her. "But not that time. That was my finest hour."

Her face burned. She yielded to his magnetic pull on her body and swayed close enough to smell his skin. Feel the delicious, life-giving heat rising off him.

"That kiss," she whispered. "At the bus station."

He looked embarrassed. "Sorry about that. It was my last chance to kiss you, maybe forever, so I took it. But after all the shit you'd been through with Kimball, I should never have touched you. It was selfish of me."

"Oh, no, no, no," she said swiftly. "It was wonderful. Innocent."

He grunted under his breath. "Not quite the word I would choose."

"I would," she said vehemently. "By contrast, I definitely would. Kimball had been feeling me up and muttering filth at me for months. It made me feel so dirty. Then you kissed me goodbye like you really saw me. I mean, me, Fiona. The person I am inside, not just my body. You kissed me like I was real. And special."

"You are special," he said. "You're incredible, Fi."

She let out a short, bitter laugh. "Thanks, Anton. But I'm not feeling it."

"Then try feeling this." He pulled her close, clamping her tight against his solid heat, and kissed her. Her head cupped in his big hand.

She kissed him back, wildly, feeling it come together. This was it. This was how she survived the darkness. This was the wild magic that could light her way.

The kiss was wildly carnal. Frenzied, urgent. She pulled back to drag in some air.

"I'm not innocent," he told her harshly. "Not at all. Not anymore."

"That's okay," she replied. "I'm not, either."

"Good. Then let me show you just how special I think you are," he said against her throat. "Let me make you come until you pass out."

"Whoa. The hell-bound bad boy comes out to play."

"If that's what makes you hot. Just be aware. This place makes me feel half-crazy. The sex will be crazy, too. Fair warning."

Yes. Her back straightened. Power filled her up. She felt taller, bigger, stronger. Ready to leap on him. Claim her prize.

She seized his shirt and yanked. "I'll warn you right back," she told him. "When it comes to crazy? Buddy, I leave you in the dust."

He let out a crack of laughter. "Competitive much?"

"Always."

Anton sank to his knees in front of her. "Let's see who begs for mercy first."

15

The buttons of her jeans yielded swiftly to his deft fingers. The hot, soft skin underneath drove him nuts. He had to cool this off. Slow this down. But not too much.

Tricky, to balance the struggle inside him. The wild animal lunging on the chain. The macho control freak with something to prove. Both of them needed to be in on the action. Fi liked that wild animal. It got her going.

Fi would always get exactly what she needed from him. Those were the rules.

Oh, fuck, where to even begin. He wanted to touch every part of her perfect body. He wanted to kiss her, lick her, fuck her endlessly. But she was tight and tense. Insanely wound up. Which meant lots of slow, juicy licking action to get her primed and ready.

Ahhh. Yeah. He was so down for that.

He dragged her stretchy panties down to bare the trimmed swatch of hair on her mound. It curled into tight reddish vortex over her clit. Her skin was so soft and hot, the damp curls silky soft against his lips. He loved her strong, shapely thighs. Loved sliding his tongue up and down her pussy lips. Endlessly. Patiently.

Slowly opening them to seek out the slick tender inner lips. Already wet and slick. He opened her wider, rolling his tongue slowly around her clit, caressing her inside her pussy with a slow, skillful thrust and swivel of his fingers. Going for the spot inside that made her shudder and moan. Opening her wider for his cock.

But not yet. First, he had to prove a point. A whole lot of points, like stars in the sky. First, he delivered that crucial message that words could not convey. Only his body could say it, burning with the need for worship her, pleasure her, and just…never…stop.

She arched back against the railing with a low, shuddering gasp as the first orgasm broke over her. Anton waited, enjoying the strong pulses of energy throbbing against his mouth and squeezing his probing fingers. The helpless sounds she made. *Yes.*

A good start. Promising. Time to get horizontal.

Fiona was so boneless and disoriented with pleasure, she barely protested when he picked her up. He carried her back through the opened door and was putting her down onto the bed before she could rally her defenses. She watched him tug off her unlaced boots, then her jeans and panties. Her long, strong legs were so fucking beautiful.

She shivered. "Brrr. Cold."

"Not for long." He lunged for the door and closed it, blocking out the chill and the eerie rush of the night wind. "I'll warm you up."

He flicked on the bedside lamp to the lowest setting,

just enough to admire the details of her. The ginger curls of pussy hair, the pale pinks and hot pinks of her pussy, in stark contrast to the milky Irish paleness of her freckled skin.

He wanted to memorize all those freckles. Kissing them and licking them. Points of reference like a star map to leading him through the dark. Her sexy juice was flowing, sticky and sweet, and her pussy was slick and hot. He shook inside with eagerness.

He helped drag the sweater off over her head and unhook her bra. Lifted off the flash grenade necklace and placed it carefully on the bedside table before ripping his own clothes off. Pulling out the condom he carried around, just because it would be tragic to miss a chance to get lucky with Fiona for something so stupid as a lack of latex.

Fiona rolled over to pull the covers down. Her ass was so beautiful like that, he grabbed her hips, holding her still. So fucking gorgeous. She stole his breath.

"Wait," he said. "Let me look at your ass. Fi. You are so damn beautiful."

She cast a glance over her shoulder through her heavy fall of red hair. A secret smile curved her lips as she worked it, giving no quarter. She widened her knees and arched her back, flaunting her luscious backside to his hungry eyes. Letting him catch a teasing glimpse of the shadowy glories between her legs. Luring him.

"Are you begging for mercy yet?" Her voice was husky and low.

He stroked his hands reverently over the incredibly, baby-smooth skin of her ass cheeks, admiring the curves and crevices. "If it would turn you on to win, I'll beg," he said. "I'm not proud."

"You don't need to beg. You need to stop fucking

around and get to work."

Ah, yes. That was the spirit. Lust had hijacked his ability to make a snappy comeback, so he got on with it. Rolled the condom on and positioned himself behind her, shaking with readiness. She rocked eagerly back with a gasp of excitement. Then the slow, careful back-and-forth, getting himself slick and shining with her sweet juice. Working himself inside her. Then, bit by bit, the rocking deepened into slow, surging thrusts.

She took him so deep, gasping as he stroked inside her plush depths, his whole length kissed and caressed by her shining pink pussy lips. Surging in. Gliding out. It was fucking killing him. She was so damn beautiful. Perfect. There was nothing else like her on earth.

They were far past teasing or talk. Fiona just braced herself against the padded headboard and held firm against his deep, heavy strokes, just gasping with each thrust. The gliding friction, the way they moved, was making them crazy. She was so hot and slick and yielding.

Fi threw her head back, moaning. He drove harder. She rocked back to take him deeper. Hotter, more frenzied. He reached around her hips and sought out the delicate pink pearl of her taut clit. Loved on it tenderly with his finger as he fucked her.

That brought her off. She came wildly, sobbing with pleasure. Her pussy squeezed at his cock like it was sucking on it, demanding everything from him.

It happened so naturally. Inevitably. His whole self, cracking wide open, to give her all of it. The good, the bad. Everything. He had no choice. No say.

After the cataclysm, he slumped over her damp body on the bed, panting. Everything he was, wide open to the wind and weather. Hers for the taking.

If she wanted it.

His face was pressed against her shoulder. She was breathing hard. He lifted himself away to let her breathe, and saw that raised, welted scar on her back, right before his eyes. The one where Kimball had hidden his microchip.

It made him fucking furious.

Fiona sensed it, turning to frown over her shoulder. "Something wrong? You're angry."

"Not with you," he assured her, kissing her shoulder. "It's nothing."

"Didn't feel like nothing."

Anton let out a sigh of trepidation. "I saw your scar," he admitted. "I had a moment. Being pissed at them. Not just Kimball for being a sleaze. Jeremiah, too, for not protecting you like he should have. For treating you like a thing that could be traded. There was no excuse for that."

Fiona slid off the bed, stretching, and tossed her hair back. She gathered the wavy mass and twisted it into a tight, fuzzy rope over her head, a look of challenge on her face.

"Maybe not," she said coolly. "But don't get all hung up on it."

He was chilled by her remote tone. "Hung up? What do you mean by that?"

She coiled the hair into a fuzzy topknot. "I don't do the 'poor Fiona' routine." She threw the words over her shoulder as she marched toward the bathroom. "The scars, the sob story, the shock value. Cults and child marriage. The ick factor. Fuck all that. I'm not interested in being anybody's poor, sad, damaged victim. I'd rather be that bad bitch with the machete. Besides, you have my same damn scars. Just more of them."

He followed her in and got rid of the condom. "So? That's different."

"Different how?" She shot him an ironic sidelong look and set the shower running. "Because you're a man? Please. You think that makes you experience pain differently?"

"Fi," he said. "Don't waste your energy being defensive with me. We have deadly enemies to fight. Save it for them."

"It's no problem, Anton." She stepped into the shower. "I got plenty for everyone."

The door slid shut. Anton just stood there, staring stupidly through the fogged glass at her beautiful wet body under the flow of water. Her back to him.

He shook himself free of his paralysis. He wasn't going to let her slam the door in his face like that. That shit ended right here.

He pulled open the sliding door and stepped inside.

16

Whoa. The shower just got really cramped and small with Anton introducing himself into it, blocking all the light, stealing all the air.

This was ridiculous. The big, steel-hard contours of his body, beaded with drops of water that slid sexily down the sculpted contours of his pecs, over his taut belly, into the dark thatch of wet hair around the root of his enormous, fully erect cock.

Oh, please. Not fucking fair, for him to be that big, that beautiful, that hot.

"What the hell do you think you're doing here?" she complained. "You're too big for this shower."

"So exert yourself. Make some goddamn room for me."

The edge in his voice made her bristle. She wiped water from her eyes and tried to retreat. Nowhere to go. Just hard, wet wall tile. "What the fuck is that supposed to mean?"

He responded by seizing her. Covering her mouth with a hot, claiming kiss.

She drew back just as a reflex from his aggressive energy, but only for an instant, because God, he tasted good. Hot and salty-sweet. She licked her lips, gazing into his hooded eyes. Drops of water trickled down the stark, perfect angles of his face.

Aw, hell with it. She grabbed him. Wrapped her arms around him and kissed him back. As ravenous as he was, like she hadn't just been fabulously pounded into a state of boneless bliss. She was still slick and soft and quivering inside from the last sex session, but if he still had more to give, she was taking it. Forget pride or dignity or bullshit man-woman games. She felt fierce and pure and raw. She wanted what was hers.

Besides. She liked him like this. Uncompromising. Hard to handle. In her face.

They devoured each other's mouths. She gripped his cock as the water beat down on them. He caressed her pussy, working her clit until she writhed against him, gasping for breath. Keening as the sensations grew. Swelling into something huge, terrifying.

She was wiped out by the cataclysm tearing through her.

When her eyes finally opened, Anton had his hands under her ass. She was braced against the tile wall, straddling his hips. His cock prodding her pussy lips. Waiting.

She reached down and gripped him at the root of his shaft, shifting herself in position. Getting him just the right angle to shove his thick, gorgeous cock inside her.

And then oh…yes. That slick, slow, gliding invasion. The bulb of his penis, shoving inside, deep and slow and stroking her, everywhere. Her body transformed into a hot glow of frantic welcome around him. Taking him in. Craving

SHANNON McKENNA

more. *Yes. Yes. Yes.*

She melted still more with each deep, gliding stroke. He stared at her with his soul in his eyes. She strained against him, reaching for it…

Exploding once again.

Anton pulled out of her. He let out a strangled shout against her shoulder as his own orgasm wrenched him.

The realization came very slowly. Tiptoeing into her mind in shocked disbelief.

No condom. Neither one of them had even thought about it.

He hadn't come inside her, but even so. That was so dangerous. So irresponsible.

Anton kept his face pressed against her hair. The water bounced off his massive shoulders. His lips moved softly against her throat, his teeth nipping her gently.

"Anton," she whispered. "What the hell did we just do? With no latex?"

He nipped her again and followed it with a kiss and a hungry swipe of his tongue. "Sorry," he said. "I didn't mean to. I've never done that. Forgotten to suit up, I mean."

She closed her eyes, biting her lip. There was nothing to say. It would be dumb and unfair to scold. It wasn't like she'd thought of it herself. She'd dragged him inside her body. He had the marks of her nails on his ass. She had to own this.

It was crazy, to have forgotten something so basic. Her better judgment was trashed. She'd let Anton Trask fuck it right out of her. Squealing with delight all the while.

Time to take responsibility for herself. By brute force if necessary.

She pushed him away. He resisted at first. "Huh? What?"

"I need space," she said curtly. "I can't breathe."

Anton set her down onto her feet.

Fiona shoved him away from herself, soaped up her hand and washed briskly between her legs. "More space than that," she told him. "I need to rinse."

Anton's mouth tightened, but he shifted back. "Really?" he said. "It has to be like this between us? Every fucking time we get it on?"

"You are too much," she said. "I'm on overload. I've already got homicidal thugs and angry ghosts riding my ass. Now I've got you breathing down my neck and banging me into screaming oblivion every chance you get."

His eyes were hot with controlled anger. "You were with me the whole way."

"Yes! I know! That's the problem, Anton! I don't want to hurt your feelings, but holy fuck! Letting you inside me without a condom? I am losing my fucking grip. It is time for both of us to back off from this. Let me have some air."

"You're panicking again," he said.

"Oh! Yah think?" She laughed at him, bitterly. "In case you haven't noticed, I'm not exactly a poster child for emotional stability even in the best of times. Stop breaking me down into pieces. I can't function in pieces, and I'm all I've got."

"Not anymore," Anton said.

That brought on a wave of panic that made her practically feel faint. She shoved again, or tried to, but the guy was rooted to the ground like an oak.

"Don't," she said furiously. "That's just more of the same. Jerking me around."

"You're not alone anymore. You've got me now. Just fucking accept it."

"Oh, God." She dragged a towel off the rack and wrapped it around herself. She tried to speak, to swallow, but her throat was one big, hot aching lump. "You're making this worse. Don't ask me for something I can't give. I'm a mess. I just can't."

"You think I'm any better?" he demanded. "Want to know something? You're the first woman I've ever had sex with in my house since I bought that place. Four years ago."

"But..." She gave him a blank look. "Where do you go to do the deed, then?"

"I keep a suite permanently rented at the Four Seasons Hotel for that. I don't bring women to my own place. Not anyone. Not ever."

"God, what a waste," she said. "Your house would make the ladies melt."

"I didn't want to melt the ladies. They didn't belong in my house. But you did. I didn't even think twice about taking you there. Fucking you there. And I didn't even realize how weird that was until right now."

"I'm not sure what you're trying to communicate to me with this fun fact, but that is messed up," she informed him. "Crazy extravagant, too, but I already knew that about you. A dedicated hotel suite just for playing with your fuck buddies? That's a man who is deeply committed to his unwillingness to commit."

"Exactly," he said forcefully. "And it worked for me just fine. Until now."

Her throat was getting that hard ache again. "You're reading way too much into this," she said. "It's all the danger, all the drama. All our history. You barely know me anymore, Anton. It's just great sex. Just be content with that."

"Too late," he said. "The damage is done. Don't be

afraid of this, Fi."

She let out an incredulous laugh. "Are you fucking kidding me? Can you even hear yourself? Don't be afraid?"

"That's what I said."

"I am nothing but afraid! Of this town, of Kimball, of being chopped up and raped and murdered. I'm trying to be brave—"

"You are brave. Incredibly brave."

"Shut up and let me finish," she snapped. "A person only has so much courage at a time. I can't be brave in all ways, at all times. It's not fair to ask that of me!"

"You're braver than you know," he said. "And we're worth the risk."

She looked away from the intense longing in his eyes. "Anton. Don't. Not fair."

"You came to me for help," he said. "You came on to me, hard. You fuck me like a runaway train. You make me want something I've never wanted in my life. And then you shoot me down. Every damn time. What is your problem, Fi?"

"If I had the answer to that, I would have solved it by now," she said fiercely. "This is not a game. I'm not fucking around. I really am exactly this hard to deal with. I genuinely am way more trouble than I'm worth. Face it. Back off. Let me breathe."

Anton grabbed another towel from the stack and dried himself with furious energy. He pushed past her into the bedroom and picked up his jeans.

"Breathe, then," he said. "The air's all yours."

"Anton—"

"Get some rest." He buttoned his jeans, and leaned to scoop up the rest of his clothes. "Busy day tomorrow hunting angry ghosts. You'll need all your strength."

The door clicked shut behind him.

Fiona pulled her sweater and underwear back on and shuffled over to the window that looked out over the terrace.

Dawn had turned the night sky to a deep charcoal gray. She could see the shape of the opposite ridge now through the window. If she went outside and squinted hard, she might even see the Upper Falls and the pool below, where they used to swim.

One of the two good things about this place was how incredibly, outrageously beautiful it was. Mountains, forests, flowers. The falls.

The other good thing had been Anton.

She closed her eyes. Miserable as she was, the intense pleasure he'd given her still vibrated through her body. A residual glow of sexual delight.

It started with that reverent, worshipful kiss at the Shaw's Crossing bus station. Spontaneous and sweet. Charged with longing and hopes and dreams.

That kiss was a beacon in the darkness. It was proof, or at least hope, that love and sex and all that stuff could be a good thing. Beautiful. Holy, even. Untainted by Kimball's filth. She'd clung to the memory of that kiss like a talisman.

And for some reason, she was doing her best to kill it.

17

Anton stood outside Fiona's bedroom door for a full minute before he could bring himself to knock. Crazy, that he knew so much about her and had such intense feelings about her and yet, he didn't know yet if she was a morning person. If she'd slept at all. If she'd bite his head off again.

He rapped on the door. "Hey. Fi? Breakfast with Eric and Demi and Chief Bristol at the café. Can you be ready in fifteen?"

The door jerked open. Fiona stood before him, fully dressed, already zipping up her coat. Her hair was tightly braided in a long, thick rope that hung over her shoulder.

Morning person. Duly noted. The flashbang necklace still gleamed, swinging below her breasts. He decided to take it as a promising sign.

"I'm ready now," she said. "Let's roll."

Huh. The flat tone of her voice told him he was still in the doghouse. Whatever. He'd been in one doghouse or another for most of his life, and had the scars to prove it.

"Before we go, can I have your microchip?" he asked. "Eric wants to take a look, so I'll put it in the file along with my notes about the Seattle attack, and the police reports from Highettsville. Eric's good at poking around on the darknet. He'll be careful with it."

Fiona unfastened the earring without protest and unscrewed the hanging bead. She plucked out the small plastic capsule that protected the microchip and held it out.

"If he burns my last password attempt, I will flatten him," she announced.

Anton took it and tucked it into the plastic envelope. "He won't do that to you."

Nate followed them out of the house as they got into the car. "Wait," he called, running down the porch stairs. "I'll come down along with you. I want to hear what's said at this meeting. Plus, I'm hungry and the food is awesome. I can nap after breakfast."

He and Fiona were locked in frigid silence in the car. Halfway down the hill toward town, Nate met his eyes in the rearview with a puzzled frown. Anton just shook his head. No way could he explain it to someone else if he didn't understand it himself.

Fortunately the drive wasn't too long.

Eric was looking out the restaurant window when they pulled up. He bounded out the front door, grinning, which was strange itself. Eric had never been the exuberant type.

His brother's face was bruised, scraped and scabbed up, and he limped as he approached them, but he had a look in his eyes Anton had never seen. Like he was flying on some buzzy happiness drug, but there was an edge of anxiety to it. As if he were all too aware that it could wear off at any moment and brute reality could come crashing down.

The look of a man who couldn't quite believe his luck.

Eric gave Anton a hard hug, and Fiona a more careful, gentle one. "Hey, Fi. Look at you, all grown up. You look great. Congratulations for making it this far in one piece."

"Same to you," Fiona said. "Sorry to say it, but you look like hell."

Eric's grin widened. "Yeah. I still can't believe we survived. Come meet Demi."

Demi Vaughan came out from behind the counter as they entered. Like Eric, she had scrapes and bruises on her face, and the same glow of terrified happiness in her light green eyes. She was short and curvaceous and extremely pretty, her dark brown hair twisted up into a thick messy bun, just a few long wisps dangling around her chin.

"Great to see you again, Anton," she said.

He embraced her carefully, mindful of her injuries. "You two look like you're just back from the battlefield."

Demi and Eric exchanged goofy looks. "Yeah, we got a beat-down. But you should have seen the other guy." She looked at Eric with a dazzling smile. "Thanks to him, of course. I can't take much credit for that." She gave Fiona an impulsive hug. "So you're the famous Fiona? I've heard all about you. What wild tales they tell."

Fiona looked alarmed. "What tales? What did they tell you about me?"

"Oh, you know. The daring escape from GodsAcre, the day before the forced wedding to the evil pedophile. You and Anton and the nine-mile hike over the Bluff and down to the bus station in town. It's a breathtaking story. You could write a book."

Fiona looked horrified. "I do everything in my power

not to think about it."

"Ah. Well. Sorry I mentioned it, then," Demi said smoothly. "Come on in and get some coffee. We've got a breakfast buffet just about ready. And there's Elisa with the cheese scones."

A slim woman swathed in a big apron deposited a platter of hot scones on the table. Golden-brown eyes, and dark curly hair twisted into a tousled up-do.

Elisa's shy smile froze as she locked eyes with Nate. She stood there, at a loss for a moment, then shook herself out of a daze. "Ah...sorry. I'll just...go back and get the rest." She disappeared back into the kitchen.

Nate followed her every move. Not even trying to pretend that he wasn't.

Anton was unsurprised. Nate had been intrigued with Elisa ever since she'd almost slashed him in to the next world with a box-cutter on their last foray to Shaw's Crossing. Which was to say, she fit right into the place's general high-tension vibe.

Anton turned back to Eric. "I'm sure the food is great," he said. "But this isn't a conversation to have in a public restaurant."

"It won't be public this morning," Eric told him. "This is the diner's day off. We have the place all to ourselves."

Anton turned to Demi as she swept past him, laden with a platter of breakfast sausages. "Demi, I was sorry to hear about your dad," he offered. "Sorry about all of it."

Demi's smile vanished, and for the first time he glimpsed the strain in her eyes.

"Thanks," she said. "But it was good to learn the truth, even if it hurts. It makes things clearer going forward. Excuse me. Gotta help Elisa get the rest of this food out."

Fiona watched Demi hurry away, puzzled. "What was that about?" she asked. "What truth? What hurts?"

Anton hesitated. Eric finally spoke. "Her asshole dad was in with whoever attacked them up at GodsAcre. Kimball, I assume. But he lost his nerve and tried to run. And he organized to have Demi kidnapped so he could defraud the ransom money from her granddad. That was supposed to be his getaway fund. Real prince of a guy, but whoever was using him killed him a couple days ago, probably with that stealth weapon, if Eric's hunch is right. I'm sorry for Demi, but I'm not shedding any tears for the guy."

"Oh, God." Fiona winced. "That's awful."

"Yeah," Eric said. "No father of the year awards given around here."

"Parents," Fiona said. "We get what we get."

After a tense silence, Anton blurted out the words on impulse. "We could do better than they did," he said. "Better than the whole worthless fucking pack of them."

Eric and Fiona were both struck silent by that bizarre outburst.

Fuck.

The charged silence dragged on and on but Anton didn't trust himself to break it. He'd only make things worse. Since he didn't seem to have any goddamn control over what came out of his mouth this morning. Where the hell had that come from?

"Ah...I hope you're right, when the time comes," Eric said slowly. "I just never thought I'd hear anything like that come out of your mouth." He gave Fiona a speculative look. "So, ah...does this mean that you two are—"

"No," Fiona said. "It doesn't mean anything. Other than he's short on sleep and not making much sense. Excuse me. I need coffee."

The two of them watched Fiona walk away. She looked just as hot in the hiking boots, jeans and Gore-Tex coat as she had in her stretchy silver mini-dress and her thigh-high boots. She affected him just as strongly.

"Well," Eric said, gazing after her with speculative eyes. "She turned out…interesting."

Anton cleared his throat. "You could say that."

"So are you two a thing?"

Anton hesitated. "It's complicated."

"Ah. Well, good. So are you. Since the day you were born. Sounds perfect."

"It's not so simple," Anton growled. "She's not on board. She's tense. Like I told you, her cousin was just murdered, and she's been fighting off mystery thugs trying to slice her to pieces ever since. It's not the most promising time to try to win her over."

"Wow. Sounds intense. Have you two, ah…" Eric waggled a suggestive eyebrow.

"That," Anton said, biting out each word. "…is none of your…fucking…business."

"Got it. Loud and clear." Eric controlled the grin, but he couldn't hide the delighted look in his eyes. "You were bored as hell with the spoiled socialites and the underwear models. They just wanted to fuck a famous bad boy and go viral. You need someone tough and smart. And real. Someone who can kick your ass to the next level."

The tension inside him rose higher. "Don't say that," he said. "I have no idea if I'm going to be able to pull this off, so don't act like it's a done deal. You'll jinx me."

Something in Anton's voice made Eric's smile fade. "Okay," he said. "I'm sorry you're having a hard time with it.

But I still like to see you this way."

"What way?" he snarled. "Fucked up, stressed out, miserable? Thanks, dude. Nice to know you care."

"I do care." Eric's eyes burned with intensity. "That's the whole point. Because so do you, finally. For the first time in I don't even fucking know how long, you're acting like you actually care. You genuinely want something. You've been playing it cool all your life, or at least since the fire. You never let yourself care about anything. Things just came to you. Money, fame, a big fancy career, blah blah blah, but you never seemed to give much of a fuck, one way or the other. But this? This, you want."

Anton couldn't deny it. "Ironic," he said sourly. "I go and pick the one thing I can't have to give a shit about."

"We'll see," Eric said. "I have a piece of advice for you."

"Oh, great," Anton muttered. "This should be good."

"It *is* good," Eric said forcefully. "Not easy, but unbeatable if you can pull it off. Just solve her problem. Raze that motherfucker right down to the ground and salt the earth around it. You'll be amazed how the new horizons will open up. Like magic."

Anton stared at his brother, then at Fiona, who sipped her coffee, stone-faced, staring out the window. As far from himself as she could get without leaving the building.

"I don't think I have any choice about that," he said. "Her problems are our problems. And if we don't solve her problems, she won't survive at all."

"Well? There you go, then," Eric encouraged. "Solve them. It'll soften her right up."

"She doesn't even know what it means to soften up," Anton said. "That's the problem. She's never had the chance.

In her whole damn life."

"So give her one," Eric said. "That's the part you can provide. Don't worry about the rest of it. Focus on making yourself useful. Let everything else take care of itself."

A ray of morning sunlight slanted through the window and hit Fi's hair as she sipped her coffee. It lit up that coppery color. So bright. It dazzled him.

He wondered if softening up was something that a person could learn with time.

Maybe. Maybe not, but who cared? He liked her just how she was right now. All sharp angles and jagged edges.

After all. He was pretty fucking hard-edged himself. Made out of scrap metal and scar tissue. Fuck it. He was tough. He could take it.

It was what he was built for.

18

"A pathogen?" Fiona looked around at everyone at the table. "You really think someone from GodsAcre exposed the town to a pathogen? I thought the Prophet's curse was a weapon of some kind."

"It is a weapon," Eric said. "A biological weapon. The only thing I can figure is that it's a two-part thing. You're vulnerable to the frequency that comes out of the death-pen only if you've been exposed to the virus. But you don't know that you're vulnerable, because the virus is asymptomatic. That's my theory."

"Sounds far-fetched," Fiona said.

"Is it any more far-fetched than your story?" Eric pointed out.

Demi hurried to fill the loaded silence. "If it's true, then we can't even begin to guess how many of the deaths in Shaw's Crossing are actually murders," she said. "We know about my mom and dad and Otis because they boasted about it to us. They also said something about a time window for contagion, and a database with names of everyone who had been exposed. That my name is in it."

The group fell silent over the clutter of breakfast dishes. Most platters were empty, and many pots of coffee had been drunk. It had taken some time to thrash through it all.

"He'll pay." Eric's voice was hard.

Demi gave him a disapproving look. "If you recall, he already did," she said. "All of those guys did. You saw to it. Personally."

"Not that guy," Eric said. "He was still breathing when we left that night. And in any case, those guys were just hired muscle. We need to cut the head off the snake."

"Agreed," Anton said.

"You boys just hold your horses." Chief Bristol's voice was stern. "There will be no snakehead cutting going on around here. We don't know exactly what we're dealing with yet, and I'm still considering options. Don't go vigilante on me. That's not how we do things in Shaw's Crossing."

"Thank you, Chief." Demi's voice was hard. "Listen to Chief Bristol, gentlemen. No pissing contests. No scoring points. No secret pacts. That bullshit does not go over here."

Eric and Anton exchanged unreadable glances.

"The virus must work incredibly fast," Fiona said.

"The guy who tried to use it on me was expecting an immediate reaction," Eric said. "I could see from his face that he was used to having it stop people in their tracks."

"But it didn't work on you," Fiona said.

"Either that particular device wasn't working, or else I'm immune to the pathogen," Eric said. "Which got me to thinking about the injections Kimball gave us that last year. Remember? Seemed like every other day he was sticking us with a new shot."

"I remember that," Anton said.

Fiona's stomach lurched. She remembered it, too. All too well. She was needle-phobic because of it. Every time she had to get a shot of any kind, she would see Kimball's flushed, grinning face hanging over her, and smell his foul breath.

He used to rub his erection against her thigh while he swiped her arm with the disinfectant. *Brace yourself, rosebud. This is going to hurt.*

She'd puked her guts up after Kimball's shots every time, and she still threw up after any kind of hypodermic injection. They made her stomach turn. After all these years.

"Hey, Fiona?" Demi was leaning forward, concern on her face. "You okay? You just got really pale."

"I'm fine, thanks," she said. "I thought my tale of woe was freaky, but this one is even weirder."

"Same tale," Anton said. "Same weirdness. Just a different angle."

"We're in over our heads," Chief Bristol said. "We need the Center for Disease Control. They have to run tests. Find out what the hell is going on."

Panic made Fiona's stomach lurch again. "I won't be anybody's lab rat ever again," she told him. "I've had enough needle-sticks to last me a lifetime."

Chief Bristol gave her a long look. "Stay calm, Miss Garrett. Right now, we're just talking options. If Eric's theory pans out, then the four of you might be immune to whatever this weapon might be, and verifying that would make everything clearer, right?"

"What about everyone who isn't immune?" Eric said. "They're still in danger. Like Demi. You, too, Chief. Everyone who's in their database. We can't have a panic. We can't have the press come down on us. We can't have local people going up there, because any one of them could be murdered just as easily as Otis and Terry and Ben Vaughan were. If those bastards felt cornered, they could use that thing to kill hundreds of people in just a few minutes. Without even getting out of their car. We have to step softly."

"Have you been back up to GodsAcre since the attack?" Anton asked Eric.

Demi shuddered. "Hell, no, we haven't. After what we went through up there?"

"But it would be different this time," Eric said. "We're on guard. We'll be a team. We know more. We'll be heavily armed." From the coaxing tone in Eric's voice, this was a topic they had discussed many times without reaching any resolution. "You and Fiona would have Murphy and Wong both guarding you. They weren't here during the contagion period, so they won't be subject to the Prophet's curse. We need to see what's happening up there before we send anyone else into danger. And with both Anton and me together, and armed? I'd just like to see them try to fuck with the two of us."

"I do not want to see it!" Demi said, through her teeth. "I don't give a damn how good a fighter you are. I don't care that you were a Marine. I don't care that you trained as a commando for your whole childhood. I don't care how many asses you can kick. I still don't want you anywhere near that place!"

"Speaking of kicking asses," Fiona said. "You can sign me up for that. I'm going up there with you."

"Fuck no!" Anton could feel how useless the words were as soon as he met Fiona's gaze.

"It's not up to you," she said calmly. "This is my fight, too. I had all the same injections you had. I was trained by Jeremiah. I can fight. I can handle a gun. I want to see the old place. There's no reason for me not to go up there with you. No logical, coherent reason at all."

"Yes, there fucking is," Anton snarled. "It's too damn dangerous!"

Fiona let out an impatient sigh. "If this is just because I'm female, don't waste our time. I'm not the little girl you put on that bus years ago."

"Moving on," Anton growled. "We'll argue about this later."

"No, we won't," Fiona said. "Because there's nothing to argue about."

An awkward pause. People exchanged nervous glances and cleared their throats.

"So, ah...let's recap," Eric said swiftly. "Something they want was buried in the caverns when we blew them up. Maybe something in Kimball's med lab, maybe something associated with the death pen. Plus they want Fiona's chip, which may or may not be connected. They're willing to kill anyone who gets in their way."

"But who?" Chief Bristol said. "Who's willing?"

Fiona gave him an incredulous look. "You're still asking yourself that? After everything we just told you? Kimball put that chip in my back! He ran the lab. He gave the injections. Of course it's Kimball! Who else could it be?"

"Kimball is dead," Chief Bristol said forcefully. "I was there when they identified those bodies. I saw them with my own eyes. The criminologists know their stuff."

Fiona shook her head. "I feel Kimball's hand in this," she said stubbornly. "I don't even know how to describe it. It's like a bad smell that's specific to him."

Bristol looked dubious. "In my experience, evil all has the same general stink," he said gruffly. "Rot is rot. Not a lot

178

of nuance there."

"Then who killed my cousin and carved her up?" Fiona's voice had begun to shake despite her best efforts. "Who keeps trying to cut that thing out of my back?"

"I don't know," the chief said grimly. "But it's hard to argue with a charred skull."

"Oh, but that's where you're wrong," Fiona told him. "That's my special superpower. I can argue with anything."

Chief Bristol's lips twitched before he could stop himself. He glanced at Anton. "You've got some interesting times ahead of you, young man."

Fiona ignored that stonily. "I want to see that charred skull," she told him. "I want to see those forensic records. If possible."

Bristol sighed. "I see. So you're a forensic scientist now?"

"No, of course I'm not. But I'm curious. And what could I hurt, just by looking? Are the records still available somewhere?"

"The bones themselves were claimed years ago," the chief said. "By a sister, if I'm not mistaken."

"I didn't even know he had a sister," Fiona said. "But what about the files? The pictures they took of him?"

Bristol hesitated for a moment. "I'll see what I can do," he said.

"You said that you saw cars up at GodsAcre," Anton said to Eric. "Did you run their plate numbers?"

"The chief did," Eric said. "They're stolen plates from random locations. Whoever these people are, they're very well organized."

"And Otis's pictures? The cars you said he saw up there?"

179

"All gone," Eric said. "They smashed Otis's camera when they attacked us."

"They have surveillance up there," Demi said stonily. "Lots of it. Hidden in all those thousands of trees. Whatever you do up there, they'll watch you. Whatever you say, they'll hear it."

Eric and Anton exchanged glances. "Bring it," Anton said. "I have a few things I'd like to say to that guy."

"Oh, great," Demi snapped. "Your brother's as bad as you are."

"Worse, actually," Fiona commented.

Demi smacked her hand down onto the table, making her coffee cup rattle. "So you two are just going to egg each other on?" she demanded. "You want to just go up there and what, spit in their eye? Offer yourself up as fucking *bait*?"

"We should break this wide open," Chief Bristol said. "Right now. Call the FBI. Turn it over to the CDC. Call the press. Make a lot of noise. Let them overrun the place and test the living bejesus out of everything. If we turn this into a three-ring circus, that'll keep those bastards away."

"What makes you so sure?" Eric said. "What if they retaliate? They have a doomsday weapon, as far as Shaw's Crossing residents are concerned. They've killed before. What would they do if they had nothing to lose?"

"I don't know," Chief Bristol said impatiently. "But that Lone Ranger stuff you fellows want to do is reckless and irresponsible. I can't condone it."

"We're the only ones who can face the death pen safely, so we should —"

"Safely, my ass!" Demi yelled. "They could still just shoot you!"

"They could try," Eric corrected softly.

"The death-pen didn't work on you, yes," Demi said hotly. "That time. It's a big leap to assume it won't work on Anton, or Mace, or Fiona. Or that it will never work on you. That conclusion is premature. Maybe that death-pen's battery ran down. Maybe he had a bum death-pen but there are eleven more in the box that work just fine. We don't know! We can't know!"

"We've waited as long as we can." Eric turned to the police chief. "Don't call the cavalry just yet. One more look around up there first. Just one last time."

The two men stared at each other. Wade Bristol's jaw was set.

"Your wife lived here thirteen years ago, right?" Eric said. "And your girls? They were little then. In primary school, right? They would all have been exposed to this thing."

"Don't jerk me around, Eric," Bristol warned.

"You think these bastards won't target your family? It's the first thing they'll do."

"Angela and the girls can fly down and visit her sister in San Diego," Bristol said stiffly. "I'll give you today. Tomorrow I call the Feds, and the CDC." He looked over at Fiona. "What about that microchip? What's on it?"

"Nothing I can use," she told him. "It's a password-protected portal. I had six password attempts. I've burned five of them."

There was a dismayed silence.

"Yes, I know. It was years ago." Fiona's voice sounded defensive. "At the time, I had no idea what was at stake. I thought it was just something in my past for me to process and hopefully move past. I never dreamed that anyone would come after me for it."

Anton pushed the envelope up the table toward his brother. "Here's the chip."

Eric nodded. He took it and slid the envelope into a briefcase beside his feet.

It felt strange to have it out of reach, as if she were giving up part of her body.

The bell over the door pinged. Nate came in, hunched against the chilling wind in his Shearling leather jacket. "Here's her new phone, as requested." He placed a smartphone on the table in front of Fiona. It was nested in a protective case of hideous lime green rubber. He set down the box next to it. "Paperwork, charger, cords and whatnot. Sorry about the color. It was that or pink, and I didn't take you for the pink type. They also had moppets, puppies or kittens. And a skull with snakes coming out its eyes, which I actually considered for you. But in the end, I didn't have the nerve."

Fiona smiled at him. "Green is fine. I'm not fussy."

"I charged it for you," Nate told her. "And programmed in all our numbers."

"Thanks," she said. "How much to I owe you?"

Nate's eyes slid over to Anton. "Take it away, pal." He looked at Fiona. "Talk to the guy whose name is on the credit card."

Fiona nodded. "Of course."

"Never mind that," Anton said. "We've got bigger things to worry about."

Nate slid back into his chair, his gaze flicking down to the table where Elisa sat, sipping her coffee and carefully not looking at him. "So? What did I miss?"

"Nothing I haven't filled you in on before," Anton said. "You and Wong will cover Demi and Fiona here at the diner this afternoon while Eric and I go up to check out the situation up at GodsAcre."

"I'm coming with you guys," Fiona said. "As I stated before."

"Goddamnit, Fi—"

"If you want to be gallant and chivalrous, give me first pick from your gun stash," she suggested. "A big-ass shotgun would suit my mood."

Eric looked impressed. "I hope you have something she likes," he said. "I wouldn't want to disappoint that woman."

19

The pick-up truck was dead silent on the way up Kettle Canyon Road. Fiona had planted her ass in the tight back seat of the truck's cab, and there was nothing he could do about it, apart from dragging her out bodily. He'd even considered that idea, and then abandoned it. That could only end in disaster, and possible dismemberment.

He couldn't control her or persuade her, which made it really fucking hard to protect her.

After one too many sidelong glances from Eric, he finally turned on his brother. "What the fuck are you looking at?" he snarled. "Watch the goddamn road."

Eric shot Fiona a glance in the rear-view. "It's the look on both your faces. Like you're being marched to your execution. Fi, if you've changed your mind, say the word. I can turn this truck —"

"I never change my mind," she said flatly. "I need to see GodsAcre. Drive on. We're not going to enjoy it, but we're tough. We'll live."

Eric stared out at the road ahead. "I don't think we'll run into those assholes up there today," he said. "I doubt they'd mobilize again so soon. I slammed them hard the other day, and you slammed them again in Seattle. We've thinned out their ranks."

"And pissed them off," Anton said.

"I can't wait to piss Kimball off," Fiona said. "Personally. Right before I shoot him in the face."

That was a conversation killer, if anyone had felt like talking.

Anton started recognizing landmarks. Rock formations that loomed above them as they rounded the final bend were eerily familiar. Eric slowed and then stopped next to the huge boulders that flanked the entrance to GodsAcre. There had used to be a gate between them. Now there was only a heavy, rusty chain lying on the ground.

Eric gunned the engine. The truck's tires bumped over the chain. They crossed the bridge, weathered and sagging but still miraculously intact, over the creek. Slightly farther down the hill that creek joined with another spring that then became the Upper and Lower Kettle Falls. They drove along the washed out road alongside the creek bed that cut through the narrow canyon. That access point had been chosen by Jeremiah for defensive purposes, and Anton and Eric and Mace had all spent many long, chilly nights perched in those rocks with a gun, wearing infrared goggles. Sentry duty. No rest for the vigilant.

They emerged into the small hanging valley beyond, and they had arrived.

Eric drove past the ruins of the Great Hall without stopping, and onto the muddy track leading downhill. He parked on the hillside and they got out of the pickup, struck silent by the strangeness of being there.

There were no signs of any people. Just the sound of birds and the rush of the wind in the trees. No vehicles. Just tire tracks in the mud and garbage everywhere.

Fiona shouldered the bag that held her pistol, spare ammo, flashlight and water and set off briskly toward the excavated pit over what used to be the caverns without even turning to look back up at the ruins of the Great Hall.

"Hey," he called after her. "Wait up!"

She didn't seem to hear him. But he knew what drove her. The memories that thronged this place were deafening. One look at the Great Hall took the air right out of him. He was skilled at not thinking about shit that bothered him, but not when it was all rolled into one big fucking lump and shoved forcibly down his throat.

He and Eric scanned the place as they followed after her, but they saw nothing but trees bending in the wind. There was a smell of snow in the air. They were high up in altitude here. The crisp, clean scent of the air was achingly familiar.

They were approaching the edge of the pit when his brother spoke again. "Their cars were parked there," Eric said, pointing at the tire tracks.

"I doubt they've been back since their clean-up crew came and went," Anton said.

"Nate's drone has been monitoring the place. We haven't seen any movement up here," Eric said. "Not yet."

"They couldn't clean up the blood," Fiona said.

Eric and Anton walked up and joined her on the hillside near the big pit. The hair escaping from her tight braid whipped around her face in the cold wind. She stared at a brownish stain on the ground, her mouth grim.

"One of them shot himself in the thigh by accident

186

while we were fighting," Eric said. "He bled out right here. Another one got knocked out right about...here." He indicated the spot. "Two of them fell into the pit. One was face down in the water when I left, and he'd been that way for a while. I'm pretty sure he was dead. The other one had a broken leg, but he was still alive when we left."

"I would have killed them all," Fiona said.

Eric shrugged. "Demi didn't want me to. They were already neutralized."

Fiona crouched down next to the bloodstain. "The vanguard of the Army of the Faithful has gotten soft," she commented. "The effect of corruption from too much contact with a decadent society speeding toward its inevitable doom."

"Or maybe it's love," Anton said. "Love fucks you up."

Eric looked like he was trying not to smile. "I'm riddled with fatal flaws," he said. "No longer worthy to be God's holy weapon. Big shame."

"We're all defective," Fiona said, prodding at the bloodstain with the end of a twig. "That's why we're all still alive."

"Don't dwell on it," Anton said. "Stay sharp."

"Like a razorblade." She stood up and tossed the twig away. "I'm glad the blood is still visible. I wish it was all visible. Like a scorecard. They got my Patti. I want to see the chalk outlines where those bastards fell."

She brushed her hands off on her jeans, and without hesitation, lowered herself over the edge of the excavated pit at a point where the drop was shortest. She dropped down, landing in a deep crouch.

Anton followed her down, a swift, jolting slip-and-slide through rocks and mud. "Damn it, Fi. Slow down."

"Can't," she said. "This place will eat us alive if we

wander around in a daze."

Anton looked up at Eric on the ledge above. "Can you keep watch?"

Eric lifted Otis's Glock. "Make it snappy. This is no place to linger."

Hard to be snappy in sloppy, sucking, ankle-deep mud. They slogged their way laboriously all around the perimeter of that big, wet hole in the ground. At first they saw nothing but rocks, brush and a whole lot of garbage.

Ultimately, the garbage was the key. Once he started to really see the cigarette butts, soda cans and pop-tops, a pattern began to emerge. Like a trail of bread crumbs, the scattered trash got thicker, on a beaten trail that finally dead-ended up against a raggedy pile of cut tree branches leaning against the side of the pit, which was deeper and sheerer on this side. Anton grabbed some armfuls of the branches, tossing them aside.

Then he saw it. A diagonal line in the mud, too long and regular to be anything but man-made. A concrete wall, partially collapsed. A weather-beaten sheet of plywood leaned against it.

He pulled the plywood aside, revealing a triangular black hole that led back into utter darkness. Near the door, the tunnel had been shored up with chunks of new lumber.

He pulled out a flashlight as Fiona joined him. Her eyes shone hot with excitement but she was playing it cool. "What did you find? A tunnel into the cavern?"

"Looks like it." He peered in, flicking the beam of light around. "Looks like it could collapse at any moment."

Fiona crouched down, peering at the ground around the opening. "I don't think so. They were using it a lot. Look at all this trash." She gestured at the shreds of cellophane, scraps of fast food wrappings, the straws and plastic tops of soft drink cups. "Bored sentries hung out here for hours while other people were inside working. Looking for that mysterious whatever-the-hell-it-is."

Anton studied the floor of the passageway. "It's covered with boot prints."

"Well, then. Good enough for me."

"What do you mean? That's your standard? If it's good enough for Kimball's goons, it's good enough for you?"

She rolled her eyes and crouched down, leaning to look deeper with her flashlight. Then she tucked the flashbang necklace inside the neckline of her sweater. "No," she said. "All I meant was, they were free to take their chances, and I am free to do the same. Ladies first." She disappeared inside.

"Fuck!" he hissed. "Wait for me! Hey! Eric!"

Eric's face appeared above him. "Found something?"

"A collapsed wall with a passageway underneath. Fiona just went in before I could stop her."

Eric looked appalled. "She's fucking insane!"

"Tell me about it," he said, as he dove headfirst into the suffocating darkness.

20

The darkness had a heavy, sticky quality to it. Fiona fought to breathe.

She was bent nearly double, sometimes crawling on her knees through mud to get through the lopsided triangular tunnel, sometimes slithering on her belly.

She stuck the small flashlight between her teeth to free her hands. Tasted mud and grit. The sickly beam bobbed and wavered over broken concrete as she wiggled past it.

A fainter light beam danced around her as Anton came up behind her. "Fi," he hissed. "For the love of fuck. Wait for me."

She didn't turn or stop. "I'm not being a bitch on purpose," she called back. "I just have to keep moving. It's like riding a bike. If I stop the forward motion, I'll fall over."

"At least let me go first! I won't block you."

"Sorry. Can't." She approached the narrowest part of the passageway yet and squirmed through it. "You'd never get past me. You're too wide for this rabbit hole, big guy."

She ignored the muffled cursing from behind her and just focused on moving forward. The bag she was carrying was awkward in the tight, irregular passageway. She had to constantly duck and turn to keep going. Anton was twice her size but he kept grimly on, closing the gap between them.

She finally felt air moving, and crawled out into a larger space. It smelled of mud and mold, and the ever-constant, eye-watering smell of piss. Anton emerged from the passageway behind her and unfolded his long body with a sigh of relief.

The two of them played the beams of their flashlights along slabs of concrete that lay at crazy angles. Rusted rebar spikes jutted every which way.

They made their way carefully and quietly, boots crunching, taking the most obvious and most heavily traveled way through the chaotic darkness.

"It's like a labyrinth in here," Fiona whispered.

"I'm keeping track of the turns," Anton told her.

Thank God. She realized that she was holding her breath as they picked their way through the place. Tiptoeing, as if there was a sleeping monster, and they didn't dare wake it. It was so quiet. The air was clammy. Water had seeped in from outside. She heard constant, hollow dripping.

At one point, they found themselves walking alongside a wall that was intact and upright. The tiny halo from her flashlight picked out faded colors, obscured by dark mold.

Recognition slammed into her. "Oh my God," she whispered.

"What is it?" Anton spun, gun at the ready.

"Look at the wall. It's TJ's mural. See? It's the Army of the Faithful entering the happy valley. This must have been the library wall."

The painted images were barely recognizable. Just a few details of stylized faces and hands were visible, a windmill, a cornstalk, a plow, showing through like ghosts. TJ's colorful utopian fantasy had once covered the entire library wall. Now it was obscured by mold and crawling roots.

Pot-bellied, gray-bearded TJ had been the GodsAcre art teacher. He'd taught drawing and drafting and painting, ceramics, glass-blowing, stained glass, art history. She'd spent a lot of time in that library, staring at TJ's mural while Jeremiah ranted about his own dark interpretations of history, philosophy, political science and economics.

She'd spent all the years since unpicking those knots. Unlearning Jeremiah's bizarre convictions. She'd been given a set of truly fucked up maps to navigate the world with.

But who knew? Maybe in the end, everybody's maps were just as fucked up as her own had been. Maybe everyone was just blundering around in the dark with their fingers crossed, just like her.

Right now, that thought was far from comforting.

The beam of Anton's flashlight wandered over the mural, and then moved down to the rubble at his feet. He kneeled down to pull something small out of the rocks.

A paperback book, or it had been once. Now it was swollen with moisture and eaten by fungus. The pages disintegrated under his fingers as he opened it.

"*Pride and Prejudice,*" he said quietly.

That slid right under her guard. Mom had read that book with her when she was twelve. She'd read it on her own many times since then. Probably that very same copy.

Pride and Prejudice tore the lid off of all her memories. They welled up all at once, overwhelming her.

It was so grim and awful. TJ's ruined mural and the ruined book in Anton's hand pierced her defenses. Because for all its faults and its bizarre eccentricities, GodsAcre had been home, and these people had been her family.

She turned away from Anton's light and fought tears. *Not. Now.* Damn it.

It took a minute, but she got herself in hand, sniffing back the moisture. The beam of Anton's moving flashlight wavered and swam in her eyes. She wiped them fiercely.

"What's over there?" she asked.

"Come and see." He waited for her to clamber up onto the heap of stones and stand beside him.

They gazed out into the huge space beyond. The flashlight's beam penetrated at least fifty meters, maybe more. It was too dark and too irregular to estimate, with all the collapsed rubble and heaps of haphazard building materials.

The explosion had destroyed the buildings constructed inside the cave, but it hadn't taken down the actual roof of the cavern, at least not all of it. The roof seemed lower than she remembered. Maybe because of the rubble piled below. But when they shone the flashlight on the ground, there were paths cleared. Boot prints in the mud.

"They're looking for the mysterious object in there," she said. "But they haven't found it yet. Or else they wouldn't be bothering us."

"We're not going to find it, either," Anton said. "At least not today. But Kimball's med lab would have been in that chamber, judging by where it is in relation to TJ's mural."

She nodded. Her throat ached, and she coughed to loosen it. "Demi said there was electronic surveillance up here."

"Yeah. Eric says they knew he was there before anyone

193

could have seen him, that night that they were attacked. He was in the trees at twilight, wearing forest camo with lots of cover. They drove up the road and called out to him from a hundred yards away. They knew exactly where he was."

"Then I imagine they're watching us right now," she said.

"I'd be surprised if they weren't."

She pondered that idea for a moment. "Then I guess we should go."

"Thank God you said it first."

She had no smart-ass comeback for him in her current state. It was all she could do to keep her shit together and not start sniveling while she followed him through the maze.

Good thing Anton's sense of direction was rock solid. He led them unerringly back to the exit and they crawled through the tunnel quickly, but this time Fiona struggled with a panicked sensation that something was pursuing her. When she came out into the open air, she dragged in huge, rasping breaths like a swimmer who'd been underwater too long.

"About goddamn time." Eric's disapproving voice came from above. "I was about to mount a search and rescue mission. I do not need this fucking stress right now, people."

"Sorry," Anton said. "It was slow going in there. Let's get out of this hole."

They crawled up out of the hole with some difficulty. Anton stayed right behind her, catching her whenever she started to slide back down.

They told Eric what they'd seen inside the cavern as they walked back up toward the Great Hall. Fiona slowed down as they passed the ruined building, and Anton and Eric stopped to wait for her. For a few minutes the three of them just contemplated the spire of the chimney that rose above the mossy, vine-choked concrete foundation.

Her eyes were blurring again. Damn. She fought it.

Wind rustled the dead grass at her feet. Some of the coneflowers had outlasted the autumn frosts, their lingering petals bright purple. Her mom had planted those. Back in the old days, the grounds around the Great Hall had been thick with flowers of all kinds and colors. Mom had planned the garden so that something indigenous and beautiful would always be blooming right up until the snows came. Everyone loved Mom's flower garden.

The ragged, stubborn remnants of that garden were now spread out all over the meadow. Most of the flowers had gone to seed, but persistent scraps of color still remained.

Fiona picked a handful of raggedy flowers and divided them into two bunches. She laid the first bunch on the mossy concrete slab below the spire of the chimney.

"I don't need to go to the cemetery," she said. "This can be her monument."

Anton nodded. He looked like he didn't trust himself to speak.

She lifted the other bouquet. "These are for your mom. She's up the hill above the meadow, right? Under the big fir?"

Eric turned and looked. "I didn't pass it last time I was here. I was trying to be sneaky and I hiked down from the far side of the ridge. Let's go find it."

But when they got to the big fir tree, Lindsey Paley's grave was nowhere to be seen.

"What the hell?" Eric stared around, baffled. "She was here. This was her favorite tree. There's no mistaking it. Where the hell did the headstone go?"

They stared around blankly at the churned-up earth as the answer to the puzzle sank in.

"They scraped the stone off with a bulldozer," Anton said finally, pointing at the huge tire treads. "For no good reason. They went out of their way to do it. Out of spite."

"It has to be here somewhere," Eric said. "They may be spiteful, but they're lazy slobs. They would never have gone to the trouble of hauling it away or throwing it out."

Without saying another word, the three of three of them got to work, picking through the piles of brush, garbage, bricks, dead wood, machine scraps. As time crawled by, their search took on a strange intensity, as if someone's life depended on it.

Time stretched on. The cold wind picked up. Rain began to come down.

"Found it," Anton called from the far side of the meadow. "It's covered with mud, but it's in one piece." He heaved the thing right side up with a grunt of effort.

Between the two of them, Eric and Anton staggered across the meadow with the heavy block of granite to the gravesite, and laid it carefully back in its proper place.

The three of them huddled around it, scraping off the thick, clay-like mud with their fingers until they could see the inscription.

Lindsey Jane Merton Paley, beloved wife and mother.
Who can find a virtuous woman? for her price is far above rubies.

Anton used a twig to scrape mud from the engraved dates of her birth and death. Fiona pulled out the water bottle from her bag, and using a handful of dried grass, slowly poured the water over the stone's surface, rinsing until the letters were clear and clean. Then she stamped out the tire-treads that marred Lindsey Paley's grave, first with her feet, then smoothing the earth carefully and patting with her hands.

She laid the flowers in front of the headstone. "There," she said. "That's better."

"Thanks, Fi." Anton's voice was rough.

Fiona rose to her feet, careful not to look at him. If she crossed eyes with anyone she'd start an emotional feedback loop that would shake her to pieces.

The blustering wind had picked up, whistling and whipping in the fir boughs.

"We've left our calling card," Anton said. "Guess we can go now."

"Damn straight." Fiona raised her voice until she was shouting. "I'm glad they're listening because I'm talking directly to them. Or to him, I should say. Kimball, you sick, twisted bastard. I am coming for you."

Only the wind answered. After a moment Anton slid an arm around her rigid shoulders and squeezed. "Take it easy."

"Why should I?" she demanded. "How can I?"

"Just pace yourself. If you go off like a bomb, you do Kimball's work for him."

She wanted to spit out something bitter, but she held it back. This vitriol was not for him. He didn't deserve it. Besides, he also happened to be right.

"Let's get the hell out of here," she said, exhausted.

On the road back to town, Eric slewed around those tight hairpin turns on the road much faster than it was safe to take them. Neither of them asked him to slow down.

Halfway down the hill, the phone buzzed in Anton's pocket. He pulled it out. "Anton Trask here," he said. "Hey, Chief Bristol."

Fiona leaned forward, straining to hear.

"Yeah, sorry," Anton said. "I forgot to message Fiona's number to you. She did? That's great. Thank Holly for us. We'll go straight there. We're on our way down from GodsAcre. Cleanup crew's been and gone, like we saw before with the drone. Cars gone, bodies gone, nothing but bloodstains up here. But we found a passageway into the caverns. They've been digging for something down there, and they've been at it for a while. Probably years. We'll tell you about it when we get there."

He ended the call. "They found records in the archives for you," he said to her. "The forensic investigation of Kimball's body. I assumed you'd want to go straight to the police station to check it out. Unless you'd rather rest. It's not like they'll go anywhere. We could do it tomorrow."

"No, let's go straight to the station," she said. "I want to see the files. I don't need to rest."

Once at the police station, they were shown into an empty storage room at the back with a big table. Fiona stared down at her hands as if she barely recognized them. She'd stopped to scrub off the worst of the mud in the police station bathroom, but she hadn't gotten all the grime from under her nails. A pile of file boxes sat on the table. Demi was at the station as well, shadowed by the vigilant Jim Wong. Chief Bristol presided, his face set in a now-permanent expression of worried disapproval.

Holly, the police station's head administrator, had gone through the boxes and pulled out all folders pertaining to Redd Kimball. All eyes were on Fiona as she leafed through them, trying not to think about her mother as she looked at photos of Kimball's charred bones. She stopped to look at pictures of the mandible. Then she looked at the dental x-rays that the forensic examiners had used for comparison. And looked again.

It took a moment to sink in, she was so wrung out from seeing GodsAcre, but the frontal panoramic X-ray made her gasp like she'd been splashed with ice water.

Oh God. Of course. How stupid she'd been.

So. Fucking. *Obvious.*

Anton leaned forward, frowning down at the film that she held. "What?" he demanded. "What did you see?"

"I…" She stopped, blew out a shaky breath and carefully steadied her voice. "These aren't Redd Kimball's teeth." She held up the X-ray. "This is Titus."

21

"Titus?" Anton leaned forward, peering at the film. "What the fuck? How's that possible? It says Redding P. Kimball, right here on the film."

"That's not Kimball," Fiona repeated. "Those aren't his teeth."

"Fiona. Please." Chief Bristol's voice had a strained air of professional patience. "How can you possibly know this, after all these years?"

Fiona pointed at the X-Ray. "Both of these front teeth are broken almost halfway off. Probably from being beaten, because I'm sure Titus was Kimball's victim, too. Kimball's teeth weren't like that. They were big and bleached and weirdly perfect."

"I remember the name Titus," Chief Bristol said. "From the monument in the cemetery. He's the one with no last name. We never did identify his body."

"No, you didn't, and this is why," Fiona said. "No one ever knew Titus's full name. He couldn't speak, so he never told us. Kimball certainly never did."

"How on earth do you know so much about this man's teeth?" the Chief asked.

"Because I brushed them, every day," Fiona told him. "And I crushed his food and spoon-fed it to him. Morning, noon and night."

Chief Bristol looked appalled. "How old were you when you did this?"

"Fourteen when it started," she said. "Almost fifteen when I ran away."

The other people in the room were talking all at once. She couldn't follow anything they said. Something had broken loose inside her. She leaned forward, put her hands over her face and dissolved.

It horrified her to cry in public. It wasn't who she was, or how she saw herself. Fiona Garrett kept her shit together and soldiered on, always. But no force on earth could have stopped this from mowing her down.

People fussed over her, trying to comfort her, talk to her, touch her. She slapped their hands away. She couldn't bear touch while this energy was raging through her. It was like a bad carnival ride. She was strapped in, no way to get off. She just had to suffer through to the bitter end.

It did finally end, at great length. When she dared to open her eyes, a box of tissues sat on the table in front of her. She grabbed some. Mopped her face, blew her nose.

Anton sat next to her, waiting silently. The others had the good sense to look away.

"Sorry," she muttered.

"Don't be," Demi said. "Crying is good. It drains the poison. Believe me, I know."

It had, in a sense. Drained was just how she felt.

Hollowed out. Like a dead tree.

"What touched that off?" Anton asked.

Fiona closed her eyes. "Titus," she said wearily. "Seeing his teeth. I knew that he died in the fire along with the rest of them. I just never let myself really feel it until now. It blindsided me."

Demi pulled her chair closer. "Were you close to him?"

Fiona shrugged. "I wouldn't say that. It's hard to explain. It's not like he could talk to me. He was brain-damaged in some way. He couldn't walk or talk or even keep his mouth sealed. One of my jobs was to wipe his drool. But I spent so much time with him, I got to feeling like he was trapped in there with me. Except it was worse for him. He was trapped in his own body, too. He felt desperate, just like me. I saw it in his eyes. Plus, I know he hated Kimball. The two of us were like cellmates with the same jailor."

Anton finally dared to lay his hand on her back. She didn't shrug him off, so he started gently stroking.

"I worried about Titus after I ran away," she went on. "I wondered if other people would take care of him properly. If he would miss me. Then the fire happened, and I just...buried all it all. Under a big rock."

Bristol cleared his throat. "I don't see how dental records could have the wrong name printed on the X-Ray," he said. "That seems improbable."

"Yeah, that is screwy," Fiona said. "We should talk to that dentist." She looked down at the film again. "It's a dental studio in Lake Oswego. Wallace Saft, DMD."

"I'll follow up on that," Chief Bristol said.

There was a long, charged silence. Fiona took a deep breath. "So, everybody," she said to the room at large. "You know what this means, right?"

Chief Bristol looked like he was bracing himself. "Tell us what it means to you, Fiona," he said.

"The stakes just got higher," she said. "Redd Kimball faked his own death. He switched Titus out for himself. He murdered thirty-seven people in cold blood to cover his tracks, and he's been killing people ever since. He's not just some creepy asshole who's dead now, and thank God we don't have to worry about him anymore. He's a mass murderer on the loose, killing at will with a powerful weapon that we don't fully understand. Are we all on the same page now?"

"You had me the first night," Anton said.

Eric spoke up. "I'm with you," he said. "Fuck that guy."

"I'm on board," Demi said. "We can't let him get away with this."

Chief Bristol rubbed his forehead. "I need to talk to that goddamn dentist," he muttered.

"Yes, but he'll probably lie, like he did when he generated that X-ray," Fiona said. "If he has any brains, he's probably terrified of Kimball. Or else he's willingly complicit."

"Maybe," Chief Bristol said. "One thing's for sure. We're calling in the CDC, and the FBI, death-pen or no death-pen. So you all go on home and get some rest." He jerked his chin at Fiona. "You in particular."

Anton wove his fingers through hers and pulled her up to her feet.

Fiona stumbled alongside him through the station and out into the parking lot, letting herself be swept along.

Seeing GodsAcre and Titus's broken teeth had shaken loose her memories. Anton's strong, warm hand was her touchstone. Without that, she would have floated off to someplace cold and dark.

Not long after, she found herself in a pretty townhouse on the lakefront. Demi's house. Food smells were emanating from the kitchen. Impassioned voices, discussing, arguing. The sound of beers being opened.

She stayed well clear of it. Just stared out the big bay window in the living room at the lakefront walkway across the street. She couldn't get near them. Too many people. Too much noise, opinions, emotions.

Demi emerged, wiping her hands on a dishtowel. "Dinner will be ready soon," she told Fiona. "In the meantime, I'm sure you'll want a shower and some fresh clothes. I came back down from GodsAcre a few days ago soaked in mud myself, so I know how it feels. Come on upstairs and I'll find you some clean stuff to put on."

"I'm okay," Fiona said. "Clammy jeans won't kill me. I've got clothes in my suitcase up at the cabin. And I don't really feel like eating any food, but thanks anyway. I'll just have some quiet time in here."

Demi's eyes flashed. She put her hands on her hips. "Quiet time, my ass."

"Excuse me?" Fiona said, startled.

"You're doing it again," Demi said.

"I'm just standing here, minding my own fucking business," Fiona retorted.

"No, you've got that no-one-on-earth-can-understand-my-pain look on your face."

Fiona recoiled. "I'm sorry I'm so annoying to you. But truthfully? There's probably not a whole lot of crossover in our life experiences."

"Yeah? Just a few days ago, I was drugged, tied up and

put in the trunk of a car. I've had a gun to my head. A knife to my throat. I was threatened with torture, and with having the man I love tortured in front of me. I found out that my mother was murdered. That my father was partly responsible for it before being murdered himself. And that was all after finding out he'd sold me out for money. Anything in this list sound familiar?"

Fiona cleared her throat. "Um...are we in some sort of competition now?"

Demi rolled her eyes. "Don't be silly. All I'm saying is, come down from your high horse. You're not the only person who's stressed and scared. Give me the satisfaction of seeing you wearing fresh dry clothes. And eat some of this goddamn food that I went to the trouble of cooking. You need some fuel. You look like a ghost."

Fiona blinked at her. "Um...okay."

Demi looked startled. "Really? Just like that?"

Fiona shrugged. "You have intimidated me into abject submission. I will obey."

"Oh, stop breaking my balls." But Fiona caught Demi's smile before she turned up the stairway.

Once she was under the hot, pounding water, she was grateful to Demi for insisting on the shower. She stayed in until the mud was soaked away from under her fingernails.

Afterward she found several items of clothing piled on Demi's bed. Demi was a good seven inches shorter than she was, and considerably more voluptuous, but sports and leisurewear was flexible and forgiving. The fleecy black leggings exposed several inches of ankle, but the thick blue thermal socks covered the gap, and they were warm and soft, if goofy looking. The floppy teal cover-all sweater was warm and fuzzy. By the time she dressed, combed the tangles out of her damp hair and put her flashbang necklace back on, she felt better. And Demi was at the foot of the stairs, calling her to dinner.

Dinner. A meal, at a table, with people. Yikes. That prospect would have given her pause any day of the week, even before all her troubles began.

Get over it, girl. She needed these people.

As she came down, she saw the travel bags she and Anton had brought from Seattle at the foot of the stairs. Anton emerged from the kitchen and followed her eyes.

"I checked out of the cabin," he told her. "I asked Nate to bring all our stuff down here. It'll be tight, with Nate and Wong staying here, too, but I think we're safer together, considering. And Demi has that bedroom in her attic for us."

"That's fine," she told him. "It doesn't really matter to me. You didn't consult with me when you picked the other place, either. So whatever."

He slid an arm around her waist. "Food's on the table."

The conversation at dinner was dominated by the arrangements to get Mace, the youngest Trask brother, at the airport the next day. They seemed to be on top of it, so she let her mind drift while they worked it all out.

The food was great. It was a stew. Big, meltingly tender chunks of beef cooked in wine, lots of potatoes and veggies. Biscuits hot out of the oven. They had lumps of melted cheese and herbs in them. And a fruit salad. She ate more than she usually managed to.

In fact, she'd consumed more food in the last forty-eight hours, in Anton's company, than she had in the entire ten days preceding it.

Hanging out with Anton stimulated her appetite. All of her appetites.

He caught her eye, as if he had read her mind, and smiled. That smile made her heat up inside. A toe-curling rush of tingly awareness.

The four of them gathered in the living room after dinner, after Nate and Wong had taken up their guard stations.

Eric fed a crackling fire. Demi curled up in a soft chair sipping herbal tea. Fiona huddled in the corner of a big couch, a cashmere afghan swathed around her. Zoned out.

So many memories. The kitchen, the mess hall, the garden, the big bonfires in the autumn. Wandering through the forest in the summertime. Gathering huckleberries with Mom. Making huckleberry pies by the score. She could taste the pie in her mouth.

Titus's watery, pleading eyes when she gently wiped his mouth with a cloth. Wordlessly begging for her help, but she hadn't known how to help him.

And then he died. His charred bones fused to the mattress springs.

She focused on Anton and Eric, leaning over a laptop on the coffee table. A familiar landing page was on the screen.

It was her portal. The last prompt, inviting them to enter the password.

Eric's voice was frustrated. "...password attempt. Everything we need to understand. Just out of reach. We need a divine visitation. Or a prophetic dream."

"I've got one," Fiona said suddenly.

Their heads whipped around. Everyone stared at her in the silence.

"Got what?" Eric said.

"A prophetic dream. Just like you just said." She looked at Anton. "Remember that dream I had about Titus when I was at your house? The recurring one I told you about?"

"Yes," Anton said. "What about it?"

"I never thought about Titus in connection with that capsule in my back," Fiona said. "But I should have. It's strange, that Kimball would haul someone like Titus around with him. It wasn't out of affection. The dental X-ray suggests that Kimball was planning this for a while. He needed a body to stand in for him when he faked his death in the fire. But maybe Titus played a role before he was impaired. Maybe Titus knew something."

"What about this dream is so significant?" Eric asked.

She shrugged. "Maybe nothing. But Titus used to call me Kitty. It was the only word I ever heard him say. And he called me that in my dream."

Demi leaned forward, her eyes bright with interest. "Kitty like a cat, you mean?"

Fiona nodded. "I told him my name was Fiona, and he seemed to understand me. Titus always seemed lucid. But he kept on saying it. And I got used to it."

Eric looked back password prompt. "You're saying, you want to use Kitty as the password? You're willing to take that risk?"

"Yes, I am," Fiona said. "I don't care if I burn the last password. I intend to get that bastard anyhow, one way or another. 'Kitty' is the only word Titus ever said. Let's give it a shot. If we burn our last login attempt, let it be a memorial sacrifice to Titus. It's as good as anything else we might try."

Eric poised his hands over the keyboard, and gave her an uncertain look. "Okay. If you're absolutely sure about this. K-I-T-T-Y, all caps? Talk about a bullshit password."

"I have no idea, but go for it. All caps sounds good. If it doesn't work, screw it. It's done, and we're free to move on and stop worrying about it."

Eric entered the letters. They drew closer, staring at the five asterisks in the box.

Eric looked up at Fiona. "You're the one who carried that thing around in your body all those years," he told her, lifting his hand. "You do the honors."

Fiona stretched across the coffee table. Her finger hovered over the key.

"This one's for you, Titus," she whispered.

She hit 'enter.'

22

They held their breaths during the time the computer took. Seconds ticked by.

A list of files appeared on a screen. A table of contents. A trefoil, the symbol for biological contamination, was emblazoned at the top.

Eric clicked one. "'Specific Electromagnetic Frequencies Possible Stress Factors Stimulating Rapid Switch From Latent To Lytic Mode in MLB-2C-15,'" he read aloud. "This is a list of research documents, all pertaining to…something called MLB-2C-15."

Fiona leaned down over Anton's shoulder, her hair tumbling over his shoulder. "'Release of Projeny Virons of MLB-2C-15 Generate Highly Toxic Compounds That Destroy Host Cells at Accelerated Rate during Lytic Phase.' That does not sound good." She looked at Eric. "A pathogen, just like you thought."

"I've never been so sorry to be right." Eric's narrowed eyes were fierce with concentration. "Look at this. 'Certain

Frequencies of Electromagnetic Radiation a Potential Stimuli Triggering Instantaneous Reactivation of MLB-2C-15 Virus from Latent to Catastrophic Lytic Phase.' Jesus."

They stared at the screen in silence, appalled.

"Remember how that last year at GodsAcre, Jeremiah got all obsessive in preaching about pestilence," Anton said slowly. "His sermons about cleansing the earth of the corrupt and unclean. Maybe he was trying to convince himself that he was justified to do the cleansing himself." He gestured at the computer. "And Kimball was helping him."

"All those vaccinations," Fiona said, shuddering. "Remember those?"

"They could account for the death-pen not working on me," Eric said.

"But wouldn't everything have been destroyed when you blew up the caverns?" Demi asked.

They sat in stunned silence, trying to process it.

"Evidently, they're hoping it wasn't," Fiona said finally. "They've been trying to dig that place up for years now. Maybe ever since the fire. But they still haven't found what they want."

"But why?" Demi asked. "What's the profit motive? From how you described him, it doesn't seem like Kimball is a religious nut who wants to cleanse wickedness from the face of the earth. He was just an evil, selfish sadist asshole."

"He killed my Patti," Fiona said. "I'll cut his throat for that."

"Otis, too," Anton said. "Too bad he only has one throat."

"And my mom." Demi's voice was hard. "When it comes to throat-cutting, we all have to take a number and get in line. What should we do? Should I close the restaurant?"

"No," Anton said. "I like having you in public, in plain sight. The whole shopping district can see you. No one's likely to make a move on you there."

"I need to get this info to the chief," Eric said. "He'll want to give it to the CDC. Maybe they can help us work out what's in the documents. I'll see if I can dig up any of these titles online, and see if they're legit. If any of them were ever published."

"Fi and Demi should stay at the restaurant with Mick and Wong while I go to pick up Mace tomorrow morning." Anton caught Fiona's look. "I'm not stashing you there," he said defensively. "It makes objective sense. I swear. Take the laptop to the restaurant. Study up on the documentation. I want you someplace safe, in plain sight of a crowd of people. Please, Fi."

"I hate crowds," she told him.

"You'll live," Anton said. "That's all I care about right now."

She just looked at him, eyebrow tilted up.

"Go armed to the restaurant, if that makes you feel better," Eric coaxed. "I'd feel better knowing that I have three trigger-happy, meaner-than-a-rattlesnake badasses keeping an eye on Demi at the diner, and not just two. More is better."

"Don't try to manipulate me with slick flattery," Fiona said. "I don't fall for that shit."

Demi let out a short laugh and got to her feet. "You GodsAcre types duke this out on your own. I'm going up to get some sleep. The bed in the third-floor bedroom is all made up, and there's towels and stuff in the bathroom cabinet and extra blankets and pillows in the closet. 'Night, all."

"I'll go up with you." Eric gave his brother a sheepish glance over his shoulder and disappeared up the stairs on

Demi's heels.

That left Fiona and Anton alone in front of the glowing embers of the fire.

"I'll just leave you here alone for the time it'll take to pick up Mace," he said. "Then we'll stand together, shoulder to shoulder, until this is all over. Come what may."

"Okay," Fiona said.

Anton was so taken aback by her swift acquiescence, he stood there, blank.

"Oh, don't look so bewildered, for God's sake," she snapped. "Just because I agreed with you? Was it the first time ever? Am I really such an unreasonable hag?"

"Ahhh...I wouldn't put it like that," he hedged. "Just that you're not used to compromising. I get that. I'm not great at it myself."

"I'm not compromising. I'm just too tired and confused right now to think of a good reason to argue, that's all. So don't get used to it."

Anton grabbed the suitcases Mick had stowed at the foot of the stairs and followed Fiona up two flights. Two doors opened off it, a big attic bedroom, a bathroom beyond it.

In it was a single king-sized bed. Eric should have known better than to assume that he and Fiona in a bed together was a sure thing, but Fiona just sank down onto the edge of the bed, staring into space.

He put down the suitcases. "You all right?" he asked.

"No," she said. "Since GodsAcre, I made myself go numb. Going back up there today put a stop to that. So did seeing Titus's teeth. And now I'm just feeling it all again. Like when I was a kid."

He took a step in her direction. "Feeling what?"

"The usual suspects." She waved her hand. "What

you'd expect. All the bad stuff. Scared, naked, helpless, ashamed. Survivor's guilt. All the clichés. I'm a live wire with the casing stripped off. Hot enough to fry. Look, don't touch."

"I'm not afraid to touch you," he said. "I can handle the voltage. You can't shock me."

"No?" She gave him a sidewise look. "Give me time."

"I will," he said promptly. "All the time you need. How about the rest of our lives?"

She squeezed her eyes shut, wincing. "Anton, don't. Not now."

"Why not?" he demanded. "And if not now, then when?"

She squinted at him. "Don't tell me, let me guess," she said. "Is this the old classic 'we-only-have-one-night-to-live' ploy? Anton. I thought better of you than that."

"I guess that would be pretty funny if it weren't so fucking true," he said.

"Oh, please," she murmured.

"Really," he said. "Be aware. GodsAcre had the same effect on me as it did on you. I'm feeling it, too. All the bad things. But I'm feeling all the good ones, too." He sank down to his knees onto the rug by the bed, laying his hand on her fleece-clad knees.

"Good ones?" She rubbed at her eyes, frowning at him. "Like what?"

"Like you," he said.

Fiona frowned at him, perplexed. "What do you mean?"

"Tell me something, Fi. Did you ever wonder how things would have shaken down for us if none of the bad stuff had ever happened?"

"Which bad stuff?" she said warily. "There was a

whole lot of bad stuff."

"All of it," he said. "Titus, Kimball. The beatings. The fire. You running away."

Fiona's gaze flicked away. "In the past, I guess I did," she admitted, without looking at him. "Then I grew up. Got over it. I mean, I never had any reason to think that we were…you know. A thing. Other than that kiss at the bus station. Which could have meant anything, or nothing."

"But you remembered that kiss," he asked. "Before you shut it all down."

Her eyes narrowed. "I don't like where this is going. You're starting in on that again. Wanting me to wave a magic wand and magically become something that I'm not."

"Just as a thought experiment," he urged. "A game of make-believe. Play along."

She rolled her eyes. "What's the point?"

"Bear with me," he coaxed. "Picture how it would have been for us if Kimball had never come to GodsAcre. I was waiting to make my move because you were younger, not even sixteen yet, and I knew the adults wouldn't approve. I was nervous and shy, and I wasn't sure you'd be into me."

"Hah." She let out a crack of laughter. "Are you kidding me?"

"Not at all. But I'd chosen you. I thought, if I got lucky, and you said yes, we'd plan our escape. We could go on out into the world together, to see what was really out there for ourselves. You and me." He paused for a moment, and then put the question to her. "If I'd made my move in time, would you have chosen me back?"

Fiona cleared her throat, and stared down into her lap, her lower lip caught between her teeth. Hesitating as if she were afraid to speak.

"Yes," she whispered.

Breath whooshed out of him that he hadn't known he was holding. "Today, when we were up at GodsAcre, I remembered how you made me feel back then. Every time I got close to you, my heart beat so fast, I got dizzy. I couldn't even think straight."

She nodded. "Yes."

"I still don't know how I found the nerve to kiss you when I left you on that bus," he went on. "I thought I was going to hyperventilate. But it was my last chance." He stroked his hands up over the top of her thighs, kneading and caressing. "It always feels like it's my last chance with you. It's always like I'm teetering on a cliff's edge."

"You think the world is going to end? That Kimball will kill us all?"

"I don't really care right now. All I care about is this."

He pressed his face down against the tops of her thighs, stroking the sides with his hands. No ploy. The words just fell out of him, along with this huge impulse to hang on to her, kiss her, claim her, if he had the strength. She was the most beautiful thing he'd ever seen on earth. She shone. So strong, so fierce, so fucking hot.

He felt her hands sliding into his hair, gripping it. Demanding that he face her.

He looked up, realizing that she wasn't pushing him away. He was charged with terrified excitement at what he saw in her eyes. The raw emotion.

She touched his face with her fingertips. It was a gentle, wondering touch, raking over his beard scruff with her thumb. Slow, hypnotic circular strokes. That half-dazed glow in her eyes made his breath catch. She looked like she was giving into a dream. Surrendering to a fantasy. It made his soul shake.

He took hold of her other hand and kissed it, feeling the battered scraped parts against his lips. Her hands were strong and capable. Long, slender fingers. Freckled, like her face. Fingers callused from her martial arts training. She'd painted her nails silver for the dress at the club, but the paint was battered and scratched, and the nails were short, trimmed off square and practical. A warrior's hands.

He pressed her knuckles against his cheek. Felt the soundless gasp, the delicate tremor that racked her. Tension released. A door opening silently that he could feel with his secret wordless senses. He kissed them again, passionately.

Instinct led him. No thought, plots or plans. Just hunger, need, desperate hope.

He tugged off the socks. Cupped both her feet in his hands. They were as beautiful as her hands, long and narrow, a high arch. Pale, covered with that tawny blur of freckles.

He leaned to seize her waist and pulled her up onto her feet. Leaned forward to press his face against her belly as he slid his hands beneath the long sweater, finding the tee-shirt, insinuating beneath it. Looking for that hot, petal-soft skin. Sinuous curves. The dips and swells of her hips, her belly. So lithe and strong.

His cock ached with clamoring urgency, but he clamped down on it with grim resolve. He was in sexual worship mode. Any payoff his body was screaming for would just have to wait. He was going for the big prize. He slid his hands higher under her tee-shirt, stroking her with butterfly-light caresses. No bra over those small but perfect breasts Her nipples were tight and hard against his palm as he petted her.

She shivered in his arm, her body vibrating. She wrapped her arms around his head, holding him tightly against herself. Not playing it cool. At all.

That was a relief. To leave the power games behind. She could hold him as tight as she wanted, as long as she wanted, just as long as she never let go. Let hell freeze over. He could never get enough of her. He was so owned.

There was a tight thrum of tension in her body, as if she were poised to jump. He glanced up, and for an instant, before she turned her face away and let a fall of hair hide her eyes, he saw two glittering tears flash down. One of them hit his face.

He touched the wet spot with his finger. Tasted it, savoring the heat of it. The salt.

"Don't," she whispered.

"Don't what?"

"Don't look at me," she said.

"That's too much to ask," he told her. "You're too beautiful."

"I can't stand it." Her voice was uneven. "It's freaking me out. It's too much."

He pressed his face against her belly, then hooked his fingers into the waistband of the leggings and tugged them down. "Distract me, then."

"Oh, yeah?" She was wiping her eyes, but a smile flashed over her face. "How?"

"How do you think?"

She snorted under her breath. "Opportunist."

"Hell yes," he agreed, dragging the fleece leggings down her thighs. "Any opportunity to make you come. I love your taste. I can't get enough of it."

She laughed, steadying herself with one hand on his shoulders, her fingers digging in. The other wound into his hair, tugging. Almost hard enough to hurt. The pressure was demanding, warning, admonishing him. "You're fixated on that, aren't you?"

"If it's you, yeah." He tugged her underwear down. "Got a problem with it?"

"Oh, God, no," she said swiftly. "Believe me. I'm not complaining."

"I love when you come against my face," he told her. "Slippery soft. Wide open."

There might have been words in the incoherent moan vibrating through her as he buried his face in her muff, nuzzling and kissing that twist of downy red ringlets, stroking the warm divide of her pussy lips with his fingertips. She was hot and slick and welcoming as he kissed his way all the way around her silken hollows and curves, the highlights and shadows. Flower-petal soft warmth of her inner thighs.

He kissed the red curls decorating her mound. Taking his time. No rush. He resisted the temptation to thrust his fingers inside her, feel the scalding wetness he craved. Part those pussy lip and make her clit pop out, and then go at it with his lips and tongue and fingers, rubbing and licking and sucking until she sobbed with pleasure and gave it up completely, yelling and bucking, coming wildly. Taking his thrusting fingers inside.

Not...quite...yet. He waited, silently promising more pleasure to come with his slow, lazy kisses and caresses.

After a few minutes of that treatment, she got impatient herself and started moving against him. Her nails bit into his shoulders, her hips moved.

"Stop playing around," she said sternly. "Get on with it."

He hid his smile against her mound, one lingering final kiss before he looked up. "I was going to wait until I heard you beg," he said. "But now that we're here, it seems like the regal imperial command vibe is just as hot. Judging on the effect it has on my dick."

"Yeah?" She dragged him closer, eyes glowing hot. "Prove it."

23

There was a keening sound in the back of her throat. Fiona couldn't seem to stop. It was just too goddamn intense. Agonizingly sweet, this shivering brightness lighting her up, making her chest so hot and soft, her throat melt and her eyes fill. And between her legs, the tender, lashing strokes of his tongue, the deep slow pull as he sucked at her clit, the liquid caress as he circled it, flicking and teasing. Hands inside her, opening her.

Still teasing, right to the brink of coming, and then he eased her back, waiting until the tension subsided, ever so slightly. Then he had at her again. Running his tongue around and around her clit, just...fast...enough to...oh God. The energy swelling. Rising.

Yes. Please.

The wave crested, broke. She lost herself in the uncontrollable power that jolted through her body and then widened out. Infinitely wide. Shivering. Achingly sweet.

After she found herself on the bed, flat on her back, no

memory of sitting, lying, falling. Every damn time he touched her, the feelings stabbed deeper, reached further. Every time, he stirred her up into fresh chaos.

She was limp and soft, her body still shimmering with delight as he kept on kissing her thighs, her belly. Cupping her pussy tenderly with his hand.

She struggled up into a sitting position. Lifted up her arms eagerly up as Anton dragged the sweater and necklace and tee-shirt off her. Kicking off the pants and underwear that still clung to one of her ankles. Tossing the wild tangled mass of hair back from her face.

Anton was wrenching off his own clothes with quick, economical gestures. He leaned over her and jerked the covers down. Then seized her and pulled her up to lie next to him. Skin to skin against his heat. The shock was a rush of pleasure all over her, like falling into water, caressing every inch of her. She fell into his kiss the same way. As long as their tongues were doing that slow, hungry dance, she would stay in flight somehow.

He'd managed to twitch the covers up over the two of them, somehow managing never to break contact with her, by some miracle of acrobatics. He pressed her down into the mattress, settling between her legs, and had rolled on a condom before she even thought about one. He'd plucked the thing out of thin air, and lucky for her, because she hadn't thought about it at all. He positioned himself, and they writhed and moved against each other, breathing hard, as he slid his cockhead between her pussy lips, caressing them with it. Getting slick and shining with her juice before he pushed slowly inside.

Breathless perfection. His cockhead caressed her, shoving in, sliding slowly out. Surging forward again. She couldn't hardly drag in enough air to whimper for the next deep, penetrating stroke. Digging her nails into his back, lifting up to demand more.

The power possessed her. Nothing mattered but getting more of him. No pride or fear, no past or future. Just his deep, slow, expert fucking, driving her absolutely mad.

He refused to give in to her incoherent urging for a long time, keeping it deep and slow, but the power finally overcame him, too. At the end, his hips pumped against hers wildly, his hair brushed her throat as he kissed his way up her neck and tongue-kissed her madly while he drove her straight into an intensely beautiful orgasm.

He shouted with his own release as he let go and came with her.

After, he rolled to the side, still panting. Pulling her to face him.

And that was it. The soaring flight was over. She hit the ground so hard, it physically hurt.

Same wipe-out. Every damn time. The more earth-shattering the sex, the harder she crashed afterward. Cold, gripping her deep inside. Something inside her was intent on punishing her for letting herself feel it. Letting herself want it.

This is what you get, you dumb little slut. This is how you feel. And this is only the beginning. It gets worse. Oh yes, it surely does. There's no end to how bad it'll get. So go ahead. Knock yourself out, bitch. If you have the stomach for it.

She rolled over onto her back, her hand over her eyes. Anton tried to tug her back to face him, but he sensed the tension in her body and let her be, rolling backward.

"Fi," he said. "Really? We're doing this now? Again?"

She looked over at him. "I didn't say a goddamn word."

"You don't have to."

She turned her back to him. "You just keep begging for it, Anton," she said. "I keep warning you. And then when we hit the wall, you still act so fucking surprised."

"Tell me about that wall," he said. "Why are we hitting it now? What did I do?"

Oh, God, there was no getting through to the man. Fiona rolled off the bed and grabbed the tee-shirt and sweater, tugging them right side out again before pulling them on. Not looking at him.

"Where are you going?" he asked her.

"I need some alone time," she said. "I'll go stretch out on a couch downstairs."

"Oh, for fuck's sake. Stay up here in the bed. I'll be the one to leave, if you don't want my company." Anton reached for his jeans. "I have to get up early to get Mace anyhow. Just let me get rid of this condom, and I'll get out of your hair." He stalked out the door, leaving her to pace miserably around the room until he came back in and pulled on the rest of his clothes. He smelled like soap and toothpaste. He kept his eyes averted.

He stopped with his hand on the doorknob and just stood there, immobile. She sat just as still. She couldn't even breathe.

"Why, Fi?" he asked. "Make me understand. This could work. We have something unique. Something I don't think either one of us will ever find again in this lifetime. And you're shutting it down. Why?"

She lifted her tight shoulders. Her throat ached. "How do I know? If I knew, I wouldn't be all twisted up like this."

"Can't you just try?" he asked. "Can't you give us a chance?"

"I keep trying." Her voice felt tight and strangled. "I wipe out every time."

"Wipe out?" He turned to look at her, frowning. "What do you mean? How so?"

She let out a sharp sigh. "You said to imagine if all the bad stuff never happened," she said. "And I did."

"Yeah, and it was amazing. So?"

"So it was a fucking fantasy, Anton! The bad stuff did happen! It's all still there, inside me. It made me who I am. I can't instantly make myself into something different just to suit you. It doesn't work that way."

"I don't want you to be different," he said. "I love the way you are."

"Hah," she muttered. "You haven't tried being me. I'd love to change. I'd do anything to make him shut up."

He stared at her for a moment. "Make who shut up?"

Oh God, now she'd done it. "I misspoke," she muttered. "Never mind."

"Bullshit. Who is this 'him?'"

She shook her head.

Anton folded his arms over his chest. "I'm not going anywhere until you tell me."

No way out of this except for through. "Kimball," she admitted reluctantly. "I hear his voice. In my head. I hear it all the time."

"Uh…okay," he said slowly. "So…"

"Not like an auditory hallucination," she said. "It's not like I'm psychotic, or anything. I wouldn't mistake his voice for a voice coming from outside myself. But I still hear him, and I can't make him shut up. He's just as disgusting and hateful and slimy inside my head as he was in real life. He makes me feel like shit. Particularly if I'm in any sort of a

225

sexual situation. He just...I don't know. Jabs at me. Constantly. Makes me feel ashamed and stupid. Polluted."

"And that's why you freeze me out after we have sex."

"I didn't want to tell you," she said. "It's embarrassing, to have a psycho sleazebag stuck inside my head. I try to just live my life as if he wasn't in there, yammering at me, but sometimes it gets the better of me. I've tried getting my head shrunk, several times. My aunt took me to a bunch of therapists, psychiatrists. I've tried different drugs. Anti-anxiety, anti-depressants, anti-psychotics. I tried talking it to death. Nothing seems to work. So." She threw up her hands. "There it is."

He nodded, thoughtfully. "I hear Jeremiah in my head," he said. "We all internalized his voice. But I know it's not the same. Jeremiah was crazy, but not a sadistic abuser."

"I hear Jeremiah sometimes, too," she admitted. "Kimball's worse."

Anton walked back to the bed and sat down. His dark eyes had that piercing quality they took on when he was aroused, or inspired. Or enraged. "So you're going to let him win?"

That rocked her backward like a slap. "Fuck you, Anton! I have done nothing but fight! I don't even know how to stop fighting! That's my whole damn problem!"

He sat there, eyes boring into her. "Kimball knew that I wanted you, back at GodsAcre," he told her. "He caught me looking at you. Pining for you."

"Pining?" she scoffed. "Please."

"Call it whatever you want. He saw it, and that was part of the thrill for him. That way, he got to fuck us both at the same time. He got his toy, and he also got to show me who was boss by hurting you right in front of me."

Fiona flinched at the thought. "Anton. Do we have to talk about this right now?"

"So you're going to let him take this, too? He already took everything else from you. GodsAcre and all its people. Your childhood. Your girlhood. Your mom. Patti."

"Stop it, Anton."

"He destroyed it all," Anton went on. "A clean sweep. But by some miracle, it looks like you and I get one more shot at this. If you're brave enough to take it."

Fiona lifted her hands from her wet eyes to glare at him, sniffing aggressively. "You're questioning my bravery? Seriously?"

"Yes." His voice rang with naked challenge. "Are you up to it?"

In the silence that followed, her automatic response was to shove him away with harsh, cutting words, but she didn't trust her automatic response.

It had been programmed by someone who was not her friend.

So she just held herself, silent and suspended, barely breathing. Then she wiped the angry tears off her face with the backs of her hands and sucked in a deep breath.

"So what am I supposed to do to satisfy you?" she asked him. "Fake a smile when I feel like dying?"

Anton pried off his shoes and came back to the bed, sitting down next to her. "You never, ever have to fake anything with me," he said. "I'm not afraid."

She snorted. "Maybe you should be."

"Maybe," he replied. "But I want you. All of you. You made me want this, like I haven't wanted anything since I was seventeen. You made me crave it."

"What, exactly?" she demanded. "Sex, you mean?

Because personality-wise, I'm not exactly little-wifey-type material, Anton. In case you haven't noticed."

He smiled briefly. "I don't care. When I'm with you, I feel like there's magic all around. Infinite possibilities. It's an incredible feeling. I'm hooked on it. Now that I've felt that, I'm starting to see the point of it all."

"Point of what?"

"All of it," he said. "Being alive. I didn't give much of a shit about anything for a long time, except for Otis and my brothers. But maybe, just maybe, the rest of this crazy goatfuck could be worth it. If you're around to kick my ass. Blow my mind."

"Whoa," she whispered. "Dial it down, lover boy. You're getting pretty flowery for a hard-assed babe like me."

"It's your own fault for being so fucking incredible."

She let out a huff of startled laughter, and that was it. That brief, whispery giggle was the first crack in the dam. The pressure had sneaked up on her, but it was all there, pent up. It overwhelmed her, suddenly and completely. A tidal wave that tore her apart from the inside.

Anton tried to put his arms around her, but that was too much. She pulled away, pressing her hands hard against her face to keep it from shaking to pieces.

Anton just waited. Eventually she found herself resting her forehead against his broad shoulder.

That point of contact was all she could stand. Her forehead glowed where she touched him, as if an inner eye had opened up while the impossible idea slowly took form in her mind. The revolutionary notion that everything she thought she knew about the world could maybe, just maybe, be re-thought. Re-understood. That maybe the world could be re-ordered, with some place in it for her. Some place where

SHANNON McKENNA

she could breathe.

This thing, with Anton. Was it even possible? It seemed so dangerous to hope for something so huge, so delicate and lovely. She'd be setting herself up for pain, humiliation, heart-crushing despair. She'd be letting them all make a fool of her again. Every instinct forbade it.

But she didn't trust those instincts anymore.

Her forehead still glowed. A light in the darkness. Anton sat patiently, witnessing her fall to pieces and apparently not freaked out or repelled by it. A quiet bulwark.

He reached out, gathering up handfuls of her hair and winding the thick locks around his fingers. Then he leaned down to drop slow kisses against her head.

No hurry. That was the silent message. She could sob for hours if she needed to. He knew he couldn't touch her yet, but he tethered her to himself gently with her hair. He wouldn't let her drift away into those dark, wild waters. He would keep her safe somehow.

Or else die trying.

Yes, that was the other face of this terror. The thought of losing him again. For good this time.

It would be the end of her.

It took a long time for the fit of sobbing or whatever it was to move through her. Years of pent-up, unacknowledged sadness. It took longer still before her throat was calm enough to produce a sound recognizable as speech.

When she got there, she pulled in a deep, steadying breath. "Okay, then."

"Okay what?" Anton's voice was soothing and gentle. And very cautious.

She shrugged. "Who knows? You want something from me, right? Spell it out for me. Be really specific, because I have

229

HELLBENT

no clue. Truly. I don't know where to even begin."

Anton placed his hand against her cheek until she was forced to meet his eyes.

"Let's keep it simple, to start with. Let's just get into bed and lie there together."

She was baffled. "What, you mean, like...lie there, not having sex?"

"Not necessarily. We just lie there. And hold each other."

She gazed at him blankly. "Hold each other," she said. "Why? What's that supposed to accomplish?"

"Have you ever done it?"

"Cuddle, you mean? You are talking about cuddling, right?"

"Yes. Have you done it?"

"No," she admitted. "By no means. Not my style. Not that I've had very many opportunities."

"That sounds like reason enough right there." Anton shifted on the bed, reaching up to the head to shove the pillows aside and pull the covers down. Then he slid between the sheets and lifted up the blankets for her in silent invitation.

Fiona just looked at him, open-mouthed. "For real?" she said. "You want a snuggle-fest in the midst of our turbo-charged doom and death scenario?"

"Given the doom factor, absolutely yes. We should take our opportunities when we can." He waited a minute. "Please, Fi," he coaxed. "Indulge me."

She hesitated for a long time, but then let out a sharp sigh and crawled up the bed to the open space under the blankets that Anton was lifting up for her. She couldn't believe she was actually doing this. It was ridiculous.

Anton scooted back, giving her the spot that he'd warmed up, and pulled her close.

Her body went rigid. Anton went still, lifting his arms. "Sorry." His voice rumbled against her ear. "Didn't mean to grab like that."

"It's okay," she whispered. "I'm just tense and twitchy. And this is kind of weird."

"I want to hug you." He just waited, patient and motionless, for her to answer. Giving her time to work it out in her head first.

She drew in a deep, jerky breath, and nodded. "Do it."

He did so, slowly and gently pulling her close to himself. Wrapping his arms around her. Not too tight, but oh, he was so big and hot and solid.

For the longest time, it didn't work at all. She just lay there, stiff as a board, feeling self-conscious and tense and nervous. Mind racing wildly with a million conflicting thoughts. The foremost of which was how silly and useless and forced this whole exercise was. How much she sucked at it. How much of a disappointment she was bound to be for him, with all her tedious tics and freezes and hang-ups and issues.

But the minutes crawled on. Nothing bad happened. And slowly, very slowly, his huge warmth and patience started to unknot some of the tension in her body.

At some point he had begun stroking her back. Lightly and tenderly, shoulder to thigh, then back up again. Soothing. No moves other than that slow caress, but the sexual tension was always there, throbbing heavy and hot between them.

Fiona shifted around in the bed until they lay facing each other. She'd finally calmed down enough so that she could look him in the eye for more than a split second. It was hard at first, not to blink, flinch away. Say something sharp to him, by reflex.

She didn't let herself do it. Not this time. She just breathed. Deep and slow.

After a while, something shifted inside her. She was floating in the midst of a deep inner stillness. His eyes, her eyes, were an open conduit. She felt so close to him. Closer than she'd ever known how to be to anyone. Not even to herself.

Everything he was shone out of his eyes. So gorgeous. She was dazzled.

He saw everything she was, and he accepted her. Desired her.

Loved her.

That last, fleeting thought was too much. It broke the magic spell. She broke eye contact and pulled away, rolling onto her back. "Wow," she whispered. "Intense."

"Yes," he said.

"Is it always like this? Cuddling, I mean?"

"I wouldn't know," he replied. "First time for me."

She looked back at him, she was so startled. "No way. So how'd you get so good at it? Beginner's luck?"

He shook his head slightly. "I think it's just specific to you."

She waved that away. "Come on, Anton. How could you have had all these famous, high-profile lovers and never lounged around in bed with them after sex?"

He looked pained. "So we're doing this now, Fi? Seriously?"

"Just tell me," she insisted.

He rolled over and stared up at the ceiling. "There's nothing to tell," he said. "I always got up and left after the sex was finished. I told you about keeping a hotel suite, right? That's why. So I could fuck off immediately afterward. No complications."

"You never wanted to stay?"

"Never," he said. "I'm not proud of it. I did everything I could during the sex to make it good for them, but afterward I had to get away. Like a compulsion."

She placed her hand on his chest, resting it over his heart. "And yet, here you are."

"Here I am," he echoed. "I finally know what my problem was."

"Yeah? Do tell."

"I was sulking," he said simply. "I wanted you. Only you. If I couldn't have you, then screw it. Why not misbehave? Why not be indifferent? I didn't give a fuck. I was a colossal dickhead."

"No wonder you had a bad boy rep."

He was silent for a moment. "It had to be you, Fi," he said. "No one else will do."

Her face was getting hot. She couldn't meet his eyes.

He tilted her chin up again. "Don't run away," he pleaded. "Stay with me."

Fiona squeezed her eyes tightly shut, and forced herself to open them. "I'm still here. So far, so good, right?" Her voice didn't sound like her own. So soft and shaky.

"I'm all done sulking," he said. "I'm all yours. Forever."

"Don't think you have to make any big promises," she said. "We've got other urgent stuff to worry about right now."

"Those aren't promises," he said. "They're just statements of fact. Now that I've found you again, you couldn't pry me away with a fucking crowbar."

She smacked him on the chest. "Oh, quit with the gooey

stuff. You're killing me."

"I can't stop," he said. "I've been waiting for this moment all my life." He paused for a moment. "Unless you want me to fake it. Pretend I don't care."

Oh, for God's sake. There would be no shutting this guy up unless she brought out the big guns. She wrapped her arms and legs around him, and kissed him.

24

So much for self-control. Once she lit that fuse, there was nothing he could do but burn. He loved her like that, strong and fierce and hungry, seeking out her pleasure. Her nails digging into his shoulders, her tongue in his mouth. Oh God, yeah.

Fiona fumbled with the buttons of his jeans in the darkness under the covers. She got them undone, dragged them down over his hips and crawled on top of him, kissing him hungrily, her hair a warm, fragrant cloak around them as she gripped his cock, stroking it and then holding it at just the right angle so she could force his cockhead inside herself. Hot and wet and wonderful. The slow, tight, suckling kiss of her clinging pussy.

She rocked and swayed over him, forcing him deeper. Rose up, bracing her hands against his chest, shoving his sweatshirt up. He held her hips, surging beneath her as she swayed. It was a rocking, gliding dance. Hypnotically slow at first, both of them sighing with pleasure, intent on every tiny slow, slick, delicious detail of their bodies joining.

Soon their hands were clamped together and shaking as they moved together, the rhythm growing frenzied. His hips surged up beneath her, pounding deep and slick. Her desire was a pure, white-hot flame, and he wanted to be consumed by it. He would give her all of it. Everything he was, offered up. Hoping it was worthy.

They exploded together, and he forgot where he ended and she began.

His senses returned sometime later. He was still inside her.

He'd come inside her.

He braced himself, wondering if another panicked freak-out was imminent, but Fiona didn't say anything. She just held him. Arms, legs. Her face pressed against his hair. At last, she pulled away, and slid off the bed and out the door, toward the bathroom.

She was back in just a few minutes, smelling of soap and toothpaste. She pulled on her underwear and leggings and slid back into bed with him.

Right into his arms. Winding her arms around him. Squeezing him. That boded well. A bright glow of hope flared in his chest as she held him tight.

He held her, reminding himself to breathe through the terrified joy.

They didn't say a word, wary of breaking the spell. Neither one of them slept. This was a miracle. He didn't dare to miss a second of it. There was just enough light filtering in from the streetlight outside to reflect the gleam in her eyes as she studied him like she was memorizing him. Learning him by heart.

She was already imprinted on his.

Dawn began to lighten the sky to gray. He waited for as long as he could before the internal pressure built up to the point where it forced him to grab his phone from the bedside table and check the time, which hovered on the edge of late. Mace's plane would touch down in just a few hours. He had to get going. Pick up his brother. The more united they were, the safer they would all be for whatever came next.

He kissed her. "Gotta move."

"Hurry back," she said. "This clusterfuck is way more fun with you around."

That might be the closest thing to a love declaration that he was ever going to get from Fi Garrett. He'd take it gladly. "Stay with our friends," he told her. "Please. Don't separate yourself from them for any reason. Not for one second. Promise me."

Her lips twitched. "Do I look stupid to you?"

That was a question best sidestepped, so he kissed her rather than answering it. The kiss inflamed him again, and he forgot what he was supposed to be doing until Fi pulled back, panting, and gave him a sharp little shove. "You tease," she said breathlessly. "You're so bad. Get the hell out of here. The sooner you go, the sooner you'll be back."

When he got downstairs, Nate was in the kitchen. He'd come in from his post on the front porch to get some coffee. He gave Anton a thoughtful onceover as he sipped his brew, and looked away with a nod, satisfied with what he saw.

Eric padded into the kitchen, yawning. All of them were early risers by nature, programmed from childhood by GodsAcre's tight-assed military vibe.

Eric studied him as he sipped his coffee. "So? How did it go?"

Anton gave him a quelling look. "None of your

237

goddamn business."

Eric was unfazed. "Excellent," he said. "You look tired, but you're all lit up. I haven't seen you like this since you put her on that bus to California."

"It's five AM," Anton growled. "Don't bug me. I know you're all drunk on love and high on soul fusion, but I need to coffee up before I —"

"You shut down after Fi left," Eric observed. "Not just because of the fire. I think it was losing Fi that did it."

Anton grabbed his jacket off the coat-hook. "I'm out of here," he said, backing away. "Mace's plane lands in a few hours."

"Have some breakfast before you go," Eric urged. "There's stuff in the fridge."

"I'll get breakfast on the road," he said.

"Hurry back," Eric said. "I've got a weird feeling. I want you back here. ASAP."

"We'll come straight home," he promised.

He could feel his brother's eyes on the back of his head as he went out to the SUV.

Dawn was just beginning to lighten the heavy, cloudy sky, but the world was still dark gray, streetlights lit and glimmering on the water of the lake beyond the moored boats at the marina. The dead leaves and pine needles drifted on the side of the road glittered with frost. The trees looked stark. The leaves that were still attached looked raggedy and sad, the ground fuzzed with a haze of dead gray grass and foliage.

He topped the ridge and came down to the long descent to the crossroad before the entrance to the highway, the one that led up toward Otis's property, and the turn-off that led up to GodsAcre. The roads were deserted, and the light at the crossroad ahead had just turned green, so he picked up some speed on the long downhill slope to give him momentum for the ascent on the other side.

A big container truck barreled out of the tree cover and cut across the road in front of him, at insane speed.

Too late to brake. He tried, but the road was slick. He lost control, spun out.

He hit the container. A huge crashing noise. Breaking glass.

He came back to consciousness, disoriented. Everything was red. Blood in his eyes. He was upside down, pressed in by the airbag. The BMV was in the ditch.

He smelled smoke and burning rubber. Tasted blood.

Sounds started to penetrate his consciousness. Blows, squeaks, groaning and creaking of protesting metal. Voices, outside the vehicle. Someone was forcing the crushed car door open with a crowbar. Trying to get him out.

It was the way they dragged him out of the BMV that tipped him off. Their hard, unfriendly grip. Fingers biting deep, yanking and hauling and wrenching.

These guys didn't give a fuck if he had a broken neck or back. They weren't medics or good Samaritans.

These assholes were Kimball's crew. And he was deep in the shit.

They dragged him free of the crumpled vehicle and tossed him down on to the freezing asphalt among the glittering pebbles of glass. He gasped in pain as they yanked his shoulders back and fastened his hands behind him. Big ratchet ties, jerked tight.

They were hooking up his SUV with a chain. Two big men hoisted him by the armpits from either side and dragged him to the back of the container. The back doors yawned open. A cold, sour smell of motor oil, shit and mold hit his nose.

They hauled him up, and tossed him inside. Doors slammed shut. Bolts slid home.

He lay there in the blackness as the truck began to move, bouncing and rattling him.

All he could think of was Fi. That miraculous night they'd just spent together.

He'd gotten that, at least. Maybe the rest of his fantasy had always been too much to hope.

But that night, God. It had been worth all the rest of his life combined.

No way to warn Fi, or his brothers. Nobody would find his wrecked car if Kimball's crew dragged it away. No one would have a clue what had happened to him. At least not until he failed to pick up Mace, which would be three hours from now.

A lot could happen in three hours.

None of it was good.

25

emi's Corner Café was too damn noisy for Fiona to concentrate, even huddled back in her corner nook near the kitchen entrance. Granted, it was the breakfast rush, and she'd tasted Demi's food so she understood their motivation. But she was not a breakfast rush person.

She avoided rushes. She shunned crowds on principle. Too damn much information for her to comfortably process. Her defense instincts went into overdrive, and sometimes the results were not socially acceptable.

She tried to isolate herself by concentrating on the documents they'd discovered in the portal the night before. Educating herself on the mechanisms by which obligate intracellular parasites relied upon their host cells for replication, etc. etc. Cellular biology had never been her strong suit, even if the whole thing didn't make her sick with anxiety.

She took a break from reading about the cellular proteins that played a role in viral reactivation to address another thing nudging her mind. The dentist who had taken a picture of Titus's teeth fourteen years ago. She had a strong sense that Chief Bristol would not appreciate her butting into his investigation, but she wasn't getting in anyone's way by poking around of her own accord. She plugged his name into the search engine.

The dental studio that had X-rayed Titus's teeth was nowhere to be found.

She found out why when she ran across an obituary in the Oregonian, dated March 28, from fourteen years ago.

Wallace Saft, DMD, was born in Bend Oregon to Philip and Gwendolyn Saft. An only child and a gifted student, he lived his early life helping his father on the family cattle ranch, but at the age of seventeen, he broke from family tradition and chose to study dentistry at the University of Oregon. He ran a thriving practice in Gresham for eight years, then in Lake Oswego for twelve more. He died tragically last week after a hit and run accident near his home, leaving behind many grieving friends and neighbors. A funeral will be held on Saturday morning at 10:30 at the Blackburn Funeral Home.

A hit and run. Damn. Yet another person had swung too close to Redd Kimball in the random trajectory of his life, and ended up unexpectedly dead.

Fiona stared at the phone that Anton insisted on buying for her. His number was up on the screen. She just had to press 'call.' She wanted to tell him about that dentist. She wanted to hear his voice. She kept reaching for the phone and stopping herself.

The man was busy. He was driving on an interstate highway. She wasn't the type who called just to coo sweet nothings. They needed to concentrate on the job at hand.

She couldn't let herself get distracted by being,

well…happy about Anton, or daydreaming, or anything stupid and unguarded like that. Under the circumstances, it seemed inappropriate.

It also felt like she'd be just begging to get an epic slap-down from on high.

She would not let herself call him, just for a fresh hit of that sweet feeling that his voice gave her. It wasn't like the news about the dentist was relevant or time-sensitive. Saft had been dead for fourteen years, after all. He would stay dead until Anton was back.

Unlike Kimball himself. That was the real issue. Not Anton, or that amazing, fabulous, epic sleepless night. Not these breathless, sweet, giddy feelings.

Goddamnit, Fi Garrett. Stay sharp.

She took a swallow of tepid coffee and stared into the laptop's screen.

So damn noisy. Cups clinking and forks clanking, the hum of conversation and laughter, orders shouted to the kitchen, the clattering of pans, people yapping and squawking and giggling. Every goddamn booth was occupied, every stool at the counter filled, and there was a line at the door snaking out onto the sidewalk. The whole damn town came here for breakfast. If they would all just shut…the hell…*up.*

Shame, to tie up a table for two for hours, but Nate and Wong had both insisted that she stay right where she was, back to the wall right near the kitchen. Mainlining coffee as she scrolled through research documents about nonintegrated, nucleosome-associated episomes in the nucleus of infected cells, and cytopathic super-infections. As if she had the faintest fucking clue what it all meant.

Nothing good, that was sure. A world of hurt. And she no longer had just herself to worry about. Danger loomed over everyone. Most specifically these people here in Shaw's Crossing, all of them cheerfully devouring their pancakes and pastries and breakfast sausages. She felt weirdly responsible for all of them. They were so clueless and innocent.

Yeah, lay on the pressure. Kimball with his goons and their magic death pens were running around out there, slaughtering at will. They could kill without shedding a drop of blood. Without making a sound. All the friction had been taken out of death and killing. All the risk, danger, accountability, had been surgically removed from the equation.

For those guys, it was like being able to kill with an unkind thought.

Crash. Breaking glass. A woman across the street shrieked something and pointed.

Fiona leaped to her feet along with everyone else at the restaurant who wasn't trapped in a booth and hurried to see what the hell was going on.

They heard an engine rev, and a car speed away. There were gasps and exclamations, a swell of excited conversation. People streamed out the door, or hurried to the window to peek out.

Fiona couldn't see over the crush of people, particularly with all the grease-pencil artwork on the huge window. When Nate came back inside, he gave her a warning frown.

"Stay inside," he said gruffly. "In the back, at your table. Please. Humor me."

"Of course," she said. "But what the hell was that?"

"Someone threw a rock through the storefront next door," Nate told her. "I couldn't catch the plates. They were caked with mud. Looked like a gray Range Rover, though. Tinted windows. Couldn't see inside. Maybe someone has security footage on this street. The cops can look into it."

Demi joined them from the kitchen, her face shadowed. "I called the police," she said. "That's so weird. Do you think it's connected?"

"It seems so childish and spiteful," Fiona said. "Like using spitballs instead of bullets. Kimball would hit harder than that."

"But it's strange," Demi said. "In broad daylight, in front of a busy restaurant? Is someone trying to freak us out?"

"Don't read anything into it that you don't have to," Nate said. "It wasn't the restaurant window. It could be random, right?"

"Everyone said the Prophet's curse was random, too," Demi said.

Fiona made her way back to her table. A crowd had gathered outside, near the shattered storefront. The police arrived not much later.

She took a sip from her much-refilled coffee cup, and then her new phone rang.

She choked, spattering coffee. The green phone, which had never rung before.

She hadn't even chosen a ringtone yet. This was a bland, medium pitched buzz. A factory default ringtone.

She picked it up and looked at the display. *Anton*, the display said.

The effect was like a happy hand grenade lobbed into some part of her mind. A crazy explosion of excitement and delight. Fireworks, popping and fizzing.

Keep a hold of yourself, girl. You have a functioning brain. Use it.

Fiona picked up the phone in her hand, savoring the buzz. Twice…three times. Oh for God's sake, stop. They were working together to defeat Kimball and possibly save the freaking world from his goddamn pathogen, whatever the hell it was, and her precious little tender romantic feelings would have to wait.

She held the phone to her ear and answered it. "Hey, Anton. What's up?"

"Good morning, rosebud."

It was Redd Kimball's low, oily voice.

26

Fiona's legs gave out. Her butt thudded down onto the chair. Coffee splashed over the laptop's screen.

She couldn't speak. Breathe. Or even hear, over the crazed thundering of her heart.

"...just spilled your coffee, you dumb-ass cunt. I thought you'd have more nerve than that. You seemed so tough. Don't make a scene and start to cry like a little bitch or I'll cut a chunk right off your fuckboy here. Clear?"

Fiona licked her lips, tried to speak but managed only a thick, strangled sound.

"Anton," she whispered. "Where is Anton?"

"You don't need to know that right now," Kimball said. "Listen carefully, rosebud. And don't try to signal to anyone. I have my eyes on you right now, this second. I see your laptop, the doughnut you didn't eat. No, don't bother turning to look. You won't see me."

Fiona stopped herself from whipping her head around. "What do you want?"

"For you to shut up, for starters. Speak if I tell you to speak. Don't move, don't turn, just listen to what I say. Nod once if you understand me. Don't make a sound."

Fiona nodded.

"There we go. Good little girl. Now we're communicating. Be aware that I can see everything you do. I am also observing you through the camera of the phone you're holding. I see everything you do. Absolutely everything. So don't try to be sneaky. Do you understand? Nod, rosebud. Show me you get it."

She nodded.

"On the phone in your hand, you'll find a chat app. It's one of the very few things on your screen. Open it. There's a message from the number that just called you. Video call that number. Do you have earphones?"

She nodded again.

"Put them in."

She plugged in the earphones with trembling hands. It was strangely difficult to get the earbuds into her ears. They kept falling, and tangling around her numb fingers.

She called, and the picture filled the screen. Anton, tied to a chair in a dimly lit, indeterminate setting. His eye was swollen shut and his face and mouth were bloodied.

Kimball leaned into the picture, head to head with Anton, as if about to take a selfie. He looked pretty much like he always had, just thicker, meatier. His neatly trimmed black beard was frosted with white, but that taunting look in his eyes was just the same.

There was a confusing flurry of pixels as Anton twisted and lunged. Kimball shrieked and jerked away, and Anton's chair toppled off the camera screen.

Kimball appeared briefly, wild-eyed in the camera

screen, holding his hand up against his ear, and his fingers streamed with blood. Blood coursed down his neck.

"You piece of shit!" he snarled. "You're going to feel that, dickhead!"

The camera field shifted again as Kimball handed it to someone. Then Kimball appeared again, farther away, but waving his hands wildly. "Point it at him, you fucking idiot!" he bellowed. "Not at me! Let her watch!"

The camera's viewpoint dipped and spun and finally fixed on Anton, on the floor on his side, still fastened to the chair. A rusty, filthy, corrugated metal floor. It looked like an old shipping container.

"You got him?" The camera swung back to Kimball's bug-eyed face. "Good. Okay, rosebud. You've been a bad girl. This is what happens when you're bad."

The camera shifted back down to Anton on the floor. Fiona's body clenched as Kimball kicked him savagely. Belly, groin, thigh, chest. Heavy thuds, boot to flesh. A huff of air escaped Anton's mouth with each blow, but he made no other sound. It went on and on. *Thunk. Thunk. Thunk.*

A tiny sound, just a wisp of air whistled past Fiona's lips. Too soft to be heard. Her throat was so tight. She felt throttled with thin, burning wire.

The camera swooped back up to Kimball's face. "Give me that!" His hands reached out, grotesquely foreshortened and marked with blood. The picture bumped, and settled on Anton's bloodied face. There was a smear of blood on the camera's view screen. "Let's see how your fuckboy feels after my first round." Kimball's voice was louder now, blaring harshly into her earbuds. "Tell your girlfriend how you're doing, shit-stain. Need a little more? I don't have all day. Look alive, fuckhead. Say something!"

Anton's swollen eyelids fluttered. He looked directly up into the smartphone's viewscreen. His bloodied lips twisted. He sucked in air, and spat something at Kimball.

The camera joggled as Kimball flinched back, but she'd caught sight of it, on his lap. A raw, pinkish ball of flesh.

"I'm good," Anton said hoarsely. "Your earlobe tastes like ass, and you're probably poisonous, but that pig squeal you made was so fucking worth it."

The picture blurred and jolted again as Kimball leaped to his feet and started kicking him again, howling incoherently.

Some endless time later, Kimball picked up the camera again. He smiled maniacally right into it. His face was distorted, his eyes rolling and bloodshot.

"This is how this goes, bitch," he told her. "No sudden moves, understand? You've been drinking coffee all morning. I've seen you. So now you need to pee, naturally. Hold the phone to your ear, and go straight to the bathroom. Do not do or say anything that will draw anyone's attention to you, understand? Or I cut off his thumb. And that's just for starters. Nod if you understand."

She nodded.

"Let me go, Fi," Anton called out. "I'm fine. Don't sweat it."

Right. Like that was an option.

Fiona stood up and moved slowly through the tables in the back of the restaurant, careful not to stumble over her own feet. The homely normalcy of the scene was a grotesque contrast to the horrors on the telephone's screen. A toddler was eating pieces of banana muffin in a high chair while her parents laughed over a shared plate of home-fries. An old guy was working through a short stack of huckleberry pancakes with a side of bacon. While Anton huddled, bloody and battered on the floor in some filthy container, being tortured for her sake. And she couldn't say a fucking word.

She felt like a walking bomb.

"Easy now, rosebud," Kimball crooned into her ear. "You're shuffling and staring like a maniac. Not a good look for you. Act natural. Try harder."

Elisa gave her a puzzled look as she walked by. "You okay, Fiona?"

Fiona saw the other woman's lips moving, but her heart thudded too loud to hear the words. She tried to smile but quickly gave up the attempt. She patted her belly and gave Elisa a small, expressive grimace. Nausea would explain the ashy color, the cold sweat, the staring eyes. She hoped.

"Almost there," Kimball crooned. "Into the corridor now. Very good. Go into the bathroom."

Her belly heaved at the ooze of his voice against her nerve endings as she pushed her way into the bathroom. It was a small one, two toilet stalls, sink, hand towels, dryer.

"So far, so good," Kimball said. "The next bit will be tricky, but if you're quick, I won't have to cut pieces off him yet." The cheery-encouragement in Kimball's voice made her want to shriek. As if she were a toddler being coaxed to eat her peas.

"Hold up the phone so I can see your face in the camera," Kimball commanded. "I'm tired of looking into your ear canal."

She did as she was told. The small square of her own viewscreen monitor showed up in the corner of the smartphone's screen, brightly lit in comparison to his murky dimness. Her eyes were huge with horror and dread.

"Poor little rosebud. You look so scared. And you

should. You've been bad, and now you have to be punished. Something for us both to look forward to."

He licked his lips, making them horribly wet. Eyes glittering wildly. The camera still had that brownish smear of blood on the view-screen. His, or Anton's. Kimball hardly seemed to notice the blood on his own face. As if he were stoned.

"Will you promise to be a good girl?" His voice had a sing-song quality.

She nodded.

"Now that we're alone, you can talk to me," he told her. "Say the words. Tell me you'll be a good girl. That you solemnly promise. Or else I take his thumb."

Her throat bumped, dry and tight as she swallowed. "I'll be good."

"Excellent. Put the phone back to your ear. Not too close. I like to see the color of your hair. I can almost smell it from here. So sweet and hot. I remember it."

She remembered that, too. He had used to trap her against the wall when they passed each other in the corridor, and sniff at her like a dog. The memory almost made her hurl the coffee and pastry. "Shall I go now?"

Kimball blinked to find his reverie interrupted. "Hold the phone up in front of your face so I can see you. Then leave the bathroom, and walk quickly through the kitchen without looking at or speaking to anyone. Go straight out the back entrance. There's a short flight of concrete stairs that leads down to the alley. Eyes on me, the whole time. If I catch you looking away, signaling anyone...the thumb goes, snip. Earplugs in. Quick, smooth and purposeful. No eye contact with anyone but me. Understand?"

"I understand."

"Good. Go."

She went. It was just like he said. The kitchen was bustling and steamy and noisy. Everyone in there had many urgent things to do. Cooks were cooking, waiters were hustling around with plates of food. She kept her eyes on Kimball's smirking face, using her peripheral vision to navigate the room and not walk into tables and counters, rolling trays and fridges. She saw a butcher's knife lying on a countertop. After a split second of frantic assessment, she walked on by. Too obvious. She wouldn't be able to hide it without Kimball or whoever else was watching her seeing it.

"Keep moving. No funny stuff. Right, left, right."

She walked past a table with a big roast beef in a roasting pan fresh out of the oven, still steaming and sizzling. A folding digital meat thermometer stuck out of it.

Without breaking stride or looking at it, she plucked it out, snapped it closed and held it against her leg. The heat in it burned through the fabric of her pants. Burned her hand.

Straight ahead. No eye contact. Face blank. Don't stop moving. Don't slow down.

Don't think about him hitting Anton. Kicking him. Cutting him.

She made it all the way through the kitchen and found the back door to a storage area, just as Kimball had said. From there, the stairway down to the alley. A dumpster, then a brick wall. Cars went by. The sun was shining, and a sharp breeze chilled her scalp, damp with cold sweat. She had left her coat behind at the restaurant table.

She squeezed the joint of the meat thermometer, breaking it. Let the electronic top fall to the ground, then lifted her foot, and in one seamless motion tucked the hot, greasy pin into her boot. It protruded, but only slightly. She barely broke stride. Now it burned her foot. Her burned hand stung.

She closed her fist around it and squeezed hard, letting the pain ground her.

"Now turn around," Kimball commanded. "Show me with the phone that you're completely alone, and no one is following you."

Fiona held up the phone and did a slow three-sixty. Turned it back so that he faced her again. "Now what?"

"Keep your mouth shut until I tell you to speak," Kimball said. "Turn to your right. Look down to the end of the alley. See the black van pulling up?"

She looked, her heart sinking, as the shiny black panel van appeared, blocking the exit to the street. It had tinted windows. It was dirty, weather-beaten, ominous. Her boots crunched on broken asphalt as she marched toward it.

When she was a few feet away, the door slid open.

She'd heard of the phenomenon of people's lives flashing before their eyes at the point of death. That brief and horrible walk to the end of the alley felt like it. Except that it wasn't her whole life. What she most regretted was not living the last few days with Anton more fully. So much time wasted trying to protect herself from the way she felt about him.

Every kiss, every smile and glance and word. So precious, but it wasn't enough. She could've had more, if she'd opened up to him sooner. Let herself feel it.

She loved him. Those words didn't even describe her bone-deep certainty. She finally understood what it meant with every cell of her body.

The shining, soul-shaking truth of Anton. His beauty and strength and valor.

She leaned forward, and arms seized her and dragged her in. The door slid shut. She was shoved down onto her belly and a hood was jerked over her head. Rough, probing hands felt her all over, ribs, breasts, back, her ass, between her legs, all the way down.

The bag stank of dust and mildew. She lifted her head, and got a stinging rap to the temple that knocked her right back to the floor. "Stay down, bitch." A low, scratchy voice. "Don't move a fucking muscle."

She did as she was told, coughing helplessly inside the dusty fabric. Seeing Anton's battered face in her mind's eye.

What a fool she'd been. She couldn't protect herself from loving Anton. It had been too late for that since time began. His pain was her pain. Kimball had a talent for inflicting pain. He found weaknesses and exploited them. And he was laughing at her. And as usual, she could hear his voice in her head. Mocking her for daring to love Anton.

I told you, didn't I? Gotcha, you dumb greedy bitch. Game over.

27

The table in the corner was empty when Nate came back inside, after talking to the police about the rock-throwing incident. He scanned the restaurant. Scanned it again.

"Where's Fiona?" he asked Elisa, who was passing by.

She glanced in the direction of Fiona's table. "The bathroom, I think," she said. "She was on the phone walking that direction. A while ago, though. She didn't say anything, but she made signs to me like her stomach was upset."

Nate relaxed slightly. A stress bellyache was certainly to be expected, and not life-threatening. "Would you check in the ladies room for me?" he asked Elisa. "Sorry to interrupt your work, but I just want to be sure she's okay in there."

"Sure. One moment."

Elisa set down the tray of salad dressings, and he ogled her back view as she made her way toward the bathroom. She wore snug black pants, a tidy white button-down shirt and her hair up high in a thick, top-of-the-head bun. Standard waiter's outfit, but on her, it looked incredibly hot. He wondered how long her hair was when she let it down.

She disappeared into the corridor, and he focused on Fiona's table…and froze.

Spilled, splattered coffee was all over the computer keyboard. A plate holding a barely nibbled maple bar was swamped with the spilled coffee. The fuck?

"Nate."

The tone in Elisa's low voice made his head whip around. "Yeah?"

"She's not in there." Elisa's topaz eyes were big and worried.

Nate stared around the restaurant. "Where did she go?"

"I just asked in the kitchen. Tasha saw her walk through there and out into the alley. That was about twenty minutes ago. She didn't say a word to anyone. Nobody in there had a clue that there was any problem."

"Twenty minutes? What the fuck?" Nate pulled out his phone and dialed the number of her new phone. It rang…and rang.

"Tasha says she was on her phone when she walked through to the back," Elisa said. "She went straight out the back like she had someplace to go."

"But it makes no sense," Nate said. "No one but me and Anton had that number, and Anton wouldn't have asked her to walk out into the fucking alley alone!"

"She could have initiated the call herself," Elisa suggested.

The pick-up pulled up outside the restaurant. Eric was back from his trip to see the police chief. "Eric might know." Nate headed for the door.

Eric spoke first, as soon as he got out. "Did you hear from Anton?"

"Not recently," Nate said. "But we have a different problem—"

"Fiona might have talked to him more recently," Eric said curtly. "I'll ask her."

"What's up with Anton?" Nate asked.

"He never showed at the airport," Eric said. "Mace can't get a hold of him. Anton's not sloppy. He knows better than to not answer his phone, or to let his battery die. All calls go straight to voicemail, and he's not—"

"Fiona's gone," Nate told him flatly.

Eric's face went blank. "Gone where?"

"She went into the bathroom with her phone," Elisa told him. "According to the kitchen staff, she walked through the kitchen and into the alley twenty minutes ago. She hasn't been seen since. She's not answering her phone either."

Demi walked out from the kitchen, her mouth tight. She held out a small elongated electronic object that Nate couldn't immediately identify.

"What's that?" he demanded.

"It's a folding electronic meat thermometer. The pointy bit goes in the meat, and then the handle has an electronic temperature display. Fi must have pulled it out of the prime rib that was resting on the counter, snapped it off at the hinge, and dropped this part in the alley. She was leaving us a sign. She only took the pin. It's small. Sharp."

The implications of that made Nate's guts chill. He hit 'call' again.

Eric pulled out his phone and tapped furiously at the screen. "We'll just follow the chip you put into her phone," he said. "Maybe she still has it on her. We can follow the—"

"Wait," Demi said. "Wait, you guys. Listen. Do you hear that?"

Demi's tone of voice made them all shut up. In the silence, they finally heard it. The buzz of a ringtone. Faint, but audible. Right near them.

Nate looked down at his own phone display. They followed the sound, and it led them to cluster around a plastic-topped waste bin that was pegged to a post next to the parking meter. *Buzz. Buzz. Buzz.*

Nate killed the call he was making. The buzzing ringtone stopped.

He pulled the lid off, and rummaged through fast food wrappings, banana peels, beer cans. He fished it out, greasy and smeared. Neon green. Tucked inside a wet, soiled paper coffee cup.

"Fuck," he said, in blank dismay.

"So that phone she was holding," Elisa said. "It couldn't have been this one."

"But how…" Demi's voice trailed off. "The vandal."

"They switched her phone while we were checking out the window," Nate said.

Eric looked up at the mountains toward GodsAcre. "That bastard has them both."

28

Light pierced Anton's brain like a hot needle. He had only the vaguest notion of how much time had passed. Pain had warped his time perception. But the light outside the cracks in the container walls was middle of the day bright.

They had hoisted him up onto his chair again. From what he could tell, it was just an old wooden kitchen chair. Something they'd found in the wreckage of the old storage sheds, maybe. The wood had weathered to dull brown-gray, the straw-weave seat was half rotted out, but the frame was sound. His hands were still fastened behind his back.

A rattling thud, and a soft grunt of air escaping. Higher pitched. A woman. *No.*

Anton twisted his aching neck and peered through swollen eyelids to see who had been flung down onto the floor.

Fuck. Those long, slim legs, clad in dark denim. Those small, muddy boots. Men were huddled around her, but he would know the shape of her legs anywhere. *Fi.*

Kimball's silhouette appeared over him, dark against the light that streamed in from the container's open door. The fresher air that rushed in was cold. Kimball's face swam into focus as he squatted next to Fiona, checked to make sure that Anton was watching, and jerked off the canvas hood over her head.

She gasped for air, coughing. Recoiling in revulsion when she saw Kimball.

"You," she spat out. "Scum."

"Of course, me." Kimball looked her over, with that grotesquely friendly smile. "You look good, rosebud."

"Don't call me that."

"Be polite, bitch." He gestured in Anton's direction. "My leverage."

Fiona turned to look at him. Her eyes were full of pain. "Anton," she whispered.

Yeah, he must look just about as good as he felt. "Fi," he croaked. "The fuck? Why are you here? You should have stayed clear."

"Fascinating question, but not now." Kimball slammed Fiona back down onto her stomach and jerked her head up by her hair. "Listen. If at any time I feel like you're not being completely cooperative, I will cut off a piece off that shithead, and I will squeeze the maximum agony out of it. I am very good at amping up pain. Do you understand?"

Fiona gasped for breath, grimacing. "Yes."

"Good. No time to waste. Your friends have already noticed that you're gone. I need to reclaim my property." He turned to his men. "Get to work," he said. "Before this place is overrun. You know what to do."

Anton locked eyes with Fiona as two of Kimball's men

grasped her under the armpits and hauled her roughly to her feet.

"Cut her arms free." Kimball's tone was businesslike. "It'll be easier to find if her shoulder-blades aren't shoved together. But watch out. She's quick."

One of the men cut the plastic cuff that bound Fiona's arms. Each man took one arm and jerked them out wide, bending her over the narrow, battered wooden trestle table that he'd watched the men drag in earlier, on Kimball's orders. Her long, tousled hair fell forward on either side.

Kimball strutted over to stand right in front of her, sidling forward until the bulge in his pants was mere inches from her face, savoring the moment. He licked his slack lips, his eyes hot with excitement.

"Get the sweater off her," he said.

Fiona struggled as they jerked her upright again, dragging the loose blue sweater up and over her head. The tee-shirt beneath was loose and soft. It gave way at a single tug. The pendant he'd given her swung wildly back and forth.

Kimball gave Anton a big, triumphant grin. He gestured to another man who stood behind him, semi-automatic pistol in hand, waiting for orders.

"Move his chair closer," Kimball said. "I want him to see everything I do to her."

Two of the men snapped to it, and his chair legs squeaked and bumped over the corrugated floor as they dragged him closer from behind. Fiona's eyes were wild as she vibrated in their grip. Their filthy fingers bit into her skin.

"Take a look, rosebud," Kimball said, opening a briefcase and displaying it to her. Inside were a various sharp, gleaming instruments. Blades, saws, clippers, hooks, scalpels, shears. "I've been busy since the last time we were together.

I've learned a few things."

Fiona stonily refused to look at them, but her lips were bloodless.

Kimball lifted up his toolkit and displayed it for Anton's benefit. Then he seized the neckline of Fi's soft, loose gray tee-shirt and yanked it down, exposing her breasts. No bra.

"That's better," Kimball muttered. "Sweet little titties. They look so youthful. You're what, twenty-eight? You don't look much different than you did back then, just taller. I wouldn't have thought you'd still stimulate me after all this time. You're full of surprises, rosebud."

One of the guys who had dragged Anton's chair cleared his throat. "Uh, boss?" he said. "After you finish up, can we have a turn?"

Kimball considered the idea, swiftly revising his fantasy. "Afterward, if there's time," he conceded. "When I'm done. But you'll have to be quick."

"Won't take us long," the guy assured him.

"Then we leave them buried in a hole," Kimball said. "Covered with mud and broken rock. Their mouths full of dirt. That's what they tried to do to me. But they failed."

"Absolutely," the guy assured him. "That's the plan."

"Bend her over the table." Kimball rolled the words around in his mouth.

They were all focused on Fiona's breasts, so no one noticed Anton rocking forward, poised on the balls of his feet.

The two guys holding Fi made a pig-like grunting sound as they forced her down, one on either side of her. Each man with one hand on her shoulder and another clamping her wrist. Kimball pulled out a knife and snapped it open. He put his fingers under her chin and jerked her face up, flaunting the knife before her eyes. "Take a good look," he said, winding his fingers into her hair. "This is what happens to bad little girls."

She looked at the knife, then at his erection, shoved in her face. Her eyebrow tilted up in a 'what else have you got' expression. His Fi. Badass to the bitter end.

"You snotty bitch," Kimball crooned. "Get ready. This is going to hurt."

"Go fuck yourself," Fiona said.

Kimball shook his head. "Have it your way." He walked around the trestle table to get behind her, leaning against her ass. Gripping her waist as he traced her scarred back with the knife tip, right over the deepest scar. Tickling it with the knife point.

"Brace yourself." He pressed the knife into her skin.

Blood welled up. Fiona gasped.

That small sound acted like a detonator. Anton heaved all his weight forward, and sprang upward, chair and all. He flung himself up, and backward.

The rotting wooden chair disintegrated beneath his back as he hit the floor hard.

29

Anton's gambit gave her the opening. Kimball stopped cutting, their grip on her arms faltered. Fiona wrenched an arm loose and twisted violently, scything her elbow back in the wild hope that she'd hit—

Thud. Her elbow hit someone square in the face. The guy reeled backward with a yelp.

A metallic clattering sound. Kimball's torture instruments had been knocked to the floor. The other guy was trying to wrestle her down again. She shoved back against him, twisting with her free arm to reach for her boot...

The meat thermometer. She braced it in her palm, twisted, jabbed—

Pop. The pin protruded from the guy's eye.

He looked bewildered. His mouth slowly opened as he figured out what had happened to him. Then he clutched at his eye, and started to scream.

Kimball was yelling, too. Anton had rolled up onto his feet. Kimball had pulled out a gun. *Boom. Boom.*

Anton dove for the floor. She couldn't tell if he'd been hit. Fiona fumbled for the necklace, jerking it to snap the chain. Her fingers were slippery, shaking.

The little ring. She struggled to pry it loose from its niche. Hooked her finger in it, just as the guy she had elbowed tried to grab her again. His nose streamed with blood.

Pull the pin. Yank it hard.

She flung the necklace toward Kimball. It bounced on the table. "Necklace!" she shrieked, to warn Anton.

Kimball glanced over, eyes widening with horrified understanding as he saw the necklace and abruptly realized his danger. He opened his mouth to yell as Fiona spun around, covering her ears, squeezing her eyes shut...

Boom.

The huge sound wiped out everything.

Some time later, Fiona felt the rough, cold container floor pressing her face. She didn't even remember falling.

She struggled to order her mind. *Do something. Now.* Urgency shrieked in her mind, but she couldn't connect it to facts, data, actionable decisions. She couldn't hear.

It swam back slowly, one small, disconnected chunk at a time. The burning in her shoulder. Hot blood, streaming down to the small of her back and into her jeans.

Kimball and his men. Cutting her. Hurting...

Anton. She had to free Anton. Fiona struggled up onto her hands and knees. Her eyes watered. So hard to see. Her eyes stung even though she'd squeezed them shut for the flash. Kimball was groping and flailing, shooting wildly, his mouth stretched open. She couldn't hear his howling voice. She saw muzzle flashes, but could barely hear the pops of his gun. Bullets punched through the container wall and the holes let in thin, slanting beams of light that sliced the dimness.

Anton was trying to get up. The ancient, weather-beaten wooden chair they had bound him to was broken into pieces on the floor. He fell heavily against the wall, sliding and stumbling to his knees.

Fiona scrambled toward where she'd heard the clatter of falling blades. One of Kimball's men tripped over her in his headlong rush and sprawled out flat on the ground. So hard to focus. She groped, feeling blindly. A knife bounced off her fingertips and skittered out of reach. She tried again, fingers scrabbling on the corrugated surface…

Her fingers hit smooth, cool steel. *Yes.* A pair of scissors. Long. Sharp.

Bam. Bam. More gunshots. She scuttled toward Anton. Hands and knees. Her hearing was coming back. They sounded like handclaps now. A bullet whizzed past her face. More thin slices of light from the holes cut through the darkness like laser beams.

Anton's eyes were squinted and straining, but he saw her coming. She saw his mouth form the word. *Fi.* He saw she scissors in her hands and twisted, holding out his bound hands to her.

The guy who had tripped over her had gotten back up to his feet. He was stumbling toward them, mouth wide in a soundless yell as she snipped Anton's bonds.

Anton sprang to his feet and kicked high. The guy bounced off the side of the container and fell. His throat had a hole in it. Blood gushed out. She looked down.

The blade poking out of Anton's boot was bloody.

Gunfire popped again and Anton jerked, staggering back against the wall. There was a hole in his sweatshirt. A dark stain on his shoulder. Oh *fuck.*

Fiona heard Kimball's maniacal howl as if it came from

miles away. Too late to evade him. He barreled into her. *Wham,* she was flat on her back and pinned against the wall, head ringing, lungs emptied, gasping for breath. She felt for the scissors she'd dropped. Her fingers closed around them, right where the wall of the container met the floor, but she couldn't pry her hand loose with Kimball's weight pinning her down.

Kimball straddled her and reared up onto his knees, throwing his head back in a howl of triumph. Lifting his bulk just enough so she could wrench her arm free.

She stabbed —

His howl of triumph choked off into startled silence.

The handles of the scissors protruded from his groin. Blood spread, soaking his pants. Kimball screamed, clutching at the blade. Fiona bucked and heaved, shoving him to the side. He fell over, and she scrambled out from under him.

Bam. Bam. More points of light from the container's wall. The guy with the pin in his eye was shooting again, but he was shooting blind. The shots were going wild.

Anton pitched forward heavily. She steadied him in his headlong stumble toward the door. They pushed it open and ran outside together, both stumbling as if they were drunk. They squinted desperately, blinded by the thin wintry sunshine.

They spun around in the forest, trying to orient themselves. The roar of the water and the lay of the land guided them. That steep slope said they were near the Upper Falls. Water leaped down some rapids in shorter waterfalls and then plunged off an arrowhead-shaped, pointy cliff in a thick spraying horsetail into deep pool below.

It was a very long fall, with brutally sharp rocks at the bottom if you didn't jump out far enough. Only Anton and his two brothers had ever done it, back when they were young and dumb and had no adults watching them.

The faint crack of gunfire caught their attention. A bullet whined off a cedar tree next to them, leaving a raw pale wound in the trunk. Men were running down the hill from above. At least three, all shooting. Reinforcements. They would be here in seconds.

Kimball shambled out the door of the container. His groin was blood-soaked, his thigh red to his knee, and he clutched it, his face contorted with rage as he lifted the gun.

Bam. A bullet hit the tree closest to them, ripping through the fir boughs.

They turned to face the empty air beyond that cliff, the thundering white water and stumbled toward the cliff's edge with all the speed they could muster.

No second chances. No second-guessing. *Go.*

They jumped, hands linked.

30

Anton's grasp on Fiona was broken when they hit the icy water. Down, down, so deep. He slowly fought back up, lungs burning. Gasping as he broke the surface.

He was yanked back underwater again. The current thundered downstream from the waterfall's overflowing pool with terrifying swiftness.

He tried to turn around, looking for Fi in the water. Didn't see her.

Fi. Oh, Fi, please. *No, no, no.*

Then he caught a glimpse of her head and shoulder, disappearing in a rush of opaque brown water that roared down between two rocks into a long sluice they used to call the Chutes back in the old days when they played there as kids. In the summer, when Kettle River acted more like a creek, and wasn't swollen with runoff from the recent rain.

He tried to move through the water in her direction, insofar as he could. He saw at least four men gathered at the clifftop above the falls. Saw muzzle flashes. Incompetent assholes. They were out of range and getting farther every second.

An attempt to backstroke toward the Chutes set him coughing painfully. He had broken ribs from Kimball's tantrum, and his right arm wouldn't respond. He did his best with his left, but the water took him wherever the fuck it wanted. And the water just wanted to go down the Chutes as fast as possible.

It dragged him under again.

Fiona flailed to keep herself at the surface. Grabbed a gulp of air at every opportunity, but always got sucked back under before her lungs could be filled. Coughing, choking. So fucking cold. She could barely move. Her feet felt so heavy. Hard to kick.

She got flung up against some rocks from time to time, like being punched by a huge gigantic fist, but the river always pulled her numb body back into action again, and now she'd been dragged into a deep, narrow channel between a canyon and she was sliding, sloping down, going faster and faster…

Right over the edge of the Lower Falls. A long, heart-stopping fall…and she plunged deep into the second pool.

When she broke the surface this time, she found the current was moving slightly slower, and the river was wider and shallower. She could just barely touch her toes to the bottom, but she didn't have the strength to brace herself against the suck of the water. She looked frantically around for Anton, and finally caught sight him. The water was chest deep now, but still brutally swift and strong. He floated face down. Oh God.

It was a slow nightmare, fighting the water with heavy, leaden limbs, trying to get closer to him.

By pure luck, Anton snagged on a boulder and was trapped there with the water beating against him, rushing and bubbling up over his still face. She fought her way across the stream. His bullet wound leaked pinkish threads of color into the brown water.

Fiona pulled herself along, scraping her numb fingers across rocks and logs for what felt like an eternity to get to him. She tried to hoist him up so his face was out of the water. "Anton? Anton! Hey! Wake up!"

His lips were bluish. He could have been bleeding out all this time.

"Anton!" Her voice felt so small and weak against the roar of the water. "Wake the fuck up! Look alive! I can't pull you out of this alone!" She slapped his face. "Anton! Goddamnit, help me out here!"

Nothing.

She screamed in frustration. The sound was lost against the roar. "Goddamnit, Anton! I love you! Don't you dare die on me before I get to tell you that properly!"

Screw this. She couldn't help him in the middle of a river. She got her back into it and pried him loose of the rock, flinging them both into the flow of the current again.

She struggled to keep him right side up, mouth above water while they swept downriver. Their combined weight made it easier for her to touch the ground more often, but never for very long.

Finally she got her feet beneath her, and got enough purchase to drag him out of the current of the deepest part of the river and into a calmer, shallower part. The water still pulled strongly at her legs, and dragged on Anton's body, trying to get it away from her.

As far as she could tell, from her sketchy memory, they were almost to the outskirts of town. A little bit farther, and they'd be close to Circle Falls, and then they would reach the spot where Kettle River dumped into Shaw Lake.

There was a trailer park built up on the hillside of Kettle Creek Canyon on both sides of the gravel road. She could see manufactured homes peeking through the trees.

The closest house was very near the river's edge. It was ramshackle single-wide, surrounded by defunct cars, and it had a thin plume of smoke curling up into the air. Someone had a woodstove fire burning inside. Anton's eyes were still closed.

She dragged him closer to the shore. Dogs ran frantically back and forth on the river bank, jumping around on the big, water-tossed smooth boulders tumbled at the bank. One, a big shaggy faced mongrel, jumped excitedly into the water and paddled toward them as they staggered closer. She hoped the animal was friendly. Fighting him off of her and Anton would be tough, with her body so numbed by cold.

"Hey," she said again. "Hey. Anton. Let's try to get out of the water. Please, wake up. Please. Open your eyes."

His eyelids twitched, trembled. He opened them, meeting her eyes, and gave her an almost imperceptible nod. She would have sobbed in relief if she had the energy to spare.

Anton tried to stay upright as she draped his arm over her shoulder. They fought the pull of the hip deep water.

He stumbled over a rock under water and went down again, splashing face first into the water and taking her down with him, and they had to start from the top all over again.

Fighting gravity, fighting to get their own shaking legs squarely under them and keep their balance. The dogs splashed and wagged and barked in wild encouragement.

Anton fell heavily onto the drifts of rounded pebbles at the shore, panting. She didn't even try to get him up this time. She just made sure he was far enough out of the water not to get swept out again, and crawled up onto the shore. Three big dogs circled them, capering and barking and yipping.

The door of the single-wide opened and a heavyset older lady with long gray hair and a black baggy track suit came out onto a sagging wooden porch, peering through her glasses. She shouted at the dogs, but Fiona couldn't make out what she said.

Fiona raised her and arm and waved. No strength left to yell for help.

The woman hurried awkwardly down the stairs and limped down the path to the creek bed. As she got closer, Fiona could finally make out the words.

"...hurt? You fell in that river? Good God, you must be froze to death! Want me to call an ambulance? You get out of the way, there, you bad dog! Go on, now! Git!"

"He's been shot," Fiona forced out, through chattering teeth. "We jumped off the Upper Falls to get away from them. If we wait for an ambulance, the men who shot us will catch up."

The woman froze, mouth open and eyes wide behind her glasses. "Holy shit." She looked at the pinkish hole in Anton's sweater. The blood seeping through it. "Is that one of them Trask boys? Oh my goodness. Are those Trasks getting into trouble again?"

"Please, could you just drive us straight to the hospital?" Fiona pleaded. "He's been bleeding since we fell in the water. And we're so...cold." She could barely get the words out, her teeth chattered so hard.

"But why did they shoot..." The lady cut herself off, lips tightening. "Never mind. Let's get him to that hospital on the double. I'm Glenda, by the way. Glenda Visser. Out of the way, you useless dog."

Between the two of them, they dragged Anton to a dilapidated Volkswagen camper van. Glenda slid the side door open and Anton thudded down heavily in the van's doorway, making the vehicle shudder and rock.

"Scoot on back in there," Glenda instructed. "Sorry about all those boxes. I was trying to get some old stuff down to the thrift store, but I never seem to have the time. Wedge yourselves on in and I'll run get some blankets and the car keys. You all sit tight."

Glenda's rattling monologue faded away as she hustled back to her house. Fiona crawled inside, helping Anton to move further back into the only free space between the stacks of dusty boxes. The biggest dog, the one who had swum out to meet them, leaped in after them, panting heavily over Fiona's shoulder and licking her face.

Glenda reappeared with an armful of wool blankets and a couple of raggedy towels, a bag of cotton balls and a silver flask. A smartphone was clutched in her hand.

"Out of there, you useless dog," she scolded, dragging at the dog's collar until the big mutt hopped reluctantly out. "Here, put some cotton balls over that bullet hole. And if you can make the call to the hospital or whoever, I'll go ahead and get us on the road. Can you manage the phone call on your own?"

"Yeah, I think so. Thanks," Fiona said gratefully.

"Sip of this Jackie D oughta warm you both up. Here,

get those feet of his inside, and I'll close up the door, and then we can haul ass."

Fiona and Glenda had to hoist up Anton's knees, one on either side, to get his feet out of the way of the door. It slid shut with a grinding crash.

And they were squished together into a dusty, breathless clinch. The poodle's face appeared again from over the seat, dangling over the stack of boxes right behind the van's passenger seat as they jounced up the road. She didn't have Eric's or Nate's phone numbers memorized, so she looked up Demi's Corner Café on the smartphone.

Demi picked up on the first ring, her voice anxious and high. "Hello, this is Demi's Corner Café. Can I help you?"

"It's Fiona," she said, her voice rough and shaking.

"Oh, thank God. Where are you? What happened?"

"Anton's been shot," she said. "Glenda Visser is driving us to the hospital from the trailer park. She's in an old Volkswagen camper van. We're on Kettle Canyon Road."

"Got it. I know where Glenda lives. I have your number memorized, and I'm letting you go to call Eric. He and Nate are headed toward you, or they might have already overshot. Call you right back."

Fiona let the phone slide out of her icy hand, and concentrated on pressing down on the wound with cotton balls. Anton jerked and gasped, which she took as a positive sign. He was in pain, yes, but he was still with her.

The camper van slowed, and ground to a halt, tires crunching in the gravel. Panic seized her. Kimball's men could have driven down from GodsAcre by now.

She stared around, saw nothing that could be useful as a weapon except for a large and hideously ugly, dust-grimed pink glass vase poking out of one of the ancient and cobwebby boxes. She shielded Anton with her body, grabbed the vase by the neck, and brandished it as the door rattled open.

It was Eric and Nate, bristling with weapons, eyes bright and battle-ready. The sight brought tears to her eyes. They were only the second-most-beautiful thing she'd ever seen. The first being Anton's eyes fluttering open in the middle of the Kettle River.

She let the vase fall from her numb hand, too choked up to speak.

31

Nate checked his watch again as a couple of nurses in scrubs walked by. Two FBI agents had been in Fiona's hospital room talking to her for the better part of an hour. Time to tell them to get lost. Come back tomorrow. Better yet, next week. Fiona had been through hell. She was battered and exhausted. Eric and Mace were with Anton in the ICU, and Wong covered Demi at the restaurant, so Eric had charged Nate with guarding Fiona from Kimball's henchmen. He could ward off overzealous Feds, too.

Things were blowing up around here, but Fiona and Anton needed to heal before joining in the fun. He was about to march in and tell the FBI agents the new rules when the elevator door across the hall rattled open.

Elisa Rinaldi stepped out, holding a big paper bag and pulling an overnight case. The gorgeous, talented and mysterious woman who worked at Demi's restaurant. Her hair was in its usual high messy bun, coiled up with a few wisps swinging loose below her chin. She was all zipped up into a puffy wine-red winter jacket.

Their eyes met, and he had his usual reaction. Partly let-me-fall-into-the-bottomless-pools-of-your-eyes, partly wishing he'd taken the time to put on a fresh shirt this morning. They'd been up all night, with one thing and another, so he'd let it slide.

Hardly mattered, though. As usual, Elisa never got close enough to him to actually smell him. She was skittish. The most he got from her was an occasional furtive, curious glance, which skittered instantly away whenever he tried to meet her eyes.

He figured she was embarrassed about almost severing his brachial artery with a box-cutter last week at Demi's house. But he didn't hold it against her. Shit happened.

And he knew PTSD when he saw it.

Something haunted that woman. It was none of his fucking business, but that didn't stop him from wondering what it was, and fantasizing about fixing it for her.

He'd love to chase the shadows out of those gorgeous eyes.

Elisa had showed up in Shaw's Crossing some months before, and asked for lunch in exchange for some fresh chalk art on the menu boards, at which she excelled. She'd ended up staying, bunking in the little apartment that Demi owned above the restaurant. She was smart and quick, and had quickly become Demi's most valuable worker. But she never talked about her life. Not even to Demi.

She stopped at her usual careful security distance and gave him an inscrutable smile. "You look tired," she commented.

Shit. He wished he'd grabbed a shower before starting sentry duty. "I'll live."

"I come bearing lunch," she told him. "I already delivered some to Eric and Mace. Demi asked me to bring you guys some sandwiches and some spicy potato wedges. There's soup in there for Fiona, too, if she's not up to gnawing on a sandwich."

"Thanks." Nate stepped forward to take the bag, stopping short as Elisa flinched back. He waited, very still, for her to move toward him before taking the bag. Wondering if she was aware of the gesture and what it revealed.

The sack was gratifyingly heavy. He was ravenous. It was afternoon and he hadn't eaten since breakfast the day before, before Fiona's abduction.

He gestured at the overnight case. "What's in there?"

"Clothes and toiletries for Fiona," she said.

Nate harrumphed, frowning. "You shouldn't encourage her. She needs to stay in that bed and heal up. If she has her shoes, there's no telling what she'll do."

"Yeah, well. She called Demi earlier and made a big fuss. Demi finally gave in and sent me over to the house to pick up some of her stuff. Fiona's difficult to argue with."

"So I gathered," he said. "Did Wong go with you to the house?"

"No, he stayed at the restaurant to cover Demi."

"You shouldn't be wandering around here alone either," he said. "This town is like a fucking war zone."

"Oh, I'm not on Kimball's hit list," she assured him. "I'm just an outsider."

"Yeah?" He studied her until her eyes slid away. "Funny, how you seem just as tense and uptight as the rest of this crowd. Maybe even more so."

Her face stiffened. "I have my reasons."

"Yeah?" He waited for more. "And what reasons are

those?"

She took a step back. "That's nobody's business but mine."

He grunted under his breath.

The room door opened, and the two FBI agents came out. Elisa spun around and walked quickly away, right past the elevators, to the end of the corridor and into the stairwell. She didn't want to share an elevator cab with the Feds. She was also still clutching the handle of the trolley that had Fiona's stuff in it.

She'd panicked. Hmm. Interesting.

He wished he could chase after her, but that wasn't an option. He'd already failed Fiona the day before at the restaurant, falling for Kimball's phone-switch ploy like a fucking idiot. He wasn't leaving her ass uncovered again. So he just waited, secure in the knowledge that Elisa had to bring the overnight case back eventually, or else face Fiona's wrath.

Sure enough, after a few minutes, Elisa's head popped out of the stairwell, checking to see if the coast was clear. She opened the door and approached him with obvious reluctance. She was careful not to meet his eyes.

She set the case down by the door and backed up a step. "Enjoy your lunch," she said, her voice frosty. "Give Fiona that, and tell her I said hi."

"You don't have to run away now," Nate said. "The Feds are gone."

Her lips tightened. "I'm not running from anyone."

"Could've fooled me," he said.

"Think whatever you want," she said. "But I have to get back to work."

Nate spoke up as she pushed the elevator button. "I wouldn't judge you," he told her. "For whatever it was you did that put you on the lam, I mean."

She spun around, golden-brown eyes blazing. "You would have no reason to judge me." Her usually low voice was crisp and carrying. "I have done nothing wrong. In my whole goddamn life."

He blinked at her. "Ah. Okay. Congratulations. Not many of us can say that."

"Well, I can," she announced. "So far, anyway. We'll see how that goes. If certain people keep pissing me off and getting in my face."

He suppressed the smile that he knew would infuriate her, and looked down, crossing his arms over his chest. "You could just tell me about it," he suggested. "Problems are lighter if you share them with friends."

"Like you guys don't have enough problems right now? Seriously? You need to fish for more? Do you crave more challenge in your life?"

She had a point, but damn, he'd take any excuse to get closer to that. She was hot when she was mad.

Aw, hell. She was hot, period.

The room door swung open and Fiona leaned out, her flowered hospital gown billowing before her. She was all battered and bruised up, but her eyes were bright. "Hey, did Demi ever send over my—oh, hi, Elisa. Do you have my clothes?"

"Yeah, the case by the door. I'm so glad you're okay."

"Thanks. Me, too. Pass me that bag, Nate. I don't want to flash my ass to everyone in the hospital."

"You've got no business getting dressed," Nate bitched. "You have to rest."

Fiona huffed out a sound of annoyance, and stepped out, bare ass and all, to snatch up her bag. "Thanks for caring,

Nate. Now get out of my way. Where's Anton?"

"Still in the ICU," Elisa said. "One floor down, and to your left. When I went by a few minutes ago, he was asleep, but they said he was going to be fine."

"Thanks." Fiona gave them a luminous smile and backed up with her case, slamming the door on them.

Nate looked back at Elisa. "So, ah…where were we?" he asked.

Elisa marched into the elevator and turned to face him, chin up. "Nowhere," she said coolly, as the door slid closed.

Ooohh, burn. He'd just been put in his place. Ka-pow.

But that meant nothing to him. He never stayed where he was put. He went wherever the fuck he wanted to go.

And what he wanted right now was to guard Elisa Rinaldi's back.

At very close range.

32

Fiona rifled swiftly through the case. Elisa had thought of everything. There were socks and the new kicks she'd packed in Seattle, to have a change from the hiking boots. Underwear, comb, brush, toiletries. She could groom herself now. Yay.

It was hard, though. Moving hurt like a sonofabitch. The wound in her back throbbed, even sprayed with the anesthetic. A grim reminder of the way it had felt thirteen years ago, after she'd been flogged. And the trip down the wild water of the Kettle River had covered her with scrapes, cuts and bruises. She was a hot mess.

But she had to see Anton. Just to lay eyes on him, even if he was unconscious, and assure herself that he was okay. No amount of assurances from third parties would do.

In the meantime, though, bending to tie her fresh new shoelaces was agony.

She made her way stiffly out into the corridor, limping. Then into the elevator. Nate bitched and moaned and followed right along like a bad-tempered shadow.

She first saw Anton through the glass. All bandaged up, eyes both swollen shut. Marks and bruises all over his face. Arm in a sling. Ribs taped up.

The nurse stopped them at the door. "You can't be here," she said sternly. "You're supposed to be in your own room. Under observation."

"I just have to see him," she told the woman. "Just for a minute."

The woman frowned. "Are you immediate family?"

"Yeah. I'm his fiancée."

Nate coughed. "I'll just, ah…wait out here for you."

Eric turned to look as she walked in, and another guy as well. He was enormous. Broad and built, dark-blond hair, laser-bright eyes. She gasped as she recognized him.

"Mace!" she said. "Holy crap. Look at you. You turned out freaking huge!"

"Yeah, pretty much. Good to see you, Fi." He gave her a gentle, very careful hug. "Thank you for saving that clown's ass for us."

"Is that what I did?"

"It is," Eric told her solemnly. "We owe you."

"He saved my ass first," she pointed out. "So many times, I've kind of lost track."

"Sounds like a good system," Mace said. "I approve. Carry on saving each other's asses. Forever."

She tried to smile, but her eyes started to leak as she studied Anton's still, swollen face. "Is he going to be all right?" Her voice sounded like a scared little girl.

"Eventually," Eric said. "They operated this morning. The bullet was no big deal, but he lost a lot of blood, and he had some internal injuries from the beating, and maybe from

285

that trip downriver. And he got some water in his lungs. But he's stable. Here."

Eric handed her a wad of tissue from a box by the bed.

Fiona mopped up her face, circling the bed until she got to the hand that didn't have the needle in it, resting on the white coverlet. All scratched and battered, like the rest of him. She placed hers on top of it, very gently.

Anton's head turned. His eyes opened, and he smiled at her.

It took all her breath. It was like watching the sun rise.

Anton heard her voice from that murky underwater place where his mind was lurking, and forced himself back up toward wakefulness.

That was Fi. He'd wake up for Fi. But oh *fuck*. It hurt. He felt so weak.

He gathered his energy and forced his eyelids up. Eric was on one side. Mace sat on the other. He was grateful Mace was here. Fiona by his bed, her face pale and scratched up, but fine. Her eyes sharp and brilliant. Tougher than the fucking Prophet's curse.

He couldn't believe that they were actually still alive. Both of them. Together.

He turned his head to speak, and abruptly remembered the disadvantages of still being alive as fresh pain knifed through him.

"Take it easy, man," Mace advised him. "Don't move. You're all fucked up."

He turned his hand around beneath hers, and tried to squeeze it, but his fingers felt boneless. "Why, Fi?" he asked.

SHANNON McKENNA

"Why what?" Her voice was wobbly. "You know exactly why you're fucked up. We don't need to tell you."

"No, not that. Why'd you let him draw you out? You ran right into his trap."

She reached up and smoothed a lock of hair off his forehead. "He had you," she said simply. "He was hurting you. As soon as he had you, he had me."

"I told you not to come," he whispered. "I told you to stay put."

"Yeah. About that. I suck at following orders, so don't bother with giving any more, going forward. Friendly warning, okay? You'll just make yourself look ridiculous."

He laughed, and his battered ribs instantly regretted it. "Oh, fuck," he hissed. "That hurts."

"I know, and I'm sorry. But you gave as good as you got," Fiona said. "I got him a good one, too. Stabbed him right in the balls. Maybe I gelded that scumbag permanently."

"Hope so. He's still alive, though," Anton said. "So we're not done."

"You're out of the game until you heal up," Eric said in a warning tone. "Don't get any crazy ideas. We'll cover you and Fi. You just get better."

"We did good," Fiona told him. "We're alive, right? He doesn't have my computer chip, or his pathogen, whatever it is. All he's got is a pile of bodies and a hole in his sack, and the cops and the CDC swarming all over his precious mystery project. Maybe not a clear win, but definitely a draw. And we're together. And that really bites his ass."

"Speaking of being together," he said. "Where are we with that, anyway?"

Fiona's eyes flicked to Eric and to Mace, self-conscious. "You're asking for a formal declaration from me now? In

287

public? In the ICU? Is this really the time?"

"Let's not waste another second," he said.

Eric hid a smile and stood up. "Um…we'll just, ah, go out and eat some of those lunch sandwiches Elisa brought us. C'mon, Mace." He grabbed the bag that sat at his feet.

Mace followed, not even trying to hide his grin. "Later, dude. Be good."

They both waited until Eric and Mace had filed out and could be seen behind the glass, talking to Nate and trying not to peek in at them. But not really trying all that hard.

"So?" Anton prompted, when the silence got too long. "What's our status?"

Fi's face was red, and her eyes had dropped. "Come on, Anton. Isn't it obvious?"

"It's been a tough couple of days," he said. "I could use a little reassurance."

"How about you just concentrate on getting better, and we save the pillow talk for when you're stronger?"

"Aw. You still can't just say it to me, can you? You just don't have the nerve. Chicken."

She laughed. "So flinging myself into Kimball's blender of death wasn't enough of a declaration for you? What do you want from me, blood? What do you want me to say? That I can't live without you? That I'd do anything to keep you safe? That I love you?"

He just waited, expectant. "Yes. So?" he prodded. "Do you?"

"Yes, I do! I, Fiona Garrett, love Anton Trask, okay? Are you happy now?"

"Yes," he said, a helpless grin making his whole face ache and sting. "I'm very, very happy now. And I love you, too. Like fucking crazy. In case you were wondering."

"No," she said. "I wasn't wondering at all. I am absolutely convinced."

"Took you long enough to figure it out," he said.

She rolled her eyes. "Well, if you think about it, Anton, we've been together for exactly four days. Four extremely busy, confusing, intense days."

He shook his head. "No," he said. "We were meant to be. From whenever time began and until forever and always. We were marked for death, but we got through it. We got another chance. Fate wants this."

"I don't care what Fate wants," Fiona said. "Screw Fate. You're what *I* want. And nobody is ever taking you from me again. I will slash, burn and stomp anyone who tries."

He wanted to laugh again, but he knew better. "That didn't even sound sarcastic."

"That's because it wasn't." Fi sniffed, brushing her eyes with her hands. Her lips shook. "I love you. Love makes you crazy. Love makes you change."

"I don't want you to change," he said, so softly she had to lean down to catch his words. "Just make some room for me. I like you like this. Smart-ass, badass. Slashing, burning, and stomping. Raising hell. Turns me on. I go for that."

"Good, because that's what you're getting," she told him. "By the truckload."

"So seal the deal," he urged her. "True love's kiss. Let's make this official."

"You have no idea what you're in for, dude," she warned him. "Not a clue."

He squeezed her hand, with the rush of strength that pure joy had given him.

"I can't wait to find out," he told her, as their lips met.

Want more? The danger in Shaw's Crossing blazes on in
Heedless, The Hellbound Brotherhood Book Four, Nate and
Elisa's story! Things are bad enough in that crazy town
when Nate realizes that the sexy and mysterious Elisa has
her own deadly problems to contend with--but anyone who
threatens her has to go through him first...

Turn the page for a tantalizing taste and a first chapter!

HEEDLESS
THE HELLBOUND BROTHERHOOD
BOOK FOUR

Find out why New York Times bestseller Maya Banks hails McKenna's books as "A non-stop thrill ride..."

Whatever it takes to protect her...

Security expert **Nate Murphy** came to Shaw's Crossing to kick ass and help the Trask brothers fight off their enemies. He didn't expect to get knocked off his feet by the elusive, gorgeous Elisa, the mysterious woman who works in Demi's restaurant. Elisa's holding something back...something big. Nate's an ex-soldier and ex-bouncer whose specialty is breaking heads...but the fear in Elisa's eyes makes him want to crush whoever put it there. If only she would tell him the truth...

Secrets and lies...

Elisa Rinaldi is on the run, hiding from a killer. The small mountain town of Shaw's Crossing seemed like a good idea at the time, but getting attached to the people there was not. Particularly the tall, hard-eyed, hard-bodied Nate Murphy. When dangerous trouble overtakes her new friends, suddenly the press is everywhere. If she shows up on TV or online, she's dead.

She has to leave Shaw's Crossing—but only after a parting gift to herself. One unforgettable night with Nate, and she'll do the right thing...even if it breaks her. The passion between them leaves Nate gasping for breath. Then Elisa vanishes. Nate can't rest until he finds her. He means to solve her problem...by any means necessary.

Elisa will risk everything to get her life back and be with the man she loves. But now her mortal enemy is playing a game of cat and mouse...

And the stakes are both their lives...

Available for preorder now!
https://shannonmckenna.com/books/heedless

Turn the page for a sneak peek of Heedless, The Hellbound Brotherhood Book 4!

HEEDLESS

1

Elisa studied the colored chalk drawing, scrubbed the board with the sponge soaked in vinegar water, and tried again. Her idea for the menus for Demi's wedding feast had been letters fashioned like cute vegetables, but the mushrooms were looking stupidly phallic today. Good for a laugh at a raucous bachelorette party, maybe, but the wedding tomorrow would be an elegant affair, taking place at the Bluff House, a gorgeous historic mansion up on the Heights.

She was going for a rustic-but-classy vibe with the chalkboard art, but it was hard to concentrate among the chaos of Demi's Corner Café, even when it was closed for business. In spite of the wild events taking place in the small mountain town of Shaw's Crossing, Demi and Eric were daring to dash away for a mini-honeymoon. Elisa and the other five members of Demi's restaurant staff had taken on the task of cooking and catering of tomorrow's wedding banquet, and there was so much to do. Elisa couldn't abandon the restaurant to run upstairs and design menu boards. She had to stay on hand to solve problems, put out fires and generally multitask.

Demi deserved a perfect wedding after the hell she'd been through. Besides, this was the last thing Elisa would be able to do for her friend. It had to shine.

That was a sad, distracting and unproductive thought, so Elisa squashed it, focusing on her mushroom chalk art. Demi would be okay now that she had her adoring Eric on hand to defend her from all danger. Anton Trask, Eric's equally tough brother, would do no less for his girlfriend, Fiona. It was something to see. All that passion and heroism and sincerity and trust in action…wow.

She wasn't exactly jealous of the lucky lovers. More like wistful. She hoped it would be real for them. Lasting and true. She herself could never risk it again.

After all. Gil had seemed to adore her, too. At first.

It was time for her to bounce. Past time. Her bus ticket was zipped into the inside pocket of her coat, along with her collection of fake IDs and her stash of cash, carefully saved over months from wages and tips. The bus left at nine-forty-five AM day after tomorrow, the morning after Demi's wedding. From the station in Tacoma, she'd pick a destination at random. Whatever bus left soonest. Maine, Florida, Louisiana. Anywhere was fine, as long as it was far away.

Leaving Shaw's Crossing made her miserable. She actually felt at home with these people, despite the trouble they attracted. The Trask brothers had a strange history. Fi and Demi had their own wild stories to tell. And of course, there was their tall, seductively handsome friend Nate Murphy, who worked with the other security staff to protect the Trasks and their women from their enemies.

Nate had developed an intense interest in Elisa after that mortifying box-cutter incident. She'd almost severed the guy's brachial artery the moment she first laid eyes on him. Eric had called on his brother for help after the first attacks a couple of weeks ago, and Anton had come running, bringing his friend Nate for backup.

No one had expected Elisa to waltz in the door early in the morning with a tray of breakfast pastries, using the key Demi had given her.

She'd seen the strange men, the guns, and panicked, lashing out with the box-cutter. Nate been quick enough to defend himself, luckily. The only harm had been to the sleeve of his leather bomber jacket. It had been a very close call.

Hell of a first impression, but Nate wasn't put off. Far from it. It was getting harder and harder to slap the guy down. He'd reawakened her awareness of herself as a woman, which had burrowed itself deep into the ground after all her troubles. She had no spare energy to be teased and tempted. This was distracting. Dangerous.

The bell tinkled, and she saw Fiona Garrett was coming through the door, Nate following close behind. He must be on Fiona guard duty today. Speak of the devil.

Fi Garrett was Anton Trask's fiancée, soon-to-be Eric and Demi's sister-in-law. Less than ten days ago, she and Anton had barely escaped with their lives from a run-in with Redd Kimball, a long-time enemy who had been presumed dead for thirteen years. Kimball was still at large with bad intentions, and Anton had been only discharged from the hospital a couple of days before, but nothing stopped those Trasks from getting on with their lives. Now that Anton was well enough, Eric and Demi's wedding was on, with a vengeance.

Fiona was bright-eyed and rosy, her long red hair tangled from the winter wind. She smiled at Elisa as she looked over the chalkboard menus she had already finished.

"That looks delicious. Sage, squash and sausage tartlets...mushroom ravioli...yum. My mouth is watering already."

"We hope it'll be good." Elisa followed Nate with her eyes as he came in the door after Fiona. "This is the first time we've done a job like this without Demi at the helm but she's trained everyone well. We should be okay."

"I'm sure you'll all be great," Fiona encouraged. "Better than great."

Even just quietly standing there, Nate seemed larger than life. Six foot two at least. Lean and taut, but very built. Wide shoulders, narrow hips, shaggy black wind-blown hair. Dark, intense eyes that examined her intently, tucking away every bit of unconscious info she let drop and missing nothing, ever. He had some dark, stubbly shadow on his strong jaw, and a big, hooked nose with a bump on it. He didn't smile often, but when he did, his sensual mouth stretched into a blinding grin, and sexy grooves carved into his cheeks. The lines around his eyes were beautiful. And that deep voice, oh God. Listening to him was like being petted by silky fur. All over.

"...to put in the freezer at the house, so it won't go to waste this week while the place is closed. She told you about that, right? Um...hello? Elisa? Earth to Elisa?"

Elisa dragged her attention to Fiona's crooked, knowing smile. "Huh?"

"The leftovers," Fiona repeated gently. "Demi said to pick them up. I hate to bug you guys while you're so busy here, but Anton's agitating for lunch, so I thought now would be as good a time as any to pick up that food."

"Ah. Um, yes," she mumbled. "Excuse me. Zoned out for a second there."

"I saw," Fiona murmured under her breath. "Can't really blame you."

Elisa's face went warm. "Let's see, I've got some squash soup and some black bean soup, some barbecued pulled pork, some prime rib, some honey ham, some eggplant parmesan, some moussaka, and a whole bunch of veggie lasagna."

"Great," Fiona said. "I'll take whatever you can give me. Days worth of food, if you've got it. Anton gets hungry as hell. He's the big foodie. I'm not much of a cook myself, but I can heat up leftovers like a pro."

"Hey, Tasha!" Elisa called to one of the wait staff. "Could you bring out the stuff Demi put in the top shelf of the back fridge? I left a cardboard box on top the freezer for it."

"Sure thing," Tasha called back from the kitchen. "I'll bring it right out."

Fiona drifted closer, glancing over her shoulder at Nate. "This is none of my business, and I'm way out of line," she said under her breath. "But when are you going to put that poor guy out of his misery? It's killing us. You know you want to."

The warmth in Elisa's face deepened to scorching heat. "You're right," she replied, her voice tight. "It's not your business. And it's not that simple."

Fiona sighed. "Yeah, I know. It never freaking is, right?" She made a lip-zipping gesture. "Not another word about it, ever. I promise."

Elisa looked away from Fiona's apologetic smile. With all the wild things happening here recently, her own private tale of woe had taken on some perspective. The Trask guys, Fi and Demi faced trouble on much the same scale as she did, and just look at them, handling it. They fought back like demons. Never gave up or ran away. Never cowered or whined or felt sorry for themselves.

It wasn't a comfort so much as a stern reality check. She wasn't the only one living under a shadow, but these people were doing it with flair. Thriving, even. Finding happiness in spite of the fear. It was the ultimate fuck-you to their enemies.

Inspiring, sure. But damn, they set the bar high.

Elisa wished she could confide in her new friends, but they were stretched to the limit with their own problems. It would be irresponsible to load her crap onto them, too. No matter how Nate pushed and pried and coaxed her to open up.

Flirted, too. Constantly making his burning interest clear every time he saw her. It was getting so hard to resist that slow, quiet pull. She felt it right now, and he hadn't said a single word.

The bell over the door jingled again and kept on jingling as a stream of people pushed inside. It was one of the tabloid e-zine camera crews that still showed up from time to time, following the news blitz about Fiona and Anton's near-death experience. The biggest flush of media interest had already passed, thank God, but smaller publications were still fishing for more lurid tidbits of follow-up.

A diminutive, heavily made-up blond woman with big hair hustled toward Fiona, holding out a big microphone. "Ms. Garrett!" she blared. "Would you tell our viewers more about growing up in that cult? Is it true that you were forced into marriage when you were just a child? How long were you married? Did you escape?"

"Excuse me, but the café is closed," Elisa called out. "Please leave. Right now."

The cameraman's lens swung toward her, as did the blonde's microphone. An icy shard of panic stabbed in deep and made her blood pressure drop, as if the cameraman were pointing a gun to her head.

"Would you like to comment, miss?" the blonde asked her eagerly.

Oh fuck no. Elisa spun around and dove for the kitchen, pushing past Fiona, Tasha. Someone tried to speak to her, but she didn't notice who or understand what they said. She just ran through the kitchen and out the back room.

She burst out the back door and onto the concrete steps that led down to the alley. Her legs buckled and she sank down onto the steps, shaking all over. There was noise in the kitchen behind her. Yelling, shouting. Nate's deep voice, responding. She couldn't make out what he said, but he was saying it forcefully.

It was unlikely that Gil would ever see this particular media outlet, she told herself. It was tabloid trash, and he had better things to do. They probably wouldn't even use that bit of footage that might or might not have her face in it. She hadn't said anything interesting. Besides, she looked different now. She was thinner, and she'd taken to wearing glasses, just frames with plain glass lenses. She'd dyed her hair back to its original dark brown, and let it spring back into its natural fuzzy state of corkscrewing frizz. Back in the old days, she'd lightened and streaked it and straightened it with expensive blow-outs twice a week. Back when she was trying to be Ms. Perfectly-Put-Together. Trying so hard to shoehorn herself into Gil's ambitious life plans without embarrassing him. Never quite getting the hang of it.

But if Gil saw her, even with a mane of dark curls and her weird, nerdy looking glasses, he would definitely recognize her.

She should have left when the TV crews first showed up,

over a week ago. She'd been sloppy. Suckering herself into staying a little longer because she liked this place, these people. She didn't want to be all alone again.

And she'd liked Nate Murphy's attention, too. His long, smoldering glances. Liked them so damn much. God, what an idiot.

Time to grab her packed suitcase and blast out of here, right now, without a word to anyone. The door creaked behind her. She whipped her head around.

Nate stood on the top of the steps, frowning down at her and wiping his wet hand on his jeans.

Elisa tried to tame the quaver in her voice. "What was the ruckus about?"

"I had a difference of opinion with the cameraman," Nate said. "He followed Fi into the kitchen. I invited him to leave the restaurant."

"And did he?"

"He did, but sadly, his camera got damaged," Nate said. "Big shame."

"Really? His camera?"

"Yeah. Funny thing, but somehow, the broken pieces of the camera ended up landing in a bucket of bleach water. Made a big mess. Tasha's mopping up now."

"Oh. He must have been pissed."

"Yeah, he was." Nate came down the steps "But he left. Smart decision on his part."

Something inside her began to relax. "So they didn't shoot any video inside the restaurant today, then."

"No, they did not." Nate sank down to sit on the steps beside her.

There was a lot of him. He took up all the available space. His hips were lean, but muscular, and his thighs were thick and steely. The big Shearling coat made him look even bigger. The alley was a small wind tunnel, ruffling his thick, shaggy dark hair. Hers, too.

Nate reached out and brushed aside a lock of hair that had blown across her face. "Your hair looks nice down. First time I've seen it when it's not up, or in a braid."

"Yeah, well." Her face was getting hot. "I, um, wasn't serving customers, or cooking, so..."

"Yeah," he murmured. "Relax, okay?"

"I'm relaxed. I just didn't want to be filmed. Thanks for getting rid of them."

"You've always been publicity shy. Since you hauled ass when FBI agents came to see Fiona at the hospital," Nate said. "You've been hiding out in the restaurant kitchen ever since then. You won't even wait tables or seat people anymore."

Her tension started to build again. "I like my privacy," she muttered.

Nate waited for more. "I drowned that dickhead's camera for you," he prompted when she didn't elaborate. "Come on. Tell me what gives."

"I appreciate the gesture," she said tightly. "And I don't want to seem ungrateful. But I don't owe you anything. And I don't feel like sharing."

Nate sighed. "Fine. Will you at least come back inside the restaurant now that they're gone? The last time a woman I was protecting came out into this alley, she got abducted by a mass murderer. I'd really like to avoid a repeat performance."

Elisa cringed at the thought of confronting Fi or any of the other restaurant staff in her current rattled state. "Ah...not quite yet."

"Please," Nate said, steel in his voice. "It's not safe out here. Indulge me."

"Actually, I'm not going back inside at all," she said, rising to her feet. "I'm going to run up to my apartment for a while. I need a time-out. So I'll, ah, see you all later. Really, you don't have to worry about me. The door is right around the corner. Nobody's going to abduct me between here and there."

"I'll walk you." He rose up to his feet, towering over her. "No problem."

In her rattled state, Elisa could think of no good way to dissuade him, so they walked in silence down the narrow alley. Around the corner. Through the breezeway in between the buildings to her entryway.

Elisa inserted her key, and stopped breathing when Nate put his hand gently on top of hers. "Tell me something."

"Um...what?" she asked nervously.

"Are you uptight with me because of that thing with the box-cutter? Don't give it another thought."

She winced at the memory. "I could have killed you."

"But you didn't," he said. "It's not your fault. We startled you. I'm a combat veteran myself, and so are Eric and Mace, and with his background, Anton might as well be. We've all had stress flashbacks. Nobody's judging you." He paused. "About that, anyhow. You won't tell me what's going on. I do judge you for that."

She snorted. "There's plenty of drama to go around in Shaw's Crossing. You guys don't need mine. Trust me on this."

"That's exactly what I want," Nate said. "For you to trust me."

Elisa's reply died away in her throat as she looked into the hypnotic depths of his dark eyes. He was drawing her slowly into a seductive trap. She shivered as tendrils of warmth slowly stole around her like an invisible embrace.

She was being pulled from the inside. This instinctive longing to tell him all of her troubles. But she remembered every detail of what had happened the last time she tried to enlist someone to help her.

That disaster would be on her conscience to the end of her days.

She looked down at his big hand resting over hers, fighting the urge to turn her fingers around and grab his long, warm, callused fingers. She would twine them through hers and yank him in the door after her, up the narrow flight of stairs and into the tiny studio apartment. Her bed up there was a narrow futon mat, barely wide enough to cover a lawn recliner, but she had no intention of lying next to him. She would climb up onto that great big hot mountain of a guy and let the buzz of sexual excitement push the bad stuff in her mind away as she rode him into screaming oblivion. As she let pleasure wipe out the past, the future. Her fear.

It would be such a fucking relief to just breathe. Even for a couple of minutes.

She shook her head. Her lips formed words, but she couldn't pull in enough air to voice them. *No. Not safe.* She couldn't put Nate in danger, too.

"Tell me who messed up your life." Nate's deep voice was mesmerizing. "I want to fuck that guy up. Until he is no longer a problem. We're talking, pulped."

Elisa let out a shaky burst of laughter. "Is this your idea of seduction?"

His sexy mouth curved, and his warm breath caressed her ear as he leaned closer. "When I start seducing, you won't need to ask."

The air hummed with tension. She craned her neck to

look up at him.

Suddenly her head was cradled in his hand and she was tipping closer, as if she were floating in space and needed the faintest touch to finish in his arms —

And then she was kissing him.

Raw emotion tore through her system. Jagged lightning. It made her shake, but she didn't pull away. His lips were so warm, moving over hers so gently. Seeking, slowly asking for more, daring more. Getting bolder and bolder, until the gentle invitation blossomed into a carnal promise.

Her body lit up with urgency, with sharp hunger. All for him. So hot. So bright.

People walked by on the sidewalk. She heard muffled laughter, and rocked back, breaking free of his embrace, pressing her hand to her tingling mouth.

She'd forgotten everything. Her problems had vanished. At least for the duration of that kiss. So hot and sweet and searching. She ached for more.

"My God," she whispered. "What the hell was that?"

Nate smiled again. "Me being seductive. In case you were wondering."

She was torn by fear and longing. Struggling for words. Trying not to pant.

"I expect you need to, ah, go guard Fiona now," she finally forced out.

"Yeah. I'll take her back to Demi's house with the food. But once she's there, she and Anton will be covered by Jim and Mitch at the house right now. So I could take a break this afternoon. If you want to hang out. Talk about stuff."

The implied invitation made her head spin. She could make this fantasy come true before she left this place forever. She could do it today. She wouldn't have to wonder what it would have been like for the rest of her life.

However short that might be.

Then she saw it again in her mind's eye. She always saw it, on some level of her consciousness. Flashing lights, crime scene tape. The pool of blood on the kitchen floor tiles. Her friend Willis's body, zipped into a black bag.

Her fault, for involving him. For underestimating the danger.

"I'm not free to hang out, or talk," she said, edging away. "I have a million things to do. I need to finish those menu boards, and help finish up the ravioli downstairs, and we all have to go up to set up the kitchen at Bluff House. I won't have a second to spare today. Sorry."

Nate looked crestfallen. "See you at the wedding, then. Save me a dance?"

"I'll be working the wedding," she told him. "Working like a galley slave. That's our wedding present to Demi. A delicious, perfectly catered feast."

Nate shrugged. "I'll be on duty, too. Keeping you safe. But I should be able to swing one dance."

Oh, man, those smile lines. The charming glint in his eye, wheedling her. Not fair. "What part of 'working like a galley slave' do you not understand?" She unlocked the door and gave him an awkward little wave. "See you tomorrow."

At the top of the stairs, she turned to look. Nate was still looking up through the glass. He'd waited to make sure she got inside. He gave her a wave and vanished.

She felt so deflated, looking at the empty window frame. She wanted to run down the steps and yell after him. Beg him to come back and fulfill all her overheated erotic fantasies. Drive away the dark with his hot magic.

But she had bigger problems than unfulfilled lust. She

needed to stay focused.

Elisa unzipped her little rolling travel bag and pulled out her laptop. She needed to remind herself of what was at stake, so she opened the file of links. She'd seen these videos a thousand times, and every time they killed her a little bit more.

The one she set to play was an archived clip from a Portland TV station. Her husband, Gil, gazing into the camera as he addressed the kidnapper who'd abducted his bride.

Gil continually repeated her name. Spoke of how special she was. How unique. How much he missed her. That would have been grotesque even if he hadn't been looming right behind Elisa's younger brother, who was seated in a chair in front of him. Josh, nineteen years old next month. He was supposed to be safe and far away, studying at MIT. Gil had dragged him home and displayed him on TV for her to see.

Josh's thin, beaky face was deathly pale. He was all nose and wild dark hair, staring up at the TV camera with haunted eyes while Gil spouted his bullshit.

Gil's hands rested on Josh's shoulders. To anyone else, that would come across as an affectionate, reassuring gesture. Gil's handsome, chiseled face was solemn as he pleaded for compassion from the kidnapper who had stolen his wife.

Was she the only one who saw the cruelty in his eyes? It was as obvious to her as fangs and horns.

She had the means to take that lying, murdering bastard down. A weapon to destroy him completely. But she was frozen in place. She couldn't use it against him.

Not with Gil looming over her little brother, fingers angled toward Josh's throat. His message drowning out every other thought in her head.

Don't. You. Dare.

Available for preorder now!
https://shannonmckenna.com/books/heedless/

The saga of the Hellbound Brotherhood continues in Havoc, Book Five, coming soon!

Turn the page for a glimpse of it...

HAVOC
THE HELLBOUND BROTHERHOOD
BOOK FIVE

He's in no mood to play nice...

Mace Trask is setting a trap for the bastard who just tried to kill both his brothers, and he can't wait to spring it. Then a sexy, mysterious woman shows up and starts wandering around GodsAcre, the remote property in the mountains that he's wired to blow, putting Mace's plan in jeopardy and herself in deadly danger. There's only one thing to do—so Mace whisks her away to his cabin in the woods, determined to find out what this fiery beauty wants, and knows...

Her beauty inflames him...

Cait Lamott is terrified when the huge guy with buzzed off hair and ice-blue eyes drags her off into a remote cabin in the woods. She's on a mission to find her father, a virologist who disappeared fourteen years ago, and nobody is going to stop her. Certainly not this suspicious, muscle-bound, infuriating, fascinating man. Not even her body's traitorous reaction to him.

But as they work together to uncover the terrifying truth, they start to crave each other's touch. Mace's armor is no defense against Cait. Her sweet passion burns him, her courage inspires him, and her razor-sharp mind might just be what it takes to keep them both alive.

Because their enemy is closing in fast — and the stakes are higher than they can imagine…

Available soon!

Did you miss Demi and Eric's earlier adventures? Check out Hellion, Book One, to read the scorching tale of how it all began — available now! Or try Headlong, Book Two, where Demi and Eric finally reunite…only to have danger and violence engulf them and threaten their love once again — available now!

HELLION
THE HELLBOUND BROTHERHOOD
BOOK ONE

He's a ticking bomb...

Eric Trask is counting the days before he blasts out of Shaw's Crossing forever. He and his brothers were raised at GodsAcre, a mysterious doomsday cult deep in the mountains, and are the only survivors of the deadly fire that destroyed it. The townspeople see them as time bombs just waiting to blow, but Eric's going to prove those bastards wrong. He's an ex-Marine, fresh off a tour in Afghanistan, working three jobs and barely sleeping. Utterly unprepared for Demi Vaughan's dazzling green eyes, lush pink lips and sexy curves. She's the town princess...he's a dangerous outcast. It was a sure recipe for disaster.

But the closer he gets to Demi, the more impossible it is to resist...

Forbidden fruit is the sweetest...

Demi Vaughan has big plans for life post- college, and Eric Trask, notorious bad boy with a complicated past, is not part of them. So when he saunters into the sandwich shop where she works she tells herself he's just tall, ripped, smoldering eye candy, nothing more. Eric was damaged. Marked by violence and tragedy. He'd be the ultimate bad boyfriend, and right now she was too busy even to shop for a good one. But his hot eyes and hard body, his sensual smile and that rough, sexy voice of his shook her resolve. After all, she was leaving this place forever. A little taste of heaven...what could it hurt?

But Shaw's Crossing has deeper, darker secrets than Eric or Demi could guess. The evil that destroyed GodsAcre is lying in wait...**and it will stop at nothing to keep Eric and Demi apart...**

Available now!
https://shannonmckenna.com/books/hellion/

HEADLONG

THE HELLBOUND BROTHERHOOD

They were never supposed to leave alive... Find out why New York Times bestseller Maya Banks hails McKenna's books as "A non-stop thrill ride..."

Only one woman could tempt him to return...

Eric Trask and his brothers turned their backs on their past and forged successful futures for themselves. Only their beloved foster father's funeral could drag them back to the small town of Shaw's Crossing and its bad memories of GodsAcre, the doomsday cult deep in the mountains where they were raised, and the deadly fire that destroyed it. Only one memory still shone bright in Eric's mind—Demi Vaughan, with her lush, sexy mouth and her stunning green eyes. Their hot fling seven years ago had crashed and burned in the worst possible way. She's still mortally pissed at him...and more gorgeous than ever.

Second chances…

Demi Vaughan had done her best to forget Eric Trask. They told her from the start that he was a train wreck, and she hadn't listened. He'd broken her heart and derailed her life, and she'd be damned if she'd let him do it again, not now that she'd finally followed her dream and opened her own restaurant. But the years have only turned Eric into a more concentrated version of what he'd always been—a flint-eyed, ambitious, focused alpha male hunk. Just taller. Harder. And as intoxicating as hell.

Demi tries to withstand Eric's magnetic pull, but she can't resist the all-consuming heat between them. But an old evil still lies low in Shaw's Crossing, and Eric's arrival has shocked it back into life.

Now it's not just their hearts that are in danger. It's their lives…

Available now!
https://shannonmckenna.com/books/hellion/

If you are enjoying The Hellbound Brotherhood, you should check out Right Through Me, Book One of The Obsidian Files! Available now!

Turn the page for a tantalizing peek…

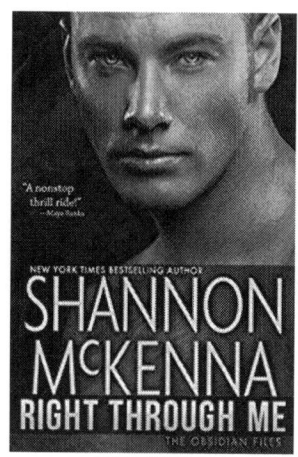

RIGHT THROUGH ME
THE OBSIDIAN FILES

Stranger, speak softly...

Biotech tycoon Noah Gallagher has a deadly secret: his clandestine training as a super-soldier gives him abilities that go far beyond human. Yet he's very much a man. When Caro Bishop shows up at his Seattle headquarters with a dangerous secret agenda, his ordered life is thrown into chaos. Caro is a woman like no other—and her luminously sensual beauty cloaks a mystery he must solve.

Caro's lying low, evading a false charge of murder. She means to clear her name, and she'll do whatever it takes to survive—but seducing a man like Noah is more than she bargained for. His amber eyes have the strangest glow when he looks at her—she could swear he sees the secrets of her heart. The desire smoldering in Noah's eyes awakens her own secret hunger, but Caro has to resist his magnetic pull. Anyone close to her becomes a target. The only right thing to do is run, far and fast, but Caro can't outrun Noah's ferocious intensity—or deny the searing passion that explodes between them.

Nothing else matters—until a vicious enemy bent on the ultimate revenge puts his murderous plan into play. Noah and Caro must battle for their lives...and their love...

Turn the page for a taste of Right Through Me...

RIGHT THROUGH ME

1

S omeone just cut the lights. What the hell?

Noah Gallagher put down his pen and looked around, startled, as drums began to thump from the hidden sound system of the penthouse conference room. Some exotic instrument joined in, throbbing and wailing.

The door to the conference room opened to a shimmery jingling sound, then a flash of fluttering purple. Everyone at the table was staring and murmuring.

Oh, Christ. Not possible. Noah rose to his feet, but the belly dancer was already halfway through the door, her hands weaving in a hypnotic pattern. Wide, light-catching green eyes laughed at him brazenly as she shimmied straight toward him, leading with one pulsing hip.

Her eyes caught him . . . and held him.

The world narrowed down. Whatever he was going to say or do stopped. Words were gone. Air was gone. Air didn't matter. Nothing moved while she moved.

She had commandeered all movement. With that smile.

Those eyes.

He was sitting again, with no memory of deciding to do so. His mind had gone blank. The woman was like a walking, breathing stun code, personally keyed to him. He'd always wondered how it would feel to be one of the unlucky chosen few at Midlands who'd gotten stun and kill codes embedded in their minds. His own brain implants had been bad enough. Stun and kill codes were worse.

But this dancer wasn't a goddamn stun code. She was just a random woman, shaking her stuff. When her act was done, he'd pull it together. Exert the fucking authority he was entitled to as the CEO of Angel Enterprises.

He had exactly until the music stopped to get control of himself.

Simple enough to figure out who'd dreamed up this unwanted birthday present. His younger sister Hannah lurked by the door. The wide-angle enhancement of his sight made it possible to see the gleam in Hannah's eyes without looking away from the belly dancer for a single second.

Not that he could have looked away.

He saw his fiancée Simone's face with his peripheral vision. She'd chosen to sit at his side for this important meeting. It was painfully obvious from her tight, expectant smile that she was waiting for him to turn to her, to smile and laugh and make light of this stupid situation. Not just for her. For everyone in the room.

He couldn't do it.

Try. Do an analog dive. Grab a hook. Concentrate.

A spotlight from somewhere gilded the dancer's body, highlighting every perfect detail. Silver anklets that jingled over her small, bare feet. Golden toenails. Shapely legs flashed between purple veils that floated from a low-slung, glittering

HELLBENT

belt. The belt and top were swagged with shining chains and dangling beadwork. Still more chains, draped from an ornate headdress, dangled over her forehead and under her chin, creating a constant soft shimmer of sound.

High, full breasts quivered, lovingly presented in the spangle-studded velvet bra. She arched back, floating a purple veil edged with spangles high in the air above herself and swishing her thick fall of of glossy black hair around. Had to be fake hair, falling to well below her ass. It brushed the curve of her hips. Fanned out as she twirled.

Everything he'd monitored in his peripheral vision was gone now. He no longer saw Hannah, or Simone, or anything else. His inner vision was too busy with the vivid fantasy of that woman straddling him. Imagining her bold, sensual smile as she swayed over him, teased him. Running her fingers through her hair, lifting it, tossing it. Coiling it around her waist like a slave rope.

He wanted to rip away all the filmy veils and all the goddamn beads and chains. See her bare-assed. Bare-breasted. Yeah.

The deep curve of her waist was perfectly shaped for his fingers to grip. The curves and hollows of her belly and her hips looked so soft. Touchable.

His hands shook with the urge to reach, stroke. Seize.

The rush of erotic images ramped up his advanced visual processor into screaming overdrive. Even with eyes shielded from eighty percent of the ambient light, even using a double layer of custom-designed shield specs, his AVP combat program was off and running, scrolling a thick column of data analysis past his inner eye.

And even that couldn't distract him from her show. Not for one instant.

His heightened senses reached out, so greedy for more that he found himself actually taking off the back-up shield specs. He'd have popped out the contacts, too, but his AVP was already going nuts at the lower protection level. Combine that with adrenaline, and a huge blast of sexual arousal—*fuck.*

The light level in this room could zap him into a stress flashback if he didn't protect his eyes. Not only that. The dark shield strength contact lenses hid the animal flash of amber luminosity caused by his visual implants. Outsiders couldn't be allowed to see that. The room was packed with outsiders. He wanted them gone.

Especially Simone. Which made him a total asshole. He tried hard, really hard, to feel guilty. Not so much as a twinge. His conscious mind had been almost totally hijacked by the dancer.

He wanted to throw everyone else out and lock the door. Study that woman with his naked eyes, dancing under the spotlight. But only for him. He wanted to gulp in the whole data flow. It was being filtered out in real time and lost to him forever, and it drove him . . . fucking . . . *nuts.*

And he couldn't do a thing. Not with an audience. His fists clenched in fury.

Heart racing, temperature spiking. Sweating profusely. No way to hide it. It was an AVP stress dump. A massive dose of fight-and-conquer energy, channeling straight into his dick, which strained desperately against his pants.

He struggled to grab onto the analog hooks that he'd established. His hooks were emergency mental shortcuts, activating an instant, deep withdrawal into the ice caves of his subconscious mind when the AVP got out of control. Best way he could devise to calm his stress reactions and stay on top of himself.

Not a hook to be had. Couldn't find them, couldn't feel them. Couldn't use his highly developed power of visualization at all, after years of grueling practice. All gone.

He was fully occupied imagining that woman naked and writhing beneath him.

His intense reaction to this spectacle made no sense. He'd seen belly dancing before and been unmoved. He did not have complicated fantasies or fetishes. He didn't even get the fun factor. He wasn't known for his sense of humor. In fact, he had no imagination at all, unless you counted biotech engineering designs, or plotting ways to grow his business, or scheming to keep his chosen family alive, secret, and safe.

That demanding enterprise left no bandwidth for fun and games.

He wasn't playful about sex, either. He was tireless, focused. Relentless in making sure that his partners were satisfied. To the point of exhaustion, even. Theirs, not his. They would tell him he was the hottest lover ever and then call him cold.

So? Noah didn't do emotions. Cold was safer for everyone concerned.

Not that he could explain that to whoever happened to be in bed with him.

He couldn't change his nature. He saw to it that his lovers had many orgasms to his one, to compensate for those mysterious intangibles. Whatever the fuck else they wanted from him, it just wasn't there. He didn't even know where to look for it.

The dancer's arms lifted, swayed. He inhaled the scent of her dewy skin as she spun closer. Fresh, sweet, hot. Sun on the flowers. Rain on the grass. His mouth watered.

Since what happened at Midlands, his senses were

sharper than normal by many orders of magnitude. He had ways to blunt the overload, but not this time. He was catching a full data load now, shields and all. Tripping out on her undulating hand movements.

He was reading her energy signature, right through the shield lenses. A cloud of hot, brilliant colors surrounded her. Her floating purple veils blended with trailing clouds of her body's energy, to which his AVP overstimulated brain assigned all the colors of the spectrum and more besides. Colors not visible to anyone but him.

Along with it a strange sensation was growing. Tension, anticipation. Dread.

He was used to being alone in an insulated bubble. Other people's drama raged outside that protective barrier and left him completely untouched. He needed it that way to stay in control. Maintaining isolation required constant effort and vigilance.

Now, suddenly, he wasn't alone. The girl had danced through his force field. Invaded his inner space. It was messy and crowded in there now.

She took up room. Confused him with her colors, her scents. Her smile was so unforced and sensual. She was bonelessly flexible, yet still regal in her diaphanous veils.

It made him jittery to have someone so close. The intimacy felt awkward. Ticklish.

He felt hot, red. No control over his face. Stuck here, sitting among colleagues and family, right next to his fiancée. Any one of them could watch him watch her. At least the massive conference table concealed his colossal hard-on.

He had not felt this helpless since Midlands.

Her luminous green eyes met his and then flicked away, but the electric buzz of that split instant of intimacy jolted him to depths he'd never felt before.

He knew he'd never seen this woman before, and yet he recognized her.

Caro narrowly missed slamming her hip into the table. For the third time.

Look away from the guy, for God's sake. Get a grip. It's just a dance.

But her gaze kept getting sucked back to Noah Gallagher, the birthday boy. Ultra-powerful CEO of the oh-so-mysterious Angel Enterprises, cutting-edge biotech firm.

The man was gorgeous. Barrel chested. A dense slab of muscle. Short hair showed off the sharp planes and angles of his face, a wide, strong jaw. He wore shaded glasses, but he'd taken them off a few seconds into her dance. It was incredibly hard to stay focused on the music and remember her moves while being examined with such blazing intensity. It wiped her mind blank. Made her lose the thread.

To say nothing of her physical balance.

Holy flipping *wow.* They said he was turning thirty-two today, but he seemed older, or maybe it was just his expression. Each time she twirled, she snagged a new yummy detail. The shape of his ears. Thick, straight dark brows. Sexy grooves framing a stern but still sensual mouth. Sharp cheekbones. His face was a taut mask of tension, as if he were suppressing strong emotion. But it was his eyes that really got to her.

His scorching laser focus made her temperature rise. She'd always been sensitive to the quality of a person's energy. Noah Gallagher's energy dominated the room. He looked like he'd tear you to pieces if you gave him any trouble, despite the elegant suit that sat just right on his huge shoulders. He didn't laugh or look embarrassed like most men did when surprised by a belly dancer. He just sat there, with the charged stillness of a predator poised to spring. Radiating danger.

Her smile faltered as she shimmied and spun. Suddenly, she was hyper-conscious of the erotic allure of the dance. His silent, very male sexual energy made it feel deadly serious. As if they were alone, and she'd been summoned for a private, uninhibited performance designed to drive him crazy.

Oh my. What a stimulating scenario.

She was actually getting aroused. For the love of God. Rising panic began to shred the sensation. Enough of this ridiculous crap. She had to get out of here, and fast.

Finish the dance. You need the cash. He's only a hot guy, not a celestial being. You're freaking yourself out. Chill. Usually she spread the wealth, bestowing flirtatious smiles on everyone. Not tonight. They weren't feeling it. Young men were usually always enthusiastic, and there were several of them here, but no one made a sound. Tension was thick in the air. No laughter, no snickering, no whistles.

Who cared. Her mind was fully occupied with the task of not gaping at Noah Gallagher's godlike hotness. Being aware of every inch of skin she displayed to him.

Her gaze bounced across the blond woman who sat next to him. A little younger, but not a colleague or an assistant. They sat too close together for that. The woman's mouth looked tight and miserable. Next to her sat a flushed, heavy older man who stared fixedly at Caro's beaded bra, nostrils flared.

Rise up, cupcake. Take back the power. This was a tough crowd, maybe, but everything was relative. The people in this room weren't trying to frame her for murder, kidnap her or kill her. And she certainly had the birthday boy's full attention.

So she'd play with it. What the fucking hell. That man needed to be humbled. To worship at the feet of her divine awesomeness. She'd dance like she'd never danced before, blow his mind, and melt away, forever nameless. Leaving him to ache and writhe.

That's right, big boy. Prepare to suffer.

But Noah Gallagher's fierce, unwavering gaze was having a strange effect on her. Ever since she'd gone into hiding, she'd had a sick, heavy lump in her belly. For months it had been sitting there, like a chunk of dirty ice that would not melt. But when she looked at him, that pinched coldness eased. It turned soft and warm and alive.

It felt amazingly good. Dancing for him, she could actually breathe again.

For as long it lasted.

The dance was ending. Caro sank to her knees, arching back in a pose of abandoned sensual ecstasy as the music reached its climax, luxurious fake hair brushing the ground in her grand finale. Dancing had never made her feel so naked before. She was stretched before him like a sacrificial virgin on an altar.

Take me.

The pose felt obscene, but only because there were other people in the room. If there hadn't been, it would have felt right. It would have felt . . . *hot.*

The sound of one person frantically clapping broke the silence. Hannah Gallagher, the girl who had hired her. Noah Gallagher's younger sister, from the looks of her. Caro rose slowly to her feet. Noah Gallagher didn't applaud. He just stared at her, as if he wanted to leap over that table and pin her down.

Tension built like an electrical charge. The other people in the room looked up, down, anywhere but at her. Caro smiled brightly. Held her head as high as possible.

Not fair, to throw a paid performer into the middle of someone else's big fat faux pas and make her swim in it. Bastards.

"That was fabulous!" Hannah's voice was a little too high. "Thanks for a gorgeous dance, Shamira! Happy birthday, Noah! Wasn't she awesome, everyone?"

Not one yes. There was only dead silence, downcast eyes, awkward looks exchanged all around. And still, Noah Gallagher's devouring eyes.

So what. She'd stay dignified. While running for her life, fighting the powers of darkness, scrambling for money. Even if it involved putting on a scanty costume and shaking her booty for rude or indifferent strangers.

Or, in this case, one single intense, lustful, smoldering stranger.

She took a slow, deliberate bow, as if she were in front of an adoring crowd. Taking her own sweet time. Rubbing their faces in it.

Take that, you rude shitheads. Like it would kill you to clap.

She didn't need any validation from these self-important bio-tech-nerd idiots. Just her fee, which she would get whether they liked her performance or not.

Fuck 'em. She had things to do. Important things. After one more hungry peek at the mouthwatering godking. Lord, he was fine.

She flash-memorized him in one breathless instant, whipping her gaze away from his face before eye contact could start the inevitable sexual mind-melt reaction. Then she swept out of the room, chin up, shoulders back. A regal sweep of purple veils.

That was it. She would never see him again. She wasn't going to feel that hot rush of opening in her chest, ever again.

Suck it up. Ignore the lust buzz. Sport sex is reserved for normal people. Fugitives do without. And don't whine.

Hannah followed her out of the room, and slammed the door harder than was necessary. "You were gorgeous," she said fervently. "You're so talented. I'm so sorry they didn't clap or anything. I'm going to tell them all off. Noah will kill me, but I'm used to it."

"I'll rather not watch that," Caro said hastily. "I'll just be on my way."

"Oh no! Stay just a minute! You have to at least say hi to Noah. No matter what he says to me, he certainly enjoyed your dance. I'm the villain here. You're just an innocent bystander. Noah's very fair that way. And I'm sure he'll want to meet you!"

In your dreams, honey. "Let me, ah, change first," Caro said, backing away.

"You remember the way to the office? Come back after. I'll introduce you."

The door flew open. A man strode out, not the birthday boy. This one was tall, blue eyed and very built, his thick dark blond hair hanging down to his shoulders. His eyes flicked over her with controlled curiosity and then turned back to Hannah.

"What the *hell* were you thinking?" he asked.

Definitely her cue. Caro took off, hurrying back toward the nondescript office that'd served as a dressing room. She didn't even want to know what Hannah's answer might be.

326

Not her family, not her fight.

Once inside the empty office, she could still hear them arguing from behind the door. Other people had gotten into the mix. Voices were being raised. Her heart pounded as she peeled off her costume and packed it up. She pulled on her shapeless street clothing, trying not to overhear. She had her own problems. Big nasty ones. Time to cruise discreetly away and let them get on with theirs.

Makeup pads got most of the paint off. She rolled the expensive dancing wig into its carrying bag, and put on her street wig, a thick brown bob with heavy bangs and wisps curling in around her face to conceal its shape. When she arrived, she hadn't worn the mouth prosthesis, which puffed out her cheeks and distorted her jawline. She'd figured that the coat and hat were enough weirdness for the client to swallow. But the job was done, and she hoped to God she could slink out unnoticed, so in went the mouth thing. Big tinted glasses finished the look, topped off by her hat with LED lights in the brim, ordered off the Internet to foil facial recognition software her pursuers might use to find her on social media.

Who knew if it really worked. At least the wide brim kept the Seattle drizzle off.

Her hands still shook as she pulled on her oversized black wool coat. The foam lining she'd sewn in bulked up her shoulders and hips. She looked sixty pounds heavier, and slightly humped.

At first, she'd tried changing the way she moved as part of her disguise, but after all the bodywork she'd done in college, she decided that the psychological toll of slumping and shuffling was dangerous to her soul. Inside her frumpy cocoon of foam and wool, she still had her pride and attitude.

Hidden, maybe, but structurally intact.

When she exited the office, she looked like a sketch that had been blurred on purpose. Noah Gallagher would stare right through her even if she were inches away.

That thought was so depressing, she could barely stand to think it.

Chin up. She'd had her fun, turning him on. Time for the disappearing act. Eat your heart out, Laser Eyes.

But disappearing didn't feel powerful to her. It just felt flat. Empty and sad.

The route back to the elevators took her right past the conference room.

Hannah Gallagher and several others were still arguing outside it. If she kept her head down, turned the corner and cut swiftly across the open space, she'd only be in their line of vision for a few seconds. Then it was a straight shot to the elevator.

One, two . . . *go.*

When she was squarely in the danger spot, Noah Gallagher came out the door.

That was her undoing. She slowed down. Not consciously, but simply unable to resist the temptation to steal one last look at him before fleeing.

His gaze snapped onto her, like a powerful magnet coupling.

Oh, God. Oh, no. He strode through the center of the group, scattering them, and followed her. Even with her back to him, his eyes burned through her layered, ugly disguise, a focused point of heat against her concealed skin. She stabbed the elevator button. He was twenty yards away. Fifteen, and closing. Picking up speed.

He couldn't have recognized her. In this dreary get-up,

she couldn't be more different from Shamira the sexy dancing girl. She barely recognized herself dressed like this. The door slid open. She lunged inside. No other riders, thank God.

"Hold the door!" Gallagher called, loping for the elevator.

Asfuckingif. She punched the close button, and the mechanism engaged.

Their eyes locked, as the doors shut in his face.

Her heart was thudding, as if she'd done something wrong and had almost gotten caught. Maybe he was just wondering who the scruffy stranger was. Dressed like that, she stuck out like a sore thumb in the muted corporate elegance of Angel Enterprises.

She hurried through the lavish front lobby. Outside, a cab was letting a passenger out. She bolted for it, waving it down.

Noah Gallagher emerged from the entrance just as her cab pulled away. His eyes locked onto hers again instantly. Even shadowed by the hat, obscured by the dark glasses, through the back window of a cab that was already a half a block away.

He started running after her. Right out onto the street. Eyes still locked. The contact felt like a wire, pulling tighter and tighter. Then the taxi turned a corner and he was lost to sight. It hurt. As if something vital had been snipped with bolt-cutters.

Her fizz of excitement died away. The cold lump of fear was back in place.

She was so sick of feeling this way. She wanted to yell at the driver to circle the block, just on the off chance of catching one last glimpse of Noah Gallagher. To feel something different than that cold, heavy ache in her core. Just for a second or two.

But she could not have this. Not even a stolen taste of it. She could not let lust trash her good judgment. She had to stay murderously sharp. Constantly on the defensive. Without rest.

Sexual frustration wouldn't kill her.

But there were other things out there that definitely could.

Available now!
https://shannonmckenna.com/books/right-through-me/

Join Shannon's newsletter mailing list to never miss a new book or a fabulous promo, and look for your free gift book when you join!

http://shannonmckenna.com/connect.php.

Follow her on Bookbub to receive new release and discount alerts!

https://www.bookbub.com/authors/shannon-mckenna

ABOUT THE AUTHOR

Shannon McKenna is the NYT and USA TODAY bestselling author of over twenty action packed, turbocharged romantic thrillers, among them the wildly popular McCloud Brothers & Friends Series, along with two new scorching romantic suspense series, The Hellbound Brotherhood and The Obsidian Files. She loves tough and heroic alpha males, heroines with the brains and guts to match them, terrifying villains who challenge them to their utmost, adventure, blazing sensuality, and most of all, the redemptive power of true love. Since she was small she has loved abandoning herself to the magic of a good book, and her fond childhood fantasy was that writing would be just like that but with the added benefit of being able to take credit for the story at the end. The alchemy of writing turned out to be messier than she'd ever dreamed, but what the hell, she loves it anyway and hopes that readers enjoy the results of her experiments. She loves to hear from her readers. Contact her at her website, http://shannonmckenna.com, find her on Facebook at https://www.facebook.com/AuthorShannonMckenna/ to keep up with all her news! Follow her on Bookbub to get new release and discount alerts!

https://www.bookbub.com/authors/shannon-mckenna

If you'd like to know when the new installments of The Hellbound Brotherhood will come out, and hear about my new releases and promos, join my newsletter at http://shannonmckenna.com/connect.php.

I'll give you an Obsidian Files novel as a welcome gift! See you on the other side!

Made in the USA
Middletown, DE
03 June 2020